**Bethel took in the four members of her new family.**

"We'll wear our Sunday best," Aaron Bontrager had said on the phone, "to make it easier to distinguish us from others at the station." Now, Bethel fixed her gaze on the tall, broad-shouldered man. Funny, but in his crisp white shirt and black trousers and suspenders, he didn't look any different from the men of Nappanee. On his right, his ten-year-old son, Sam. To his left, a pretty little girl. *Molly, age eight,* she reminded herself. The youngest boy—Matthew, the one Mr. Bontrager said hadn't spoken since his mother's passing—seemed to have a death grip on his father's hand. *How fitting,* she thought, *since they look as though I arrived on a funeral car!*

"I don't want to eat at home," the oldest boy ground out. "She looks too skinny and young to run a house or make a proper dinner."

"Hush, Sam," the father said. He ran a forefinger under the standup collar of his white shirt. "And you will address your new mother as Beth, not she."

The boy scowled. "She's not my mother."

**More Amish romance from Loree Lough**

*All He'll Ever Need*

*Home to Stay*

# LOVING MRS. BONTRAGER

### LOREE LOUGH

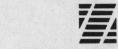

## ZEBRA BOOKS
### KENSINGTON PUBLISHING CORP.
www.kensingtonbooks.com

ZEBRA BOOKS are published by

Kensington Publishing Corp.
119 West 40th Street
New York, NY 10018

All Kensington titles, imprints, and distributed lines are available at special quantity discounts for bulk purchases for sales promotion, premiums, fund-raising, educational, or institutional use.

Special book excerpts or customized printings can also be created to fit specific needs. For details, write or phone the office of the Kensington Sales Manager: Attn.: Sales Department. Kensington Publishing Corp., 119 West 40th Street, New York, NY 10018. Phone: 1-800-221-2647.

Zebra and the Z logo Reg. U.S. Pat. & TM Off.
BOUQUET Reg. U.S. Pat. & TM Off.

First Printing: May 2021
ISBN-13: 978-1-4201-5280-7
ISBN-10: 1-4201-5280-7

ISBN-13: 978-1-4201-5281-4 (eBook)
ISBN-10: 1-4201-5281-5 (eBook)

10 9 8 7 6 5 4 3 2 1

Printed in the United States of America

*This novel is dedicated to my supportive family,
and especially to my readers, who,
for more than twenty-five years, have let me know that
they enjoy my stories . . . and look forward to more.*

# Acknowledgments

Many thanks to my dear Amish friends who have so generously opened their homes and their hearts to this silly Englisher. Your patience with my unending questions is largely responsible for the factual details and realism in my Amish stories. Heartfelt thanks to Jody Teets, too, for sharing maps, photographs, and insights into the beautiful mountain town she calls home . . . Oakland, Maryland.

# Chapter One

Despite the wide brim of his hat, Sam squinted into the early June sunlight. "She was supposed to be here an hour ago," the boy said. "If this is her idea of a good first impression . . ."

Little Matthew held tight to his father's hand as Molly elbowed their older brother. "It is not her fault the train is late. Besides, remember what we promised Daed."

Sam snorted, and the look on his face made it clear that he remembered, all right. . . .

One short week ago, Aaron had called a family meeting and confessed that he'd tried—and failed—to run his busy sawmill while caring for his children and the house, that he'd tried hiring a town woman to help with cooking and cleaning, and failed at that, too. Not that he blamed the ladies. Things were a mess, and frankly, so was he. Why else would he have blurted out, "If the three of you had helped Aunt Stella more, I might not have been forced to take such desperate measures"? Now, faced with his son's resentment, he admitted: *A man cannot get much more desperate than to hire a wife.*

His sister had done her best, trying to balance her

household and his . . . until four months ago, when her twins were born. Her husband's plea still rang in Aaron's ears: "If Stella keeps traipsing from our house to yours this way, I fear I will lose her." That's when his brother-in-law began singing the praises of his unmarried cousin, who'd likely jump at the chance to leave Nappanee behind. Even before the meeting with Bishop Fisher, Aaron had known what would be required—if she agreed to come to Pleasant Valley: "We have relaxed many of the Old Order ways," Fisher had said, "but we cannot condone a woman living under your roof without benefit of marriage."

The distinctive clatter of steel wheels grinding along the polished tracks broke into his thoughts. The train would screech to a stop any minute now, and when it did, he'd stand face to face with Karl's second cousin . . . . the soon-to-be Mrs. Bontrager.

Molly grasped his forearm. "Tell me again," she said, shaking him back into the here and now, "what is her name?"

"Bethel Mast, but she told me on the phone that she prefers just plain Beth."

"Will she let us call her Maem? After the wedding, I mean?"

"What does it matter?" Sam ground out. "She is *not* our mother. Never will *be* our mother. And I will never, *ever* call her Maem!"

Matthew clung to Aaron's leg as Molly crossed both arms over her white-aproned chest.

"There is no cause for that attitude, Sam. When Bethel gets here, I expect you to treat her with respect."

The sun glinted from the Silverliner's lead car. Sam,

seeing it, stiffened, stared at the toes of his boots. "I will be polite," he mumbled, "but I will not call her Maem."

"No one asked you to," Molly bit out. "Tell me again, Daed, why our new mother limps."

"How many times do I have to say it! She is *not* our mother," Sam snarled. "She is here to cook and clean, take care of Matthew, and feed the animals. And that is *all*."

"Daed, make Sam stop saying mean things!"

"Your sister is right, son. Bethel is not our servant or a hired hand. Karl says she has a big, caring heart, and I believe it, based on all she is giving up to help us. We will welcome her and treat her like family, because that is exactly what she will be. Is that clear?"

The boy hung his head, but Aaron could tell that he'd made up his mind not to like Bethel. Aaron hung his head, too, and said a prayer for patience. And strength. And above all, guidance. Things wouldn't be easy, especially not at first, but they'd be a lot harder until Sam came around. *If* Sam came around.

*Lord, I have a feeling I will call upon You a lot in the coming days.*

"You never answered, Daed. Why does Beth limp? I only ask because I do not want to be rude and stare."

"Why not just ask her?" Sam said. "Since she is so big-hearted and all, I am sure she will be happy to tell you."

Aaron chose to ignore the boy's latest outburst. "The way I understand it, Bethel was born with one leg shorter than the other. No one knows why, but Karl says she gets around as well as the rest of us."

He watched as people who'd come to meet the train's passengers moved closer to the platform's edge. It wasn't enough activity to blot his own words from his mind:

*She will be family.* In a week, two at most, he and Bethel would become husband and wife. Their union must appear traditional in every sense . . . on the surface. First chance he got, Aaron intended to take her aside and gently explain that he still felt bound by his vow to love Marta until death. Bethel was smart, or so Karl said, and hopefully he'd never have to explain that while he'd happily share his name, his home, and even his bed, he couldn't share his heart.

Aaron chuckled to himself. *What makes you think she wants your too-old, cold heart?*

"Are you looking forward to meeting her, Daed?" Molly asked.

"I . . . well . . ." He cleared his throat. "What makes you ask?"

"You are smiling."

"Yes, I suppose I am looking forward to having her with us." *And living a somewhat normal life, for a change.*

"And you are sure she is nice, right?"

"When I spoke to her, I found that Karl was right. She sounded very nice."

"Two phone calls and the word of a henpecked husband," Sam griped. "Oh yes. *That* is all the proof we need."

"How many times must I tell you . . . I love you more than life, itself. That's why I gave the matter so much thought and prayer, and why I discussed it at length with the bishop. I would never subject you to this if I didn't believe it is God's will for our family."

Sam stared at the space between his boots, and Matthew hugged Aaron's legs tighter, still.

"We will be fine. I will see to it." He met each child's eyes. "You have my word."

"But . . . what if she has a terrible temper?" Sam asked.

"And what if Karl is wrong, and she's a terrible person?" Molly worried.

"Then I will send her packing." He paused, searched their faces for signs of disbelief. Satisfied that they believed him, Aaron added, "Now, I don't want to hear another word about any of this. Is that understood?"

Even little Matthew nodded.

"I hope she has a nice voice," Molly said.

"She probably sounds like a screech owl."

"Samuel," Aaron warned . . . and remembered the slight tremble in Bethel's voice, how edgy she'd sounded asking and answering questions. Despite her nervousness, she had laughed several times, and the music of it had given him hope that as they worked together, providing a stable home for the children, they might one day develop a companionable partnership.

"I talked to her, remember, so I can say for certain that she sounds nothing like Sam described."

He'd learned a few other things about Bethel during two hour-long phone conversations. For starters, she wasn't a whiner. She hadn't complained about the businesslike arrangement between her father and himself, the hurry-up nature of the final decision, or anticipation of a twenty-six-hour train ride from Indiana to Maryland. It had been her agreeable attitude that had prompted him to reserve the sleeper car for her, rather than a regular seat.

"I hope she can cook," Sam said. "I am hungry."

"You are always hungry. Why, you eat more than Daed's horse! I am sure she can cook. But if not? She will learn." Molly looked up at Aaron to add, "And I will help her!"

They didn't call her Molly the Peacemaker for nothing, Aaron thought, grinning at his daughter.

"Smile, children. It will be terrifying enough for Bethel, arriving in a strange new place, without being greeted by a bunch of sour faces."

"No one forced her to come here."

Aaron wasn't so sure of that. According to Karl, her father and brother—Beth's only blood kin—treated her like an employee, and even though she practically ran her father's store single-handed, they often called her an unmarryable parasite. "Don't know how she put up with them this long," his brother-in-law said upon hearing she'd agreed to make the move. *Isn't her fault,* Aaron thought, *that she was born with one leg shorter than the other.*

He had meant to tell the children about that sooner, but what with planning her trip, figuring out where she'd sleep before the wedding, and keeping up with routine household chores and orders at work, there hadn't been time. He felt bad, having sprung it on them during the trip to the station, but better late than never. "Oh great," Sam had grumbled. "Your substitute wife is a *cripple*?"

"Disrespectful insults like that are not to be repeated. Ever. Do I make myself clear?"

Molly, true to her nature, had said, "I won't even look at her foot, Daed. I would never want to hurt her feelings!"

"Good girl. Sam?"

"I will not mention it again, Daed." He lowered his voice. "At least, not where *she* can hear it."

*Lord, give me strength,* he prayed.

Molly looked up at him. "Tell me again . . . what will we call her, Daed?"

Sam shot an imploring glance at Aaron, and in that

moment, he looked like the innocent boy he'd been before Marta's death. "Please, Daed, do not make me call this stranger Maem."

"Karl calls her Beth." The children had been through so much already that he didn't mind repeating himself. "That, or Bethel will do. Once she has been with us a while, we can ask which she prefers." Aaron had already decided that as soon as they'd exchanged vows, *he'd* call her Mrs. Bontrager, a factual title that would ensure a respectful . . . unemotional distance between them.

When the train slowed, little Matthew gasped quietly and pressed his cheek to Aaron's knuckles, pressed so close that he couldn't tell whether it was he or the boy who trembled.

"Relax, kids." *Who are you reassuring? You, or them?* "She will be good for us. We just have to give it time."

Even Molly, the eternal optimist, looked doubtful. "How can you be so sure, Daed?"

"Because, sweet girl, as I've said all along, I have prayed on it, long and hard, and believe it is God's will." *For us, and hopefully, for Bethel, too.*

The train came to a halt, and as passengers disembarked, laughter and good-natured greetings filled the brisk June air. There were men in business suits, ladies in colorful spring dresses, teens in blue jeans, children in ankle-high white sneakers, but no one who was dressed Plain.

And then he saw her, looking small and lost among the milling crowd, the hem of her apron billowing, white cap ties snapping in the breeze. She scanned the platform— *looking for you*, he realized. Even from this distance, he could see terror in her big eyes. Peripheral vision told him that the children had spotted her, too.

"Hello!" Molly shouted, waving. "We are over here! The Bontrager family!"

Those huge eyes zeroed in on them, rested on *him*. Then she bent at the waist, picked up a small suitcase, and moved toward them.

"Why, she hardly limps at all, Daed," Molly whispered.

If she heard the girl's comment, Bethel showed no sign of it.

"What a pleasant greeting," she said, stopping a yard from where the family stood. "You were very kind, and very generous, Mr. Bontrager, to reserve a sleeper car for me. It made the long trip much more bearable. So thank you."

Silhouetted by the early-afternoon sun, she reminded him of the angel statue he'd seen in the front window of Oakland's Favorite Things Gift Shop. But instead of the harp that dangled from the store angel's hand, this one clutched the handle of a beat-up cloth valise.

"I am pleased to meet you," she said. "All of you."

Little Matthew clung more tightly to his thigh, and seeing his reaction, Molly said near his ear, "Isn't she pretty? And doesn't she look sweet!"

Sam snorted. "Can we stop at McDonald's on the way home, Daed? I'm starving."

"If you have the proper fixin's, I am happy to cook supper for you," Beth said, "just as soon as we get settled in at . . ." She licked her lips. Blinked. Swallowed.

"At home?" Molly finished for her.

"I . . . well . . . yes. Home."

In time, he hoped, the word would come naturally to her. Until then . . .

*Lord, give me strength, and show me a sign that this truly is Your will.*

Bethel took in the four members of her new family. "We'll wear our Sunday best," Aaron Bontrager had said on the phone, "to make it easier to distinguish us from others at the station." Now, Bethel fixed her gaze on the tall, broad-shouldered man. Funny, but in his crisp white shirt and black trousers and suspenders, he didn't look any different from the men of Nappanee. On his right, his ten-year-old son, Sam. To his left, a pretty little girl. *Molly, age eight,* she reminded herself. The youngest boy— Matthew, the one Mr. Bontrager said hadn't spoken since his mother's passing—seemed to have a death grip on his father's hand. *How fitting,* she thought, *since they look as though I arrived on a funeral car!*

"I don't want to eat at home," the oldest boy ground out. "She looks too skinny and young to run a house or make a proper dinner."

"Hush, Sam," the father said. He ran a forefinger under the standup collar of his white shirt. "And you will address your new mother as Beth, not she."

The boy scowled. "She's not my mother." He crossed both arms over his suspendered chest. "Mark my words: By week's end, we will be here again, waving good-bye as she goes back where she came from."

Such anger for one so young! Did he intend to make her so miserable she'd beg them to send her home? Bethel squared her shoulders. *He is big for his age, but still just a child. And you are a God-fearing adult. Mr. Bontrager brought you here to take charge, so might as well start, right now.*

Squaring her shoulders, she looked the father straight in the eye. "Mr. Bontrager?"

His blue-eyed gaze traveled from her polished black boots—the regular one, and the one with the thick, chunky sole that made her legs the same length—to her cap. Why did he stand so stiff-backed and silent? And what thoughts caused frown lines on his handsome forehead? Did he agree with his son, that a woman her age and size could never run a household? That her limp would drain her of the energy required to earn her keep? She'd learned very little about the man during their brief introductory phone calls: He owned a four-bedroom house one mile from his sawmill; in addition to caring for his children, the house, and the garden, he expected her to tend a dozen chickens, one horse, a milk cow, and three goats. He'd also promised that his widowed mother, unmarried brother, and sister had offered to help any way they could. Beth had no choice but to take him at his word, just as she'd trusted her bishop's assurances that Bontrager's stellar reputation was the reason he'd endorsed the arrangement between her father and her husband-to-be.

*The arrangement.* Beth didn't think she hated any two words more than those! But what good would come of grumbling? Because she had been born with a limp, no man had ever shown any romantic interest in her. Here, at least, with a *Mrs.* in front of her name, she could pretend to be normal.

She stood as tall as her five-foot-four-inch frame would allow and met his dark-lashed blue eyes. "Mr. Bontrager, most farmers do not inspect cattle at auction with as much scrutiny." Arms akimbo, she lifted her chin. "I assure you, I am stronger than I look."

He blinked several times, then pointed at the frayed cloth bag near her feet. "This is all you brought?"

"It is."

Should she tell him that she'd worn her best shoes and dress and packed the other two—one blue, one pale yellow—a black skirt and white blouse, a new apron, everyday shoes, a crocheted shawl, and her black hat, leaving just enough room for two nightgowns, a robe, and underclothes? Quick as an eyeblink, she decided that the contents of her bag were not his concern.

He thumbed his black hat to the back of his head. "It is warm now, but June is quickly coming to an end. Before we know it, the leaves will turn red. Then the snows will fall. And winters in Oakland can be brutal."

"It gets cold and snowy in Nappanee, too. I know quite well how to protect myself from the elements."

"Is that so."

A statement, she noted, not a question.

"I am curious to know how you managed to stuff a warm coat, mittens, a wool hat . . ." He pointed again. ". . . into that little thing."

Beth cringed. "Those items would not fit, so I left them in Nappanee." She had tucked her savings into a draw-string purse, instead. The money would pay for a coat, and anything else she might need in the event Mr. Bontrager turned out to be one of those Amish husbands who didn't believe in giving their wives an allowance.

"Fat lot of good they will do you in Indiana," the boy said. He looked up, into his father's face. "I suppose she expects *you* to buy her new cold-weather clothing." He snickered. "On second thought, she will probably be gone before the weather turns cold, so . . ."

Bontrager silenced his son with a stern stare. "Sam, that is enough. I will not warn you again." Facing her, he softened his tone. "I assure you, he is not always so disrespectful. And I believe in taking care of my family. If you need something, anything, say the word and it is yours."

"I appreciate your generosity, but I have money, earned while working at my father's store. As for Sam's . . . attitude, I believe you." And when it looked as though he doubted her sincerity, she quickly tacked on, "Your boy has a kind face."

Bontrager only shook his head. "We had better get on the road. It will take forty minutes to drive from here to Pleasant Valley. And I have a meeting scheduled for mid-afternoon, so no McDonald's, Sam."

That meant she'd be on her own, alone with his frightened, resentful children, almost from the get-go. Beth could only hope Pleasant Valley lived up to its name.

She fell into step beside him and noticed right off the way he slowed his pace when he saw her struggling to match his long-legged stride. One of her father's many sayings echoed in her head: "Street angel, house devil," was how he described men who treated their wives and children with kindness in public and turned into bullying brutes behind closed doors. *And who would know that better than you, Daed!* She decided to lock away the memory of her father's abuse. She'd block Bontrager's seeming thoughtfulness, too, in case he changed his tune on the other side of his threshold.

He drew her attention to a dusty black pickup, parked about fifty yards away. He hadn't yet introduced her to the children, but surely once everyone was settled inside it, he would. Bethel forced joy into her voice that she didn't feel. "Are the rest of you as hungry as I am?" When no one responded, she looked over her shoulder at the train that still sat idle on the gleaming tracks, at the passengers who boarded. Oh, how tempting it was to join them! "This has been quite a day for all of us. So much to take in, especially for little children."

"I am *not* a little child."

"Sam, watch your tone."

"He meant nothing by it, Mr. Bontrager. I am certain of it." Directing her next words at Sam, she added, "In the future, I will take care not to speak to you—or of you—as a child. All right?"

Sam lifted one shoulder and blew a puff of air from the corner of his mouth.

By now, they'd reached the truck.

"You kids will sit in back," Bontrager ordered, tossing her bag over the pickup's tailgate.

Despite his insistence that he wasn't a little child, that was exactly how Sam sounded when he said, "But Daed, since Maem died, *I* always ride up fr—"

Bontrager interrupted with, "It is only fitting and proper for Bethel to sit up front now."

The boy looked hurt. Angry. Disappointed. *Because he believes you are here to take his mother's place.* "Mr. Bontrager, if it is all the same to you, I prefer to sit in back."

"Oh? Why?"

"It will take time to get used to your many modern conveniences. Watching through the windshield as traffic hurtles toward me will take some getting used to." Not the whole truth, but not a lie, either.

He blinked, as if the possibility hadn't occurred to him. "Oh. Well. All right then."

A flicker of victory flashed across Sam's features, and for the first time since she'd stepped off the train, his eyes twinkled with a genuine smile. Bethel hoped it meant she'd chipped a small chink in his surly façade.

"So tell me, Sam, what would you like me to fix for your supper?"

"There is ham in the refrigerator. If you have half a brain in your head, you can think of something to do with it. And the name is *Samuel*."

He stared straight ahead, probably wondering if Beth intended to point out that his sister and father had called him Sam.

"Do you know how to make gravy?" he asked.

"Why yes, I do. Which is your favorite? White or brown?"

"White, if it's made right. And what about biscuits? Can you bake?"

"I love baking. Cakes, pies, cookies, biscuits, cobblers . . ."

"If any of that is true, I might let you call me Sam."

Bethel laughed. "I look forward to the challenge . . . Samuel!"

He seemed more determined than ever to make sure she understood: *You will be a guest in our house . . . until . . .*

This was only the first hour of the first day. In time, surely the family would let down their guard. Until then, she'd pray. Nothing in life was certain, but at least in Nappanee, she woke every morning knowing today would more or less be a repeat of yesterday, that tomorrow would echo today. Her father had never been demonstrative, in word or gesture. The same was true of her brother.

She had never imagined it possible, but barely more than twenty-four hours since they'd waved good-bye from the station in Elkhart, she missed them, despite their hair-trigger tempers and dour moods.

If this much fear beat in her heart, how much more must pulse in these motherless children's? In their sad-eyed father's?

*Put their needs ahead of your own. And stop asking yourself . . .*

*. . . will you stay or will you go?*

# Chapter Two

All the way home, Molly asked rapid-fire questions about the Amish in Nappanee, Indiana: Why didn't they believe in modern conveniences, like cars and phones and appliances? Why weren't they allowed to speak using contractions? Why couldn't children attend school past age fourteen? And why would anyone prefer an outhouse over indoor plumbing!

"How did you learn so much about Old Order rules?" Beth asked, laughing.

"Daed told us we might need to teach you to use things like the vacuum cleaner and the washing machine. And . . . other stuff."

"Well, he is right. I will probably need your help, at least at first."

During a moment of blessed silence, Aaron thought her calm, patient replies had satisfied his little girl. Until Molly said, "Are you looking forward to finally becoming a wife?"

Aaron's fingers tightened on the steering wheel, and in the rearview mirror, he watched as Bethel's eyes widened, as the healthy glow of her cheeks darkened to a rosy blush.

Her embarrassed reaction was his fault. If he'd been strong enough to carry his weight and Marta's, too, Bethel wouldn't be in this position. As he searched for the right words to rescue her, she said, "Why . . . I . . . yes, I suppose I am."

Molly exhaled a relieved sigh. "Good, 'cause my father sure could use one." Leaning around Matthew, she explained: "He knows how to unclog the kitchen drain and shoe a horse, and fix the tractor and his truck and even broken fence hinges, but cooking and cleaning or laundry?" Molly exhaled a loud sigh. "Let's just say that getting you for a wife is his best fix yet!"

Aaron gripped the wheel tighter still, bracing for whatever character-revealing flaw Molly might blurt out next.

"What a magnificent view," Bethel said. "Mountains. Blue skies. Puffy white clouds. Why, it reminds me of the picture postcards in the revolving rack at my father's store."

He glanced into the rearview mirror and saw that the width of her lovely smile proved the sincerity of her words.

"I imagine all of you thank God daily for blessing you with such beauty."

Whispered yesses and of courses followed the comment. And then Molly wanted to know, "Was your father's store big?"

"Not really. It took up the first floor of our house, and we used the shed and basement to stock products that didn't fit on the shelves."

"Finally!" Molly said. "Something the Old Order Nappanee people have in common with us! A lot of people in Pleasant Valley have shops inside their houses, too."

Aaron grinned to himself and waited to hear what short-comings his little girl would reveal about the neighbors.

Instead, she brought Bethel's attention to colorful signs that invited locals and tourists alike to shop for quilts, baked goods, bicycles, homemade candies, and more.

"See that great big sign there? The one that says 'Bontrager's Mill'? That is my father's sawmill. He built it before I was born, and runs it, all by himself." Leaning forward, she rested a hand on Aaron's shoulder. "It is the best sawmill in all of Maryland, right, Daed!"

Aaron patted her hand. "I would not go that far, but we do all right, despite the competition. That's due to the fact that we have good help. Your uncle Karl. The Miller brothers. The Schwartz boys and the rest all share in our success."

Now, Bethel leaned forward slightly. "Perhaps in a day or two, you can give me a tour. I would love to learn how boards are made from trees."

The suggestion was a welcome distraction from Molly's revelations. "It is only a short walk from the house to the mill, so unless I am—"

"There it is," Molly interrupted. "Our house . . . your new home! I can hardly wait to show you around."

But *Aaron* could wait. Two years of neglect had taken their toll on the place. Marta had never developed a knack for growing flowers, but she'd kept the weeds from climbing the foundation and fence posts, and creeping over the front walk. He wouldn't have called her a fastidious housekeeper, either, but he'd always gone to work in clean clothes, and never came home to a sink full of dirty dishes.

None of that was true today, and he was in no hurry to see Bethel's reaction to the place.

He took his time parking in his usual spot at the top of the horseshoe drive. Took his time walking around to the back of the pickup, too. Molly, by comparison, hadn't matured enough to feel embarrassed by their home. She raced up the walk and flung open the door.

"Come in, Beth! *Wellkumm!*"

Sam led Matthew inside, and for a moment, Bethel stood on the porch, almost as if crossing the threshold, not their upcoming marriage, had the power to cement her future. Aaron, just behind her, watched as she stepped tentatively onto the small braided rug just inside the door. Her shoulders sagged and she pressed a small hand to her chest. Shocked by the disarray, no doubt, and the thought made him wince.

"My, my, my," she said, and removed her cap. "What a big, bright, sunny room."

He couldn't see her face, but Molly's wide smile told him that Bethel had not winced. Perhaps her eyesight was poor, and she couldn't see the mugs, plates, and flatware scattered on the end tables. Maybe arriving in this new place had overwhelmed her so much that she hadn't noticed winter boots, jackets, and hats still strewn across chair arms, the sofa, even the floor.

And maybe Bishop Fisher had been right, and this decision was God's will, after all. He was still smiling a bit at the possibility when she walked right up to him and relieved him of her bag.

"You have a meeting, as I recall. There is no need to worry. I am sure Molly will show me around."

"Oh, yes," the girl agreed. "I'm happy to!"

Bethel patted the tiny satchel suitcase. "Then, just as soon as I have found a place for my things, I will get busy around here."

She looked around, and Aaron would have sworn he saw her flinch. And who could blame her, faced with the daunting work that lay ahead? But, just as quickly as her dread appeared, it disappeared.

"May I fix you some lunch before you leave, Mr. Bontrager?"

"No, but thanks." In her shoes, he'd want to get rid of him, too, the sooner, the better! "We had a big breakfast on the way to the station."

"All right, then . . ."

During their final get-acquainted phone call, he'd asked her age, and she'd said twenty-eight. Although she stood chin up and shoulders back, he found it hard to believe. Soft curls had escaped her bun and now framed her delicate face, and Aaron caught himself reaching out to tuck them behind her ear. He slapped the hand to the back of his neck, instead.

"Supper will be ready at five, unless you prefer to eat sooner. Or later."

"Five is fine." He gave a quick nod and faced the door. "Sam, don't forget to feed the chickens and the goats. And Molly, take Matthew with you when you check on Domino's feed and water."

"I thought stuff like that was *her* job now," the boy grumbled.

Aaron was about to remind Sam that he'd promised to treat Bethel with respect when she said, "Tomorrow, first thing, I would like you to do me a favor, Samuel, and show me around, teach me how to properly care for each animal. I promise to give you my full, undivided attention, so that you will not have to do it again."

Sam bobbed his head. "Well. Okay."

"Right now, though, I think I will straighten up around here." She paused, frowned a bit. "Do you have a root cellar?"

"Yes," Molly said, "but it's a scary, dirty place. No one has been down there in months and months."

Beth waved away the warning. "As long as I can find a few things to fix for supper, that will not matter."

"You're going down there?" Sam asked. "*Alone?*"

"Unless you want to fetch some vegetables for me . . ."

The boy grinned. "No, that's okay."

Was it possible that, already, Bethel had begun to thaw his son's icy attitude?

Aaron was half in, half out the back door when he said, "If you need anything, the kids know how to reach me on my cell phone." He tipped an imaginary hat and added, "See you at five."

Donning his hat as he approached the truck, he heard her say, "Where can I find a big basket, Molly? I will need something to hold all these . . . *things* as I pick them up."

He pumped the gas and turned the key in the ignition, and couldn't help thinking yet again that maybe, just maybe, bringing Bethel to Pleasant Valley *was* God's will.

"Let it be so," he prayed, and turned onto the road. "Please, Lord, let it be so."


Molly pushed one of six chairs into place under the round oak table. "This is our kitchen."

Beth grasped the handle of the refrigerator. "We did not have one of these in Nappanee."

"Fair warning," the girl said. "Last time I opened it, the stink of rotting oranges nearly made me faint."

The prospect was enough to stop Beth in her tracks. There'd be time to peek inside after she'd donned her housedress and work apron.

"Sorry about all those dirty dishes." Molly plucked a glass from the top of the heap and turned on the faucet. "Daed asked me to wash them, but we left for the restaurant so early, there wasn't time." She gulped the water, ran the back of her hand across her lips, then held out the filmy, fingerprinted tumbler. "Are you thirsty?"

As a matter of fact, she was. But not thirsty enough to drink from *that!* "Thank you, but I should probably get to work."

"Okay." The girl put the glass back into the sink and pointed to the room behind Beth. "That is our parlor." She stood in front of a big leather chair. "Daed's," she said, patting its arm. "Very comfortable. If you pull that handle, a footrest pops up!"

At the bottom of the stairs, Molly opened the first of two side-by-side doors. Coats, scarves, hats, and mittens spilled onto the girl's shoes, and it took three kicks to stuff everything back inside. She opened the second door. "Daed calls this wasted space. Maem called it a powder room." Striking a stiff-backed pose, she tried to emulate her mother's voice. "'There ought to be one clean place for our guests,' she used to say."

Beth was tempted to hold her nose. "There is nothing

here that cannot be fixed with elbow grease." *And time. Bleach. And a stiff scrub brush . . .*

"There are two more bathrooms upstairs."

Karl had told her that Aaron Bontrager was well-set, financially, but three bathrooms . . . indoors?

At the top of the stairs, Molly said, "This is where Matthew and Sam sleep."

Rumpled bedcovers, dingy curtains hanging from bent curtain rods, wooden toys, and clothing covered the floorboards, making the room seem small and dark. In two hours, she estimated, the room could look big and bright again.

Things were only slightly better across the hall in Molly's room. Another hour's work, minimum.

The girl patted her mattress. "This is where you will sleep. Until the wedding, anyway. Daed said I could pile quilts and blankets on the floor and make a . . . a pallet I think he called it, and sleep there."

Even if the linens hadn't looked as though they hadn't been laundered in months, Beth couldn't in good conscience take the child's bed. "Thank you, Molly, but *I* will sleep on the pallet."

The girl's eyebrows disappeared under blond waves. "But why?"

"I appreciate that you are all trying to be good hosts, but I will be fine on the—"

"Host?" Molly echoed. "That would make you a guest, and Daed said you're family. Family members should have their own beds!"

"Technically, I will not be family until after the wedding." The girl had said *wellkumm* and had tried hard to prove she'd meant it. Smiling, Beth said, "I will be fine until then."

"When will it be?" Molly asked and led the way to the end of the hall.

"That is something, I suppose, that your father and I will need to discuss with your bishop."

"He'll be your bishop soon, too." She opened the door on her left. "The main bathroom," she announced. "We *all* have to share it. Lucky you. After the wedding, you'll get to use Daed's bathroom." Wrinkling her nose again, Molly pointed out fingerprints on the mirror, toothpaste streaks in the sink, and wet towels on the once-white tile floor. "The boys are very, *very* messy."

Molly hadn't exaggerated. *Another hour,* Beth thought. "Do not worry. I will clean it up and make sure it stays clean enough . . . for a *girl.*"

Molly clasped both hands under her chin, and beaming, said, "Oh, Beth, I think I'll love having you here!"

In time, Beth hoped she'd feel the same way. Nodding at the door on the girl's right, she said, "Is that your father's room?"

Opening it, Molly stepped inside. "Soon, it'll be your room, too. You can come in!"

Beth looked from the neatly made bed to the bare dresser top and the night table that held one small lamp. A warm puff of wind parted the plain white curtains, inviting a ray of sunshine inside. Beth's gaze followed it to the big wardrobe across the way, and she wondered what was inside. As if in answer to her unasked question, Molly opened the double doors to expose black trousers, hanging from three wooden hangers. Beside them, two white shirts and two blue. A short wool coat. Hooks held spare suspenders, and on the shelf above, a wide-brimmed black hat, another made of straw. And on the floor, two pairs of clean black boots. Odd, she thought as she used the toe of her shoe to straighten the small braided rug beside his bed, that he'd put such effort into keeping his space clean and orderly, but let the rest of the house fall into disarray. But, as Molly had pointed out, this would soon be Beth's room, too. Perhaps he'd cleaned it in preparation for her arrival.

"As you can see," Molly said, "Daed is a neatnik." Moving closer, she whispered, "Can I trust you with a secret?"

"Of course . . ."

"*I* think the reason he spends so much time at the mill is because he can't stand the mess in the rest of the house."

During the initial phone call that set everything in motion, Karl had told her that Bontrager often complained that he'd grown weary of nagging the children to pick up after themselves. "There are only so many hours in the day," he'd said, "and Aaron can't run the mill and the house, too." Guilt combined with frustration, her cousin added, left his brother-in-law in a perpetual state of confusion.

Now, Molly patted the threadbare handles of Beth's bag. "Let me show you where to put your things." She made her way back down the hall, opened the top drawer of her bureau and the wardrobe door, and said, "Would you like me to help?"

Empty hangers dangled from a wooden dowel in the wardrobe, more than enough to hold the few items Beth had brought. "It can wait. Right now, I should get busy in the kitchen." She paused. "Sam said there is ham in your refrigerator?"

"*Our* refrigerator. And yes, there is ham, but it might be a little crusty. Daed always forgets to cover things."

"How long ago did he bake it?"

"He didn't. Groosmammi sent it home with us after Sunday dinner."

Sunday . . . three days ago, Beth thought. "I am sure that I can salvage enough for supper."

She left her bag at the foot of Molly's bed and followed the girl again, this time, into the kitchen. The girl hadn't exaggerated about the condition of the meat, but God willing, a sharp knife lay at the bottom of the piled-high sink, and Beth could cut away the dried meat.

"Would you mind showing me to the root cellar?"

"Yes, but . . ." Molly shivered. "Are you afraid of the dark?"

"Only if there are spider webs!"

"Oh, there are. Lots and lots of them!" A nervous giggle escaped her lips. "I will find one of Daed's flash-lights. Maem's broom, too."

Somehow, the girl managed to find both amid the chaos, and as they walked outside, Beth said, "While I clean up and get something on the stove, you should go outside and play while you can. I saw storm clouds over the mountains as we parked in the driveway. You will be stuck inside if they move this way."

"If they do, it's all right. We love running around in the rain."

"All right, but we will keep a close eye on the sky, because—"

"Oh yes. Lightning is very dangerous. Last summer, a

bolt hit Sam's friend Adam during a baseball game. Knocked him right out of his shoes, and his hair was smoking when the grownups carried him off the field!"

"Dear me," Beth said. "Is he all right now?"

"Oh yes. Although his mother likes to say it was a blessing in disguise, because now she can blame the lightning for his crazy behavior, instead of her mothering skills!"

Laughing quietly, Beth followed her out back, where they found the boys, crawling along on the low, gnarled branch of a huge oak tree.

"I know what you're thinking . . ." Molly began.

Beth said, "You do?"

"You want to tell them to be careful."

"Why yes, I do!"

"Don't bother. They won't listen, anyway. Well, Matthew might, but only if Sam does, too. And Sam . . ." She raised her hands, let them slap against her sides, as if to say, *He's impossible.*

Beth made her way up the long, weedy flagstone path. In the days to come, she'd clean it up, too, and if she could find flowers to transplant . . .

She spotted the slanted cellar doors and gave the top one a hard tug. Its hinges squealed in protest as a musty odor rose up from the dark. Bending at the waist, Beth squinted into the gloom. "How long since anyone has been down there?"

"I don't know. Years, maybe. Once, Maem came up covered in cobwebs and told Daed that from now on, if he wanted something from down there, he'd have to get it himself." The girl paused. "Stella went down there a few times. Once, she threw out a whole bunch of jars, and

Daed wasn't very happy about that . . . until she said 'Fine! Pick them from the trash and poison your children!'"

"And did she replace them with freshly canned foods?"

"Oh yes! She made them herself. But . . ." She shrugged. "But no one has been down there since before the twins were born."

Beth hoped Bontrager's sister had dated the jars. Lifting her skirt, she eased onto the top step and pushed the button of his flashlight. Nothing.

"Batteries must be dead," Molly said.

"Is there a lamp?"

"There's a light bulb, but you have to pull a string to turn it on."

Holding her breath, she descended the remaining four steps, and the instant her feet hit the dirt floor, spider webs clung to her cheeks and hair. As she flapped wildly to free herself of them, the back of one hand hit the string that, according to Molly, would turn on the light. One tug was all it took to brighten the space. Turning slowly, she inspected sagging wood shelves that held dusty jars of beans, corn, tomatoes, and something that resembled peaches. There were bins, too, filled with onions, carrots, and potatoes that had sprouted foot-long eyes. "Amazing," she muttered, "how quickly dust accumulates!" *And how quickly spiders work!* Making a sack from her apron, she filled it with vegetables and jars, turned out the light, and hurried up the steps. Oh, how good it felt when the sunshine hit her face and the breeze riffled her hair!

"Told you it was creepy down there."

"And you were right!" Hugging the apron's contents to her chest, she stooped to close the cellar doors, taking care not to loosen the jars' seals. Straightening, Beth noticed

Molly grinning at her brothers. "I will be all right on my own. You should join them."

"Really?"

"Just be sure to keep an eye on those clouds . . ."

The girl skipped toward the boys, and Beth made her way back to the kitchen to face the mountain of greasy pots that teetered precariously on the counter. After placing the jars and vegetables on the table, she faced the stove. It probably hadn't seen a proper scrubbing since before Mrs. Bontrager's death.

Mrs. Bontrager.

Soon, it would be her name, too . . .

She glanced down at her apron, at grimy cobwebs and streaks of dirt left behind by the potatoes. A little scrubbing would take care of that. But bacon grease and . . . only the good Lord knew what else clung to the pots and plates and spoons . . . might not. Beth hustled upstairs, closed Molly's bedroom door, and changed into her gray work dress and apron.

Next, she searched for cleaning supplies, and found them on a lopsided shelf unit between the laundry machines. Each appliance boasted knobs, dials, and buttons. How would she ever learn which to push and what to turn!

But that, like the dirt and debris in every room, was a problem for another day.

Beth grabbed a galvanized bucket, dumped a scoop of soap powder into it, added a bottle of bleach and a scrub brush. After tearing up two old towels to use as cleaning rags, she added them to the bucket and headed back upstairs. As her feet hit each step, she made a mental list of things she'd need in the days to come: A lesson in operating every gadget powered by electricity. Oil for the squeaky cellar door hinges, and insecticide to eradicate spiders . . . and other bugs they'd been feeding on down there in the dark. A small hand shovel for digging up and transplanting flowers, and a watering can or hose to ensure they'd take root.

Once she'd placed the bucket beside the canned vegetables, Beth rolled up her sleeves. Nothing else could happen until she got those dishes done.

Two hours later, she stood back to admire her work, and noticed that the room had grown dark, thanks to menacing, low-hanging clouds to the west. Lightning sliced through them, followed by rib-rattling peals of thunder. Stepping onto the porch, she shouted, "Children, come inside, quickly!"

She half expected Sam to gripe and groan, but he'd seen the bright flashes, too, and signaled his siblings. "Inside, you two, before you end up like Adam Stoltz!"

Wind bent the trees and sent leaves and twigs skittering across the shin-deep grass. It tousled the children's hair, too, and as they entered the kitchen, it slammed the screen door behind them.

Matthew clung to Molly's hand as Sam sniffed the air. "What is that smell?"

Molly sniffed, too. "It's bleach," she said. "Our Beth has been cleaning!"

*Our Beth*. She rather liked the sound of that.

Sam walked around the kitchen, inspecting the shining stove, the gleaming pots that lined the cupboard's low shelves, the sparkling dishes and tumblers neatly stacked behind the china cupboard's glass doors. "What's that in the pot?" he asked, nodding toward the cast iron skillet.

She'd trimmed the ham, cubed and arranged it over thin-sliced onions, potatoes, and carrots, and topped it all with dumplings. Something told her that with this boy, the less said, the better. "Supper. It is nearly five o'clock, and your father will be home soon. Go upstairs, please, all three of you, and wash your hands and faces."

Beth stopped his intended protest with, "You have two choices. Wash up, or take a bath."

"Shouldn't-a showed her the tub," he whispered to Molly. "Where she comes from, they have to pump water out of a well, carry pots to the stove, then dump hot water into a horse trough."

Molly made her way to the staircase. "That's the way the Yoders do it. Not *everyone* in Pleasant Valley has indoor plumbing, you know."

"Yeah, well, now that *your Beth* knows about the tub, she'll probably make us take baths every day."

Molly paused on the landing and stood, hands on hips. "Can't you ever do as you're told without moaning and groaning?"

Sam went around her. "Wasn't moaning."

"Yes, you were."

"Wasn't."

"Were too."

For a few blessed minutes, all was quiet in the Bontrager house. All too soon, though, thunder in the sky blended with the thuds of young feet, pounding down the steps.

Molly knelt on the parlor sofa and peered out the windows behind it. "I thought I heard Daed's truck."

"He needs a new muffler," Sam teased, "but not so bad

that it sounds like thunder!" He faced Beth. "It stopped raining. We're gonna play catch while we wait for him."

His expression made it clear: He wasn't asking permission. The screen door banged as he went outside. Banged twice more as Matthew and Molly joined him. Beth carried a stack of dishes to the table and put them down harder than intended. *Patience,* she told herself. *He's just a child* . . . In time, he'd figure out that accepting her wasn't a betrayal of his mother. She'd make it her business to learn as much as possible about Marta and do her best to keep the woman's memory alive. With God's help, she'd find other ways to win the boy over, too. *Not* sitting directly across from Bontrager might be a good place to start.

At home in Nappanee, her father's seat near the back door was known as "the head." Her mother's seat, at the opposite end, "the foot." Not an easy feat at Bontrager's oval table.

"Just pretend it *is,*" she muttered, and positioned the plates accordingly: Matthew on his father's left, with Sam beside him; Molly to his right; and finally, Beth. Leaving the sixth chair empty should send the message, loud and clear.

Now that the table was set, Beth stepped onto the back porch. While looking for cleaning supplies, she'd spotted two bentwood rocking chairs in the basement. After scrubbing them, she'd carried them outside and arranged them on the freshly swept floorboards. She'd found a small table down there, too, and placed it between the chairs. It would have looked lovely with a small doily and a potted plant on it, but for now, the dented watering can, filled with daisies she'd plucked from the weeds out front would have to do.

As she had after cleaning the kitchen, Beth stood back to admire her work. *You will have to pray twice as long as usual at bedtime,* she thought, *to atone for the sin of pride.* Lost in thought, she didn't realize just how far back she'd stepped. If Bontrager hadn't shown up when he did, Beth would have toppled down the painted steps. His quick reflexes saved her from scrapes and bruises, but didn't spare her from feeling like a nincompoop.

Strong hands gripped her biceps and Beth blamed gravity for the way she leaned into him.

He turned her to face him, but didn't let go. "Are you all right?"

She stared into his eyes, bigger and bluer and longer-lashed than any she'd ever seen, trying to decide if he was annoyed or concerned.

"I am fine." *Stupid. Clumsy. But fine* . . . Why hadn't she heard his truck making its way up the drive? Especially since, as Molly had pointed out, the muffler rumbled like thunder!

The question went unanswered as she watched his gaze, sliding from her hairline to her eyebrows, from her cheeks to her lips. Instinctively, she licked them, and took a deliberate step back. When he released her, Beth noticed a distinct chill where his big, warm hands had been.

Matthew appeared, and wrapped both arms around Bontrager's thighs. He tousled the boy's hair and, smiling, said, "Something smells good. Is supper ready, then?"

Beth smoothed her apron. Smoothed her hair, too, and hoped he hadn't noticed her trembling fingertips. "It is."

"Should I call the children?"

Nodding, she said, "And if you would, ask them, please, to wash up. Again."

One eyebrow lifted at the word. "Again?"

"It was raining. Pouring, actually, when they came in from playing earlier. I asked them to clean up a bit. And they did. But then the rain stopped, and . . ." Beth remembered the way Sam had announced his plans to go outside, like a boss issuing an order to an employee. *Which is precisely what you are.* Would that change after the wedding?

Bontrager said, "I ought to prepare myself for protestations then. . . ."

"I will put supper on the table," she said, and hurried inside. Why she'd expected to feel safer here than on the porch, Beth didn't know. During her hours of hard work, she'd touched every piece of furniture, every pot and pan and eating utensil, and yet it all looked unfamiliar and unwelcoming.

"Come inside, kids. It's time to eat!"

The suddenness of his shout startled her, and cupping both elbows, Beth willed herself to calm down. Silently, she prayed, searching for confirmation that she was right where she ought to be.

*Lord, bless this house and those who call it home. And open their hearts to me, Father,* she added silently, *as proof that I am here in obedience to Your will . . .*

. . . and not because Beth's secret prayer, for as long as she could remember, was to feel that she *belonged.*

# Chapter Three

Aaron looked around the porch, taking in the two rocking chairs and a table Bethel had scrubbed and carried up from the basement. Shortly after Matthew's birth, Marta had insisted that he stow them down there, because "I haven't time to dust the old things every time the wind blows." And although he'd miss sipping his morning coffee out there, he'd obliged.

Bethel must have an eye for detail, for she centered the old watering can on the table and filled it with daisies. The effect was welcoming.

"Looks good," he said as Matthew joined him on the porch.

Peering through the screen door, Aaron took a moment to survey the changes she'd wrought in the kitchen . . . the empty white sink, sparkling tumblers, shiny flatware and stoneware bowls on a sharply creased tablecloth, the sweet scent of ham in the air.

Then he led Matthew down the porch steps. "What do you say, little man, can you call your sister and brother to supper . . . save me from bellowing again like a bull moose?"

The boy looked up, then shook his head and hid behind one hand.

*How long can you hold your silence, son?* Squatting to make himself child-sized, Aaron rested his hands on the boy's shoulders. "Remember when you used to beg me to take you fishing down by the creek?" he began, smiling. "And how you'd go on and on until I said yes?"

One shoulder rose slightly and the child nodded, once.

"You'd talk and talk all the way there. After we got there, too, even after I said 'Shh! You'll scare off all the fish!' And then you'd get a bite, and scare every bird from every tree, yelling, 'I got one, Daed . . . I got one!' Remember that?"

Matthew glanced toward the big oak, where Sam and Molly dangled from the tire swings.

"Look at them, hanging upside down like silly monkeys." Matthew grinned a bit.

"If it wasn't suppertime, you'd be right there, swinging with them, wouldn't you?"

Another silent nod.

Aaron gathered him close. "Ah, son, do you know how much I miss hearing the sound of your voice?"

The children ran up just then. "What are you two doing?" Molly said, dropping a kiss on his cheek.

"Time to eat," he told her, straightening. "And if it tastes as good as it smells, we're in for a treat."

Sam went in first, and after a quick look around, faced Beth. "You did all this, all by yourself, in . . ." He glanced at the clock. ". . . in *three hours*?"

Closer to five, Aaron thought, since he'd left for the mill. Still, he had to agree with the boy. If she could get this much done in one afternoon—

"With the right mindset, a person can accomplish much."

The kids stood side by side, considering her simple statement: Sam shrugged, as if to say *whatever.* Molly nodded, and so did Matthew. A bit early to call their reactions a breakthrough, or proof that Bethel would be a good addition to the family, but not too early to hope.

"Wash up for supper, kids. I don't know about you, but I'm as hungry as a bear in spring."

The children formed a short line at the sink, waiting their turn at soap and water. He was tempted to stand behind them, so that he could hear their whispered comments.

"So, how was it?" he asked as Sam dried his hands.

"How was what?"

"Being able to use the sink without starting an avalanche of dirty dishes."

For a second, there, Aaron thought the boy might commend Beth's efforts. But just as quickly as it appeared, his appreciative expression vanished. "That's why she's here, right?"

Aaron considered his options: Deliver a stern reprimand. Ignore the boy's rude words. Deal with his disrespect later.

"Thank you, Bethel," he said instead, "for your hard work today. It has been a long time—a very long time— since our house looked like a home."

"Yes, thank you, Beth," Molly chimed in.

Even little Matthew was smiling.

Sam rolled his eyes, then began pulling out a kitchen chair.

"No, Samuel," Beth said softly, "that is the head of the table. Your father's seat."

"There can't be a 'head' at a round table." He slid the chair out farther. "I sit here all the time."

"Fibber," Molly said. "Nobody sits anywhere all the time, because the table is always so full of junk, we can't eat here!"

Aaron was about to put a stop the nonsensical bickering when Bethel's fingers tapped the chairback, one seat to Sam's left. "Matthew will sit here, with you beside him. Molly, across from him. And I will sit next to her."

She'd left an empty space, directly across from Aaron's . . . for Marta, he presumed. *What a thoughtful thing to do,* he mused.

Bethel didn't wait for their approval or agreement. Instead, she went to the stove, then unceremoniously placed the big skillet on the trivet that sat dead-center on the table. Using the hem of her apron, she removed the lid. "Please, have a seat."

He half expected Sam to pipe up with some smart-alecky crack, and Aaron was mildly surprised when the boy helped his little brother get settled before sitting down himself.

One of the bishop's sermons came to mind, based on a verse from Psalms: "I am fearfully and wonderfully made." He'd been too young, perhaps even too self-centered to understand that it referenced the incredible miracle of God's creation of man . . . and woman. After witnessing what Bethel had accomplished in such a short time, and now watching her add a basket of golden biscuits to the table, he appreciated its meaning.

"Pass your bowls to me," she said, one hand extended, the other holding a serving spoon, "I will fill them for you."

What was wrong with the men of Nappanee, judging her unmarriable, simply because she walked with a slight limp!

She'd turned on the light above the sink, and it drew his attention to the way she'd displayed Marta's small collection of salt and pepper shakers on the windowsill. . . . The white ceramic rooster and chicken. Mug-sized aluminum tins, one engraved with a large P, the other, an S. Tall wooden grinders with faded labels that said SALT and PEPPER. Each had been scrubbed free of years' worth of grease and grime, and now shone bright from their new perch.

"Mr. Bontrager?"

One hand still extended, she waited for him to pass his bowl, first to Molly, then to her.

Now that the family had been served, Bethel sat down and, eyes closed, bowed her head and folded her hands.

The children looked confused, and it shamed him to acknowledge how long it had been since he'd set the example of thanking God for the food He'd provided. Aaron mouthed, "Pray," and one by one, they emulated Bethel's actions. Was it yet another reason to believe he'd made the right decision? Or proof of the old adage, "If something seems too good to be true, it usually is"?

*Lord, clear my mind of such thoughts!* he prayed. Their relationship wouldn't include physical love, but let it not begin on a foundation of doubt and suspicion. . . .

"I noticed that you have started work on a tree house," Bethel said to Sam. "How soon before it is complete?"

"I need more lumber. Nails, too." He met Aaron's eyes. "But I have some chores to do before I get them."

"Ah, I see . . ." Beth buttered a biscuit and, after taking a sip of milk, said, "Molly, I saw a little quilt in your room and—"

"*Our* room," the girl corrected, smiling. "Until the wedding, that is." She looked at Aaron. "When will that be, Daed?"

He felt the heat of a blush creeping into his cheeks as four pairs of eyes waited for his reply.

"We, ah, Bethel and I need to speak with the bishop about that. But my guess is that he'll schedule it soon. A week, two at most."

Now, the children stared at Bethel, no doubt to read her reaction.

And she continued as if Molly hadn't interrupted. "Is the quilt for a doll?"

"Oh, no. It will be a gift." Hiding a giggle behind one hand, she met Aaron's eyes. "For someone very special."

She'd started the project a week ago, upon learning that he intended to add Bethel to the family. "It will be scary for her," Molly had said, "living in a place where she doesn't know anyone." The quilt, she'd explained, would help Bethel feel less afraid. "And if she gets homesick, she can look at it and know that we care about her."

Aaron thought she must have inherited the kind-and-thoughtful trait from his mother, who never passed up a chance to do a good deed. *Lord knows she didn't get that from you. . . .* He hadn't done or said anything to welcome Bethel. *Too late?* he wondered.

"The stew is delicious," he said. "And so are the biscuits."

"Why . . . thank you."

The surprise in her voice and on her face made it clear that she hadn't expected compliments. Karl had told him that her father and brother treated her like property. Hearing that, Aaron had made up his mind to make sure she never felt that way under his roof . . . under the roof that, soon, would be *theirs*.

"I found several jars of peaches in the root cellar and made pie for dessert."

A tiny, happy gasp issued from Matthew. Molly clapped. Even Sam was smiling as he said, "We only have dessert after Sunday dinner, and on holidays."

"I thought . . ." She folded her hands on the table. "This has been a . . . a very . . . a challenging day for all of us. So I thought a special treat would make us all feel better."

"Challenging?" Sam echoed.

"Well, yes." She looked directly into his eyes. "It is not every day that a stranger comes into your home and starts changing things—including where you sit at the table— even before she is officially a family member."

The boy paused. Mulling over what she'd said, Aaron decided. And then he tensed. What curt, hurtful thing would he say in response?

"Yeah, you make a good point." He glanced over his shoulder, to where the pie sat on the cupboard. "Is it still warm?"

"Yes, I am sure that it is."

"Too bad we don't have any ice cream," Molly said, sighing.

Bethel winked. "Milk will do in a pinch. Especially if I warm it up a bit . . . with a spoonful of sugar, maybe a sprinkling of cinnamon . . ."

It seemed to Aaron that she'd succeeded in making the "way to a man's stomach" saying work with children, too, and the idea made him smile.

"There will be a price to pay for the dessert," she said, pointer finger aimed at the ceiling. "All of you must bring any soiled laundry lying around into the basement, so I can sort it. And one of you needs to teach me how to use the automatic machines. We had nothing like them in Nappanee. . . ."

"I will teach you," Molly said.

"And the rest of us will gather up the dirty clothes." Meeting each child's eyes, he added, "Won't we, kids?"

"Are any of you familiar with using the iron? I have never seen one quite like it."

"Good grief," Sam said. "How did you wash and iron clothes where you're from!"

While Beth described the way she'd done things in Indiana, Aaron sat back, pushing away his empty bowl as outside, the storm churned, whirling dust and dried leaves into miniature cyclones that skittered across the porch and pelted the screen door. Darkness shrouded the house, but thanks to Bethel's forethought, the kitchen and parlor lights wrapped them in a warm yellow glow. Was she feeling a hint of pride at having figured out how to turn them on?

The question made him smile. But on its heels came a troublesome thought: Yes, it seemed that Bethel had the drive and determination to turn the Bontragers' chaos into order. Could she also calm the confusion beating in the hearts of his motherless children? Could her presence calm his own harried heart?

It was a selfish thought. Aaron looked forward to some time alone, to examine his conscience and ask forgiveness of the Almighty.

"Would you like milk on yours, too, Mr. Bontrager?"

It seemed impossible that his mind had wandered long enough for her to heat and sweeten the milk, slice the pie, and deliver generous servings to the children. The *oohs* and *ahhs* that followed their first bites prompted his distracted "Yes, yes, that sounds good."

"Coffee, too? I made a pot earlier. . . ."

She'd filled the old percolator, used only during power outages. Easier than trying to figure out the coffee maker, he decided.

"That might be nice."

She poured milk into the kids' glasses, then poured a mug of coffee for him. Its rich brown hue reminded him of polished, aged hickory.

"Black?" she asked, placing it at the ten o'clock spot beside his pie.

"How did you know?"

Beth's back was to him when she returned the pot to its burner. Too bad, Aaron thought, because he would have liked to see the expression that accompanied her to-the-point "You strike me as a no-nonsense man."

Life promised to be a whole lot different in the days, months—*years*—to come.

*God, grant me the strength to endure it in accordance with Your will. . . .*

\* \* \*

Last time she'd peeked into the parlor, she'd seen Matthew in Aaron's lap, with Molly and Sam pressing close to his sides, listening as he read from *The Long Winter.* As a girl, she'd read it herself, and credited Laura Ingalls Wilder with encouraging her love of books. It was good to know these children were being raised in a similar atmosphere, and that Bontrager wouldn't have a problem with her continuing the tradition.

After putting away the last of the dishes, she swept up biscuit crumbs under Matthew's chair. As she bent to brush them into the dustpan, Beth felt the all too familiar ache in her right leg. Experience had taught her that pushing herself to get lots done in little time would cause cramping long into the night. When it happened, she'd remind herself of how the Bontragers had gobbled up their supper. Dessert, too.

"Why are you limping?"

For the second time that day, his voice startled her. This time, she nearly dropped the metal dustpan.

A nervous giggle popped from her lips. "I hope to find a bell as I continue organizing your house."

Both eyebrows rose high on his forehead. "A bell?"

"You know, the way farmers 'bell' a cat?"

"Oh." He grinned. "I'll try to make more noise entering rooms from now on." He relieved her of the broom and dustpan, stood them in the corner. "Know what I hope?"

Beth had no idea.

"That, as you continue organizing, you'll think of this as your house, too." He paused. "Because it is."

"I . . ." In her opinion, that would take a small miracle, but he looked so sincere that she said, "Thank you."

Molly skipped into the room. "What's going on?"

"Do you have time," Beth said, "to teach me how to use the laundry machines?"

"Now?" The girl sounded as surprised as her father looked. "But it's nearly bedtime!"

"For you, maybe, but I have never required the usual amount of sleep." Beth hid both hands in her apron pockets. "I might as well make good use of my awake time, getting started on the laundry."

"But . . ." Molly looked up at Bontrager. "She asked us to bring our dirty clothes down to the basement. Should we do it . . . *now*?"

"Yes, you should." He took her hand, led her into the parlor. "I'll help."

And with that, the children followed him upstairs.

Beth passed the next twenty minutes by refolding the afghan they'd mussed while reading, by repositioning lamps and doilies on the end tables, and rearranging candlesticks on the mantel. Tomorrow, she decided, frowning at the layer of dust around the woodstove and hearth, she'd shovel out the firebox and empty the kindling basket. Bontrager had made a point of telling her that, all too soon, winter would be upon them. She might as well be prepared.

Heavy footsteps drew her attention to the staircase, and she saw Bontrager carrying a basket piled so high with clothes that he could barely see around it. The children followed, each carrying armfuls of laundry. As they paraded by on their way to the basement, Molly said, "I hope you weren't planning to get all of this done before morning!"

Beth joined them in the basement in time to see each empty his or her arms.

"This is what you do," Molly began, and opened the washing machine. "Turn this knob to choose the size of the load. Large, most of the time. This knob," she said, pointing, "sets the water temperature. Warm for most things. Hot for whites." Wrinkling her nose, she looked to Bontrager for help. "Anything else, Daed?"

Smirking, he said, "Um, Start?"

"Oh yes! Then you push this button! But first, you put soap powder into the tub. One scoop for each load. And then you add the dirty clothes. And then you make sure the lid is shut. And *then* you push Start." She smiled at Beth. "Got it?"

She'd already started sorting: White aprons, shirts, socks, and underclothes. Dark trousers. Molly's dresses. Sleep clothes.

"Yes, I think so."

"It takes about half an hour for the washer to do its job," Molly said. "Then you put the wet clothes in here." She opened the dryer's door. "Throw everything in and slam the door. Turn this knob to fifty minutes, and push Start. If you leave the clothes in there too long, though, they get all wrinkly. And you don't want that to happen, because then you'll have to iron them. I hate, hate, *hate* that job!"

"I see. Thank you for the lesson. You were very thorough!"

Beth wondered how a girl of eight had learned so much about washing clothes. Had Marta taught her? Bontrager's mother or sister?

"All right, kids, upstairs to bed."

"Aw, Daed, can we read another chapter first?"

"One chapter," he told Molly, "then lights out."

Sam exhaled an exaggerated yawn, and Matthew stretched. Had they stayed up past their bedtime? Oh, but she had so many questions! Had Bontrager established fixed rise-and-shine times for his children? What time would he get up every morning? Did he work on Saturdays? Would he like her to pack him a lunch? And when summer ended, would the children attend school in town? If so, would they walk there and back, or ride a bus, like many of the students of Nappanee's Oak Grove School? Did their father see it as his duty to oversee their homework, or would he expect her to help them?

Halfway up the stairs, Molly leaned over the banister. "Will you tuck us in, Beth?"

"Of course, if that is what you want."

"Oh, it is! It is! And you'll listen to our prayers?"

Bontrager had just placed one big foot on the bottom step, and she met his eyes. "Something you prefer to do, yes?"

"I can skip it for one night."

A guilty look skittered across his features. Should she take that to mean he didn't make a practice of hearing the children's bedtime prayers?

She thought of what Bishop Lantz had told her, day before yesterday. "It is a strange and challenging thing you are doing, dear Beth. The children are young. Their father, a confused and, I would expect, lonely man. You must exercise patience as each of you adjusts." The bishop of Nappanee squeezed her hand and added, "I will be praying for all of you."

Beth sighed, and hoped God was listening to Bishop Lantz.

Once the family was out of sight, Beth followed Molly's instructions. When the machine began churning, she whispered, "You did it!" and applauded.

While the machine worked, she'd pass the time in Molly's room. What began as a prayer turned into a litany of quiet questions: Had Beth left a beau in Indiana? Did she have a favorite flower? A favorite color? While they talked, Beth assembled the pallet that would serve as her mattress until . . .

The thought of sharing a bed with Bontrager cut the thought short. *Do not think of it!* she told herself.

When it seemed the girl was ready for sleep, Beth sat on the edge of the bed. Taking Molly's hands into her own, she said, "Thank you, sweet girl, for making my first day so enjoyable."

"And thank *you* for coming here. Daed and the boys might never admit it, but I will: We need you."

"What a lovely thing to say." She finger-combed the bangs from the girl's forehead. "Sleep well, Molly."

As evidenced by the girl's understanding of laundry, Molly had likely assumed many of her mother's duties. Beth hoped that her own presence would encourage the empathetic, too-old-for-her-age girl to relax and enjoy her childhood.

Molly watched as Beth slid her nightclothes from the satchel.

"Are you going to bed now, too?"

"Not just yet. I thought I would change in the basement, so as not to wake you, and add my clothes to the things I will wash."

"Daed says I sleep like a rock, so don't worry. You won't wake me." She rolled onto her side, stretched, then slid under the sheet. In no time, she was fast asleep.

"Good night, Molly, and may God bless you with happy dreams."

Beth tiptoed toward the boys' room. The door was slightly ajar, and she saw Sam on his knees beside Matthew's bed.

"Soft as the voice of an angel," he sang, "breathing a lesson unheard. Hope with a gentle persuasion, whispers a comforting word."

*He* sounded sweet as an angel, Beth thought, clutching her nightclothes to her chest.

"Wait till the darkness is over, wait till the tempest is done," Sam continued. "Hope for the sunshine tomorrow, after the darkness is gone . . ."

What little she knew of the boy told her that if she made her presence known, he'd resent it. Only a boy with a great capacity for love could lull his little brother to sleep with a sweet song.

"May God bless you with happy dreams, too, dear Sam," she whispered, and tiptoed down the stairs.

The creaking floorboards outside the boys' room alerted him to movement across the hall. "Those kids," he muttered, placing his Bible on the chairside table. Evidently, they hadn't taken him seriously when he'd sent them to bed with a ". . . straight to sleep" warning. Determined to repeat the directive, he made his way to his own door. But even before he grasped the knob, Aaron saw Bethel, clutching a small bundle of clothes to her chest as she leaned toward the slight opening. It surprised him a bit to hear his son, perfectly crooning every word of the song that had been handed down from his great-grandmother to his grandmother and mother. Had it brought back happy memories from her own childhood? Was that why she stood so still, eyes closed and smiling serenely?

She straightened, took a step back.

And Aaron, not wanting her to know he'd been eavesdropping, did the same.

When he next peeked through the narrow opening, the hall was empty and quiet, telling him that the boys had settled in for the night. Bethel, on the other hand, had descended the staircase. He knew, because she'd hit every squeaky step.

He looked at the wind-up alarm clock on his nightstand. Ten minutes past ten. After her long trip and the hard work she'd put into getting the kitchen in order, shouldn't she be fast asleep by now?

On the other hand, he thought, settling back into his chair, Bethel had faced so much today: New town . . . and so far, she hadn't met a soul. New home . . . which had been anything but welcoming. New family . . . strangers, from the oldest to the youngest, and not all of them friendly. When overworked or stressed, he couldn't sleep, either.

In the distance, he heard the washing machine's agitator, churning quietly. It didn't seem right for him to relax here in the peaceful familiarity of his room while she toiled away in the basement. It didn't seem fair, either. Aaron made his way downstairs, thinking that, together, they could finish the job in half the time. And while they worked, he'd introduce the subject of the wedding.

Not wanting to frighten her again, he stood at the top of the basement stairway. "Bethel? What are you doing down there?"

She peeked around the railing. "Laundry, Mr. Bontrager."

Looking up at him made her appear smaller, younger than her twenty-eight years. "I thought . . . let me help," he said, joining her.

"Thank you, but the appliances do all the work." Bethel gestured toward the ironing board, where she'd stacked neatly folded towels. "I would not call them speedy machines, but they are getting the job done."

"I can see that." Aaron looked at the dozen or so knee-high piles of dirty clothes on the floor near his feet. He looked up, too, at nails he'd hammered into the support posts to hold extension cords and coils of rope. She'd used them to string a clothesline.

"I am told that electricity is expensive, so once I have caught up with the laundry, I will hang sheets and towels outside." She tilted her head to add, "I did not notice a clothesline out back. . . ."

"There's one at the back of the lot, but it's been so long since anyone used it that it's probably rusty."

"If you have sandpaper, I can—"

"No need for that." She flinched a bit at his terse tone, so he gentled it to say, "I'll build a new one with scrap wood, install it closer to the back door so you won't have to carry the wet clothes so far." The distance, Marta had always said, was the reason she didn't use the existing one, and why she'd insisted that Bertram put his plumbing skills to use, installing pipes in the basement for the washer and dryer. It was enough to wake a sour memory, and he pushed it away by adding, "This will do for the time being. And when the weather keeps you from hanging things outdoors."

She nodded, then lurched when the dryer's buzzer sounded.

Grinning, he walked over to the machine. "I've never liked that noise, either. We can turn it off if you like."

"Oh yes. Please. This place makes me jittery enough without . . ."

She put her back to him and, on her own, found the knob that controlled the buzzer and turned it off. "I am sorry, Mr. Bontrager. I did not mean that as an insult."

"No need for apologies." He watched as she made quick work of folding more towels. "I've been coming down here since I built this house more than twelve years ago," he said as the stacks grew, "and I'm still not used to how . . . creepy it feels."

She laughed a little at that, and again, he was struck by the lovely sound.

"One of these days, I'll hang drywall. Build some proper shelves." Every time he'd offered to make the improvements, Marta had told him not to waste his time, because she'd rather spend the money on quilting materials. Quilting materials that were probably growing moldy in the plastic tubs that lined the side wall.

Aaron blamed the peculiar machinations of the human brain for the negative feelings he'd been having about his wife. In truth, the attitude had begun long before his decision to bring Bethel to Pleasant Valley. In fact, it had begun long before her death, two years ago. Since confirming the wedding plans, however, the negative thoughts had doubled. Tripled, even. That had to stop, immediately, for everyone's sake.

"I'm happy to help, if you'll just tell me what needs doing."

"Really, I only need to wait for the machines to do their jobs. They are slow, but thorough." She smiled. "Thank you for offering." The smile disappeared. "I understand that household chores are my main responsibility here, and hope you do not think I expect your help with them!"

"I think nothing of the kind. And chores," he echoed, "are not the main reason you're here. There are several new housing developments going up in Oakland. Single-family homes, townhouses, apartment complexes . . . so things at the mill have never been busier. It's a sorry excuse, I know, but . . . Filling contractors' orders has kept my men employed and paid my bills, but in the process, I've let too many other things slide. The children, mostly." Aaron tucked both thumbs into his suspenders. "I'm sure that was apparent, immediately."

She blinked a few times. Was she thinking of Sam's surly demeanor and Matthew's refusal to speak?

"They are beautiful children, Mr. Bontrager, blessings from the Almighty. I trust Him to show me ways to reach them, and give each of them what they need, when they need it."

He chuckled. "A good swift kick in the pants from time to time!"

"I know you are joking, but rest assured: I will never, under any circumstances, raise a hand to any of them." Another smile, and then, "Not even Samuel!"

He believed her, and said so. But her disciplinary tactics hadn't been the reason he'd come down here.

Aaron had stored four wooden folding chairs between the furnace and water heater, and he walked to the far end of the basement to fetch two.

"Have a seat," he said, opening one. "Aw, c'mon now, don't look so frightened." He sat across from her. "I thought we could talk for a few minutes about our . . . ah . . . about our future."

"Future?"

"The wedding, of course. It's been nearly a month, now, since we first discussed our, the, um, arrangement."

Was it his imagination, or had she frowned at the word?

"I remember how much my sister Stella talked about her wedding. Not just Stella, but her friends, too. Years of wishing and planning, talking and giggling. It was a relief when each took a husband!"

Aaron didn't know what to make of the faraway look on her face. And then something Karl had said came to mind, about the way the men of Nappanee had decided a woman with a limp wasn't worth their time. Or their respect. And, according to Karl, her father and brother were no better. *You'd best watch your tone* and *your words,* he told himself, *to prove you don't feel the same way about her.*

"Have you given any thought to . . . *ours*?"

"Our wedding?" She blinked a few times. Licked her lips. Took a deep breath. And as she exhaled, relaxed a bit. "I know what I do *not* want. . . ."

He watched, waited, as she searched his face. Looking for proof, perhaps, that he'd respect her wishes.

"I do not want five hundred people in attendance."

"Even if every resident of Pleasant Valley showed up, there wouldn't be that many!"

"In Nappanee, the ceremonies are held in November. It's farm country, and by then, the harvest is over. Everything takes place in the bride's home, starting at eight-thirty in the morning . . . well, the parents of the bride, to be more accurate."

A sermon from the Old and New Testaments, she explained, was followed by hymns from the *Ausbund,* and then simple vows were exchanged.

Vows.

The word echoed in Aaron's memory as he recalled his own: "Can you both confess and believe that God has ordained marriage to be a union between one man and one woman?" Bishop Fisher had asked. "Do you have confidence that the Lord has provided you with this partner?" Both he and Marta had promised to care for one another, to have patience with one another, never to part from the other until God separated them by death. A tall order, he'd thought at the time, because even during the preparation sessions, she'd made no secret of her displeasure with the "no wedding bands" rule. "I will have my way about something. This is *my* wedding after all!" she'd said the day before the ceremony. If he'd known what she had in mind . . . *Oh, who are you kidding? Even then, you couldn't control her!* True to her stubborn, often rebellious nature, Marta had answered yes to Fisher's final question, then sparked a chorus of shocked gasps and whispers of admonishment when she'd pressed a long, passionate kiss to his lips. Even the bishop's hands were shaking as he concluded the ceremony by placing his palm atop their clasped hands.

"I would prefer something small. The church officials, two of us, and the children."

"But . . . Pleasant Valley overflows with friends and family. They will want to share the day with us."

Bethel squared her shoulders. "I would like it better if they shared other things as the years pass."

Compromise, his years with Marta had taught him, accomplished more than bickering.

"What if we keep the ceremony small, and let friends share in the reception, then?"

"I know no one here. It will be so uncomfortable, meeting them for the first time as they deliver food, as they sing throughout the meal. . . ."

He hadn't considered that. "We will have time," Aaron said slowly, "between our meeting with the bishop and the wedding. I could introduce you at Sunday services. And if, for some reason, a few of the community aren't present, then we can visit their houses."

Her shoulders slumped and she stared at her tightly clasped hands. "If that is your wish . . ."

In other words, she'd go along with his decision, even if it hurt. And if the defeated look on her face was any indicator, it would hurt quite a lot.

"It's a relief, don't you think, that we don't go along with the Englishers' honeymoon nonsense."

"Oh, yes. I could never fly in a plane!" She shuddered. "A few years ago, some tourists came into my father's store. I heard them talking about a friend of theirs . . . the woman had fallen overboard from a cruise ship, just two days after her honeymoon began. Can you imagine how devastated her new husband was, losing her at sea that way!"

Aaron was thinking more of the cost of airline tickets, hotel reservations, restaurant food, and transportation to and from the airport, but kept that to himself. He could hear Marta's voice, echoing in the back of his mind: "You pinch pennies so tight, Lincoln cries!" Bethel would find out soon enough if there was any truth to his wife's accusation. *Your* former *wife, Bontrager*! He'd better get used to saying that—to thinking that—or risk hurting Bethel's feelings.

"I suppose we can keep the reception guest count to a minimum." *And maybe invite friends and family to a gathering later, at Thanksgiving or Christmastime.* The house and yard would be presentable by then. It might feel good, letting them see for themselves that he'd made the right decision, bringing Bethel here.

"Will you want your father and brother to attend?"

"No."

Her reply was quick and curt, and seemed final.

"They would consider train fare a waste of money."

"I am happy to purchase their tickets."

She shook her head so hard that a curl came loose from her bun. "That is kind of you, Mr. Bontrager. But even if *I* used the last of my pay to get them here, Daed would never leave the store unattended. Besides, I could not in good conscience subject you and the children to their . . . ways."

First chance he got, Aaron intended to ask Karl to help him understand the strange relationship between Bethel and her family.

"Then . . . do you object to my family being present?"

"Oh, no! Of course not!" She clenched and unclenched

her hands. "I never meant to give you that impression. Forgive me, please, for behaving like a selfish brat."

Bethel stood so suddenly that the flimsy old chair collapsed, nearly taking her with it. Instinct made him reach out, and, as he had on the porch, he steadied her. This time, they stood face to face, and it took a concerted effort not to draw her close in a comforting hug.

If he had so little self-control on her very first day here, how did he hope to adhere to his self-imposed 'marriage in name only' rule!

"Thank you," she said, "again." She stepped back. *Way* back. "It will be hard for you to believe, but I am not normally clumsy."

He extended both hands, palms up. "See those scars?"

She tilted her head to get a closer look.

"They are the result of pushing myself to keep working when I'm tired. Leave the laundry," he said, "and go to bed. Even if you don't sleep, you need the rest."

Her gaze moved across the piles of laundry, sorted and scattered across the floor. If he were a gambling man, Aaron might bet on what she'd say next. . . .

"You may have learned the lesson the hard way, but is a good lesson, all the same. And you are right. I have often thought that rest is a form of God's peace."

*And you would've lost . . .*

"Will you go to the mill tomorrow?"

"I might, but not until after lunch. Maybe not even then." He'd promised to build her a clothesline and aimed to keep that promise. A good chance to reinforce some measuring-cutting lessons with the boys. With Molly, too. Unless she'd rather help Bethel. . . .

"I saw eggs in the refrigerator and saved a few slices of ham. I can use the leftover biscuits, too, to make a breakfast casserole. Are you and the children early risers?"

Aaron nodded. "Seven, eight o'clock at the latest."

Nodding, she placed the chunky shoe on the bottom step. "A good hour to start the day." She moved up a step. "Would you have an extra alarm clock that I could borrow?"

"I do. But I'd rather not give it to you. Let the good Lord wake you when He will. We will enjoy the casserole as lunch."

Halfway up the stairs, she stopped to face him. "Are things at the mill busy on Saturdays?"

Lately, he'd needed to work the men in three eight-hour shifts to meet the needs of building contractors in Grantsville and Deep Creek. And Max had stopped by earlier, asked if he could pick up four pallets of plywood in the morning for the housing project he'd started in Cumberland. But Karl could handle the Saturday crew and Max's order, too.

"Things are a little slower."

"Slow enough to show me around later in the day?"

He almost asked why the tour couldn't wait until next week. Better still, until after the wedding. But thoughts of the gentle razzing he'd taken from the guys told him it wouldn't matter when Bethel walked through the mill. He trusted them to keep civil tongues in their heads while he showed her around, but first chance they got, he'd hear echoes of "Bontrager's making so much money, he went an' bought himself a wife!" and "If the boss is doing well enough to import a wife, where's our raise!"

"Anything's possible."

Few things irked him more than people who made promises they didn't keep, so he'd chosen his words carefully. But based on her narrow-eyed expression, she'd noticed his noncommittal response.

"Good night," he said.

"You, too, Mr. Bontrager."

He hoped Bethel would sleep well, because she'd certainly earned it.

Something told him it would take every trick in the book—reciting the twenty-third Psalm, counting sheep, writing The Lord's Prayer on an imaginary chalkboard, deep breathing techniques—for him to fall asleep tonight.

Because, for reasons as yet unknown to him, Aaron felt strangely drawn to the quiet and sad-eyed Amish woman from Nappanee, Indiana . . .

. . . even though he'd made up his mind *not* to.

# Chapter Four

"I hope you don't mind the surprise visit," the young woman said, "but I just had to meet you! I'm Stella, Aaron's sister."

Beth had instantly noticed the family resemblance. Same reddish-blond hair, same blue-green eyes, same freckles across the bridge of the nose. She held open the door while Stella pushed the two-seater stroller into the kitchen. "Left to his own devices, that brother of mine would put off the introductions indefinitely." She glanced around the kitchen. "Where are the children?"

"In town with their father. They have outgrown their shoes again, it seems."

"This is what I have to look forward to," Stella said, gesturing toward the twins. "If only children took their time growing up, so we could enjoy them longer."

Now, Bontrager's sister turned a slow circle in the middle of the room. "Goodness gracious sakes alive, will you just look at this place. Why, last time I was here, there were pots and pans piled halfway to the ceiling."

She'd done her best, Stella thought defensively, trying to manage Marta's mayhem. But midway through her pregnancy, Dr. Baker had told her that unless she refrained from heavy lifting and stayed off her feet as much as possible, she'd have no choice but to order bed rest. When her brother had found out, he'd all but barred her from his house.

Now, Stella faced Beth. "Does the rest of the place look this good?"

How did the woman expect her to answer without sounding prideful! "I have done a little work in every room."

"A little! You underestimate your skills, dear Bethel." She flicked her fingers, as if to turn the page on the subject. "Anyway, as I said, I hope you don't mind that I'm here, uninvited. If I'd waited for my brother, who knows how long it might have been before we met."

In answer to similar questions she'd asked herself, Beth had compiled a list of excuses for Bontrager—time spent repairing his gas-powered mower, driving to Oakland for supplies, sorting nuts and bolts in his garage—but in the end, only two seemed likely: Either he was ashamed of the desperation behind his decision to bring her here . . . or he was ashamed of *her*.

Stella flung back the stroller's gray awning and bent over the identical twins inside it. "Meet your nephews, Bethel. And Mark and Micah, this is your Aunt Bethel."

"How old are they now?"

"Four months."

Bending at the waist, Beth took a closer look, and the babies rewarded her smile with damp-lipped, toothless grins.

"They favor Karl, don't you think?"

Yes, they seemed to have inherited his quick smile,

almost-brown hair, and eyes that couldn't decide if they were brown or hazel.

"That might change as they grow older," Beth said, although she hoped not.

Unlike the rest of Nappanee's male population, Karl had always been kind to her and he was dear to her. She'd shared in his joy the day he had overcome his fear of heights and repaired his father's barn roof single-handedly. He'd overcome his fear of horses, too, by teaching himself to ride the Millers' huge plow horse. When he had completed his eighth year of schooling, she had given him a hand-stitched quilt, and it was one of the few things he had taken with him when, after his parents' tragic deaths, he'd sold the nearly bankrupt farm to start fresh in the Maryland mountains. At first, he'd written weekly, sharing tidbits about the town, his job, the one-room apartment behind the mill provided by his boss, and new friends. Before long, the letters arrived fewer and farther between, then stopped altogether. She decided to counter her disappointment by seeing it as a sign that God had blessed him with a happy new life. One of those friends had become the wife who'd given him two strapping sons.

"He feels horrible about not meeting you at the train," Stella said, "and asked me to tell you he'll stop by soon to make up for it."

"Nothing to make up for," Beth said and meant it. As Bontrager's next in command, Karl's job came with a lot of responsibility. "I know how busy he has been with work at the mill." She smiled at the twins. "And with his beautiful family!"

Blushing, Stella shrugged. "So anyway, the *real* reason

I'm here is . . . I'm nosy." She giggled. "Do you have a day and time set for the wedding?"

"Not yet. We visited Bishop Fisher day before yesterday, and after many prayers and dozens of questions, mostly for me, he said it would take a few days to get final approval from the deacons."

"Oh, now, don't look so worried. I'm sure your former church leaders were just as picky. My guess is, he'll stop by today, at lunchtime if I know him, to deliver the good news."

Bontrager's sister had referred to Nappanee in the past tense, telling Beth that she believed her brother would move forward with the wedding plans.

"May I ask you a question, Stella?"

"Of course!"

"How does your family feel about the peculiar circumstances that brought me here?"

Stella's expression grew solemn, her voice less cheery as she began. "It has been a long time since Aaron was happy. Before his marriage to Marta, he was a joy to be around, always smiling, cracking jokes, doing his best to raise others' spirits. Afterward . . ." She exhaled a slow, sad sigh. "It is wrong to speak ill of the dead, so I will answer your question this way: Karl and I talked often about Aaron's state of mind, about how his personality changed and he avoided people whenever he could. We did our best to keep it from my mother, because her health is frail, but we could not let him go on that way, for his sake as well as the children's. So we prayed. Every night and every morning and every chance we had in between, we prayed. The answer seemed God-sent that day at the mill, when in frustration Karl blurted out his suggestion that Aaron bring you here to help with the children and the house." Her serious demeanor relaxed a bit when she tacked on, "If it seems he's a bit standoffish, it's probably because Bishop Fisher backed him into a corner." She lowered her voice in an attempt to duplicate the older man's voice: "'We have relaxed many of the Old Order ways, son, but a woman, living under your roof without benefit of marriage? We have not relaxed *that* much!'"

He'd tried hiring a woman from Pleasant Valley. He'd placed ads in local papers, tacked notices on message boards outside the town's stores, Stella told her. "But the minute they got a look at that house and those children . . ." She shook her head. "Well, you can understand why they were reluctant to take the job."

So when, Beth asked herself, had he decided that marriage was the answer to the problem?

"If you're thinking that Aaron could turn down orders at the mill and free up more time to take care of things himself, you're wrong. He tried. I watched him. Karl did, too. Even when we were children, Aaron was an 'everything in its placc' person. If you ask me, he just plain didn't know where or how to start. I tried my best, so I understand that only too well!"

Until now, Beth didn't understand why it seemed he'd been avoiding her. The self-pity she'd been feeling faded away, and in its place appeared compassion. It couldn't have been easy for a man like him, who'd built a business, a home and family, to admit defeat.

"May I ask *you* a question, Bethel?"

"Of course," she said.

"I can trust you not to tell anyone what I just shared with you, right?"

"You have my word. I would hate to be the cause of hurt feelings."

One of her twins began fussing. "I knew you would say that." Within seconds, his brother joined in. "That's my cue to leave. Oh, I nearly forgot!" Stella removed a round plastic tub from the stroller's basket. "I baked a cake. Aaron's favorite. I hope you like chocolate, too."

"Yes, I do."

"Now, before I go, I want you to know that if you need help, any help at all, I'm right up the road."

An easy two-mile walk, according to Molly, but Beth had no intention of testing the distance or asking for assistance with wedding preparations.

"I'm not just offering because Aaron is my brother. I enjoy organizing things, like rounding up the ladies who will cook and bake for the reception. I love braiding hair, too, and I know it sounds crazy, because no one likes to iron, but I love it." She paused. "If you don't have a dress, you're more than welcome to borrow one of mine." Another giggle. "Oh, what am I saying. You can *have* one of mine. I have more than a dozen!"

Why would any woman need that many? Beth wondered. And then she said, "Before leaving Indiana, I bought a dress at my father's store. Pale blue. A new bonnet, too, and I have not worn either." *Yet.*

"Wait. You bought a dress from your own father?" Stella shook her head. "My dear *daed* was a furniture maker. I can't count the number of things—tables, chairs, our bed, cribs for the twins—I asked him to build for us, and he refused to accept payment. I'd think yours would give you a dress as a wedding gift if nothing else!"

*You would think* wrong, Beth wanted to say. "I appreciate your offer, though," she said instead.

"Will he be at the wedding?"

Although she'd just met Stella, the look on her face told Beth that, given the chance, she'd have a few words with her father!

"No. He has never left his shop for more than a few hours." *And being present at his only daughter's wedding is not worth the price of a train ticket.*

Now, Stella looked sympathetic. She'd seen that expression all her life. Every time she stumbled on the school grounds. Whenever she lagged behind the other students. If she couldn't climb the ladder quickly enough to reach something from a high shelf in her father's store. And she hated being pitied!

"Oh now, it will be all right." Stella patted Beth's hand. "I have a feeling you and I will soon be good friends. I can't wait to show off my pretty new sister-in-law." She tipped the stroller so that it rolled easily down the back porch stairs. "Tell that brother of mine that I expect an in-person announcement once the wedding date is decided!" Then she secured her bonnet ties and hurried toward the road.

Leaning against a porch support post, Beth surveyed the yard, where the late June breeze had plucked leaves and scattered them beneath the swaying tire swings. It had been a pleasant visit, and she hoped Stella had meant it when she'd said that soon, they'd be friends.

There were towels in the dryer and a load of sheets in the washing machine. Lunch to prepare and supper to start. Bontrager's work shirts and trousers to iron. "And you cannot get any of it done, dawdling out here in the sunshine."

"Bethel? Oh, Bethel?" Micah Fisher waved from half-way up the driveway.

As he made his way closer, Beth returned his wave. "How nice to see you, Bishop."

He was slightly winded when he said, "A good time to visit?"

"Of course. I made lemonade. Would you like a glass?"

He looked toward the top of the drive, where Bontrager usually parked his truck. "Aaron is not home?"

"He drove the children into town for new shoes."

"Mmm-hmm. I'm sorry. That can be expensive."

It was almost word for word what the orthopedist had said, five years ago. She'd walked miles to the hospital in Goshen to discuss an article she'd found in a magazine in her father's store. The article described a surgical procedure that might correct her condition, *limb length discrepancy*. The doctor had performed an examination, then explained that if her parents had sought medical advice when she was four, or six, even, there might have been a chance of success. But the surgery was expensive. "Expensive?" she'd repeated. "Mmm-hmm. I'm sorry," he'd said. And every time she'd heard those words since, Beth's heart lurched.

"I am glad to have a few moments alone with you," Fisher said, and held open the screen door.

She filled two tumblers and joined him at the table. *Get straight to the point,* she told herself, and said, "What would you like to know about me?"

"Nothing. Nothing at all." He took a long, slow sip of

the lemonade. "After several discussions with your bishop, I am convinced that you will be a wonderful addition to our community."

Then why did he want to talk to her, alone?

Fisher told her what to expect on the wedding day. Scriptures. Sermons. Vows. Prayers. The lemonade was half gone when he leaned back and said, "Before I leave you, I feel it is my duty to suggest that you ask some hard questions of the man you are about to marry. . . ."


"Hey look, Daed," Molly said, pointing, "it's Bishop Fisher!"

"Oh no." Sam scrubbed a hand over his face. "Now we'll have to sit here in the driveway, listening to him go on and on *forever* about . . . who knows what. And it's hot as an oven outside."

The boy had a point. Micah's talent for idle banter had inspired the good-natured joke, whispered when Pleasant Valley residents saw him approaching: "The man means well, but his head is stuffed so full of small talk, it is a wonder it is not ten times bigger!"

"Sam . . ."

"I know." He sighed. "I will mind my manners."

Aaron brought the pickup to a slow stop. "'Afternoon, Bishop. What brings you here on this blistering June day?"

Fisher touched a forefinger to the brim of his straw hat. "'Afternoon to you, too," he said . . . and continued walking.

"Well now, doesn't that beat all," Aaron said, mostly to

himself. Leaning out of the driver's window, he called over his left shoulder. "Can we give you a ride back home?"

"Thank you, no. See you on Sunday at church!"

Sam, on his knees in the passenger seat, faced the back seat. "What is wrong with him, Daed?"

According to the dashboard clock, Aaron and the children had been away from home for two and a half hours. How much of that time had Fisher spent in the house?

*Long enough to tell Bethel about . . .*

*No. He wouldn't.*

Or would he?

Releasing the brake, Aaron steered the truck toward the bend in the drive. "He probably stayed so long talking with Bethel that he made himself late for his next visit."

Sam, still staring through the rear window, shook his head. "Maybe, but I don't think so. From that look on his face, she musta said somethin' to make him mad."

In his opinion, Fisher looked guilty, not annoyed, and only one thing could explain that: He'd told Beth about Aaron's darkest secret. He'd planned to come clean with her before now, but between handling the surge of new orders and making and installing Bethel's clothesline, there hadn't been time.

But that wasn't true, and he knew it. Aaron hadn't told her because . . . because what if the truth made her decide that she couldn't spend the rest of her life with a man like him?

"Now *you* look mad," Sam said. "I would have been nice to the bishop, honest I would, if he had stopped to talk."

"I know you would, son. I'm not mad." *At least, not at*

you. And to prove it, he tousled the boy's hair. "Now, why don't the three of you go inside, show Bethel your new shoes, while I check on the animals."

"I still wish we had asked what size she wears," Molly said, "because I just *know* she hasn't had a new pair in years and years. And she really ought to have a decent pair to wear on her special day."

"You are right, and tonight, after supper, I'll talk to her about what she might need for . . ." Aaron couldn't bring himself to call it "her special day." After hearing the truth about him, it was more likely she'd ask for a ride to the train station, not shoes for the wedding.

She leaned forward and whispered into his ear. "Matthew likes his new boots."

"How can you tell?" he whispered back.

"Because . . ." Using her chin as a pointer, she drew his attention into the back seat, where his youngest smiled and stared at his own wiggling feet.

"You ought to take them off," Aaron said as they climbed out of the truck, "put them back into their boxes and slip into your everyday boots."

"Aw, but Daed," she started to complain, "they are . . ." Then her face brightened. "Oh, I get it. You want us all to look nice and neat at the wedding. And you want to look that way, too. It is *your* big day, too, after all!"

His big day . . .

He'd bought himself boots, new shirts for himself and the boys, and a pale pink dress for Molly. He'd been meaning to do that for a while now, too. So even if the worst happened—and Bethel returned to Nappanee—it would be one less thing on his plate when summer ended and the community school reopened.

"We must be careful, though," Molly continued, "not to let 'looking nice' turn into vanity."

"Or pride," Sam agreed.

Aaron held out his arms, and all three children filled them. "I hope you are happy." He kissed the tops of their heads. "You make me so proud that I will need to ask forgiveness!"

Sam looked up into Aaron's face. "If this idea of yours turns out to be a big mistake, will you have to ask forgiveness for that, too?"

Once, while trying to break up a fistfight on the school playground, Aaron had taken a punch to the gut that knocked the breath right out of him. Sam's words made him feel a little like that, right now. A dozen questions tumbled in his head: Too late to cancel the wedding? What would the bishop think? Would he become a laughing-stock in the community? Was it possible that Bethel felt the same way?

Matthew pressed his cheek to the back of Aaron's hand, reminding him for the thousandth time since Marta's death how much the child missed his mother. Sam and Molly missed her, too, of course, but Matthew . . .

Aaron exhaled a weary sigh and repeated what he'd been saying for the last month:

"It is God's will."

*Lord, if it is not, please send a sign. . . .*

He closed his eyes for a moment.

*. . . before it's too late.*

# Chapter Five

Stella slid a final hairpin into Beth's braid. "You have such thick hair," she said, standing back to admire her work. "And so shiny. Such a blessing!"

Almost word for word what her mother had said every morning while twisting Beth's hair into buns or braids. After Elizabeth's death, trying to complete the job on her own had driven Beth to tears. And then one day, in a fit of frustration, she'd squinted, *hard,* and pretended that her fingers were her mother's. Since then, she'd cherished those moments—overlapping, weaving, tucking, pinning— because for those moments, it seemed as though her mother wasn't gone, after all, and the sensation eased the ache of missing her favorite person in all the world.

"Seems a shame to hide it under a cap." Stella shrugged. "Rules are rules, yes?"

Beth smiled. "Yes, they are. Thank you for this trial run. It will make things easier tomorrow."

"Are you afraid?"

"No." She'd been in town slightly more than a week, spent very little of that time with her future husband. So why *wasn't* she afraid?

"Nervous, then?"

"No, not really." Thanks to her attendance at a dozen or more weddings back in Nappanee, Beth more or less knew what to expect, and Bishop Fisher's description made it clear that even here in a New Order Amish community, the ceremony would be much the same.

"Oh, I was terrified! I mean, I loved Karl, and looked forward to sharing my life with him, but I had so many questions."

Beth's pulse quickened. "Questions? About what?"

Stella blushed, tried to hide her embarrassment behind her hands. "The wedding night, for one thing. My mother would only say 'Just close your eyes and relax, and before you know it, it will all be over.'"

Stella continued, but Beth heard only every other word. Something about an argument over who'd sleep on the right side of the bed. The cold, dark night. And somewhere between complaints about bad breath and snoring, her sister-in-law promised to offer motherly guidance on an as-needed basis. Beth didn't know which shocked her more . . . that Stella thought she could take Elizabeth's place, or that Aaron hadn't told his sister about their in-name-only arrangement. Admitting it now would end this awkward, well-intended advice . . . if she was willing to betray her future husband.

The twins' quiet babbling interrupted her thoughts. "Who will mind the boys during the ceremony?"

One eyebrow rose high on Stella's forehead. "Hmm. All right. I can take a hint. We will change the subject. I didn't mean to make you uncomfortable." She winked, then said, "My cousin Rachel will stay with the boys. I can't wait for you two to meet. You are going to like one another. I am sure of it! Next week, on the very first good-weather day, I will tuck the boys into their stroller, and the four of us will visit the neighbors." She paused. "Aaron has been so secretive about, well, about everything related to you and the wedding, I'm sure everyone is looking forward to meeting the mystery woman."

Secretive? Beth ran through the list of possible reasons, then shook her head. "In his defense, there was very little he could have told them about me, because—"

Stella frowned slightly. "It is good of you to defend him. Life has been a struggle for Aaron since Marta died, but just between you and me and the mailbox? Loss is no excuse for the way he let things slip. It's as though he thinks no one but him has ever lost a spouse! What happened was God's will. My brother needs to exercise his faith, pray for strength, come to terms with life as it is now, and move forward."

Karl had said pretty much the same thing: No one, not family and friends, not the bishop, not even his own children could convince Aaron that he needed outside help. In a desperate, last-ditch effort to help right his friend's life, Karl had put the "hire a wife" idea on his boss's desk. "It had taken weeks, and hours of prayer," her cousin had said, "but once Aaron admitted I was right, he didn't waste a minute setting things in motion. . . ."

First, meetings with Bishop Fisher and the church elders, Karl told her. Next, telephone discussions with her father and the bishop in Nappanee, followed by conversations with Beth, herself. Then, travel arrangements. Sharing his decision with the children. And finally, her arrival, which had changed nearly every aspect of his world. None of that could have been easy.

"Not to be argumentative," Beth said, "but wouldn't you agree that my presence here is proof he has started moving forward?"

While Stella considered the question, Beth added, "I never married, as you know, so I have no idea how it might feel to lose a spouse. Never had children, either. But I can imagine how difficult it must be for him, coping with the death of his beloved wife, all while trying to be mother, father, and breadwinner for his children . . . children still struggling with the loss of their mother."

Perhaps this time, Beth hoped, Stella's silence meant she'd decided to change the subject.

"You are the most understanding woman I know. When you heard of my brother's needs, your first instinct was to help him, at great cost to you. Such selflessness amazes me, and it tells me, Bethel Mast, that you will be good for Aaron and the children." She held up a forefinger. "Correction. Bethel *Bontrager*."

Allowing Stella to believe she'd come here solely to help the Bontragers wasn't just unfair. It was dishonest. "I need to explain, Stella, that I had my own reasons for agreeing to come here."

Stella's brows drew together, and for a minute there, Beth thought she might ask for more information.

"Seeing everything you have accomplished in the house and yard already is all I need to know. Your enthusiasm tells me that my brother made a good decision after all."

After all? Exactly how much *had* he shared with Stella!

"I can't tell you what a relief it is, knowing that my niece and nephews are in good hands. I care about them almost as much as my own baby boys."

"I know. Mr. Bontrager told me on the telephone how much you did for them."

Now, one of the babies grasped a marble-sized wooden ball and slid it back and forth on the metal rod attached to the stroller's tray. Seeing this, his brother reached for it, too, and for a moment two pudgy, dimpled hands grappled for the toy. Stella ended the mini dispute by handing each a teething biscuit.

"It has been too long since Aaron and the children have been properly cared for," she said, meeting Beth's eyes. "It has also been too long since they've felt loved, but something tells me you'll provide that, too."

Beth had already developed protective feelings for little Matthew, and she'd grown quite fond of personable, helpful Molly. Sam hadn't gone out of his way to connect, but at least the snide comments and angry glares had stopped. Yes, Beth could see herself loving all three, and God willing, they'd love her, too. As for their father . . .

Stella walked a slow circle around Beth. "Lovely." Then, feigning a stern expression, she said, "Please don't tell the bishop what I'm about to say, but all of us—Karl and I, my brother Seth, our mother—will feel proud as you become part of our family."

Had she deliberately left Bontrager off the list? Beth glanced out the window, where the children were trying their hand at building a tree house. Perhaps this was a good time to ask if Stella knew what the bishop had meant when he'd suggested that she ask her prospective husband some hard questions.

She might have quizzed Stella if she hadn't noticed Matthew limping across the lawn.

"I will be right back. There is something wrong with Matthew." She didn't wait for a reply, but hurried outside.

"Matthew?"

He stopped running and, looking confused, faced her.

Beth quickly caught up with him. Stooping, she took his hands in hers, and thanked God when he didn't pull away. "Do the new shoes hurt your feet, sweet boy?"

One shiny tear puddled in the corner of his left eye, and when he pointed at his left foot, it slowly tracked down the round, freckled contour of his cheek.

"Oh, I am sorry." Sitting cross-legged now, Beth said, "My feet hurt quite often, so I know how uncomfortable it is. Here." She patted her lap. "Sit with me, so I can have a look, see if I can figure out what the problem is."

Again, she sent a silent thank-you heavenward, because not only did he comply, but he leaned into her as well. "It is probably only a pebble. Or a wrinkle in your sock." Beth untied the thick black laces and tugged at the leather tongue, then gently slid the boot from Matthew's foot. "May I look under your sock?"

In place of a reply, or even a nod, the boy bent his leg, making it easier for Beth to reach his foot. Slowly, gently, she slid off the sock. "Well, Matthew, turns out you have a blister." She hugged him from behind. "You must be a very strong, brave boy. . . ."

He turned, looked up into her face, awaiting an explanation.

"That is quite a blister. If I had that one that big and red, I probably would have cried and cried!"

One corner of his mouth lifted in a tiny grin.

"How about if we go inside, so I can put some ointment and a bandage on it?"

Matthew climbed from her lap and stood, one shoe on and one shoe off, watching as she scrambled to her feet. A peculiar glint flashed in his eyes. Worry? Commiseration? Both?

He willingly allowed her to take his hand and lead him to the back porch. "You know," she said as they walked, "we have a lot in common, you and I."

Again, he looked up at her, and she read the unvoiced question in his eyes: *What do we have in common?*

"I have an imperfect foot, and you . . ."

His lips formed the words, *"And so do you."*

". . . and you," she finished, "have an imperfect voice box." Leaning down, Beth tenderly touched his throat. She'd half expected him to recoil. To jerk back his hand and run away from her.

A nod, instead, and the same faint upturn of his lips as he squeezed her hand.

*Help me, oh Lord,* she prayed silently, *to help this sweet child find his voice.*

"What's going on out here?"

Beth stifled a tiny scream. "Mr. Bontrager. I did not see you there." She glanced around and, not seeing his pickup, added, "Did not hear your truck come up the driveway, either."

He struck the pose that had already become familiar to her, feet shoulder-width apart, shoulders back, thumbs tucked behind his suspenders. "Sorry that I scared you. Again."

His slanted smile told her he meant it. Again.

"You didn't hear or see the truck because I came home an hour or so ago." He aimed a thumb over his shoulder.

"I'm parked beside the shed, where I stacked some scrap lumber for the kids' tree house."

Bontrager focused on his son, who'd placed his bare left foot atop his right shoe. "You remind me of a rhyme I read as a boy." Squatting, he placed a hand on his son's shoulder and recited, "'Diddle-diddle dumpling, my son John, went to bed with his britches on. One shoe off, and one shoe on, diddle-diddle dumpling, my son John.'"

The entire yard brightened in the light of the boy's smile. And then, as quickly as it had appeared, it was gone, and in its place appeared a look that Beth could only describe as *guilty*.

Disappointment dulled his father's eyes.

"His new shoe wore quite a blister on the side of his foot," she said, hoping to ease Matthew's discomfort. "He was very big and brave. Why, if I had not seen him limping, I never would have known he was in pain." She smiled at the boy, then met Bontrager's eyes. "We were just about to look for ointment and a bandage."

He pulled the boy onto a bent knee to get a better look. "My, my. Bethel is right. That is quite a blister, isn't it?"

A glimmer of pride sparkled in Matthew's blue eyes as he glanced from Beth to his father and back again. Then, straightening to his full six-foot height, Bontrager relieved her of the boy's shoe. Turning it over and over in his big hands, he examined its interior. "Well, here's the problem," he said, stepping closer, so she could see. "A knot in the thread that binds the upper to the shank."

Leaning forward, she peered inside. "I had no idea what one called the parts of a shoe!"

His concerned expression relaxed. "Let's get him inside so you can tend to that blister. Want me to carry you, son?"

He looked mildly surprised when Matthew took her hand instead of his and fell into step beside her. Bontrager began walking behind them, and as they neared the house, he murmured, "Well, I'll be." And unless she was mistaken, she heard a note of joy—or was it relief?—in his soft voice.

Stella backed out of the kitchen door just then, muttering as she dragged the twins' stroller with her. "I would love to stay and visit with you, dear brother of mine, but if I don't get these two home soon, they will frighten every bird from the trees."

Bontrager helped her maneuver the double-wide carrier down the steps, wincing slightly as the boys squawked and squealed. Bending at the waist, he leaned both palms on the stroller's side arms. "Now, now boys," he crooned, "is all this racket really necessary? You are hurting poor Matthew's ears!"

The boy took a step closer to his cousins and raised his right hand, smiling as he wiggled the fingers of his left hand in silent greeting. Though he'd imitated his father's posture—feet shoulder-width apart, back straight, the thumb of his left hand tucked behind a black suspender—Matthew still looked like a sad, confused six-year-old boy. She resisted the urge to hug him, to press tiny kisses to his sun-kissed, pudgy cheeks and promise to help him find his voice: Out there in the yard, when it was just the two of them sitting on the lush lawn, he'd allowed her to hold him, but here, with his father, his aunt and cousins watching . . .

Stella, still muttering, hurried down the driveway as Matthew made his way into the kitchen. Bontrager climbed the porch steps and grasped the screen door handle, and

Beth, unaccustomed to chivalry, nearly plowed right into him. Feeling clumsy and in the way, she suppressed a giggle and waited for him to open it. She'd barely crossed the threshold when he leaned close and whispered, "After supper, may I have a few minutes of your time? Once the children are asleep, that is?"

The scent of his line-dried shirt surrounded her. Fresh-sawed wood, too. The aromas, combined with the rasp of his baritone, nearly stopped her forward motion. "Why, yes. Yes. Of course. I will be in the basement, ironing the boys' new shirts. Yours, too. Molly's dress. And mine. I would not want your family, or the bishop, or . . . or anyone who might be there tomorrow to think I—"

*. . . to think I am not pulling my weight,* she almost said. *If you sound this much like an empty-headed ninny to yourself, how must you sound to* him!

"Good." He nodded, once, and when he did, a lock of reddish-blond hair fell across his forehead.

Beth lifted a hand to finger-comb it back into place, but smoothed her apron, instead. *Why would you do such a thing!* Wifely gestures served no purpose in a marriage like theirs.

Bontrager must have read her intention, and the reason she'd stopped herself, for he drove his fingers through his hair.

Mere seconds had passed since they'd entered the house, but to Matthew, who'd been waiting patiently, it must have seemed like minutes.

She pulled out a kitchen chair. "Would you like some milk while I fetch a bandage?" she asked as he sat.

He shook his head.

After rearranging the kitchen cabinets, Beth had found

herself with an empty upper cabinet, and she had filled it with liniments, rubbing alcohol, gauze pads, and adhesive bandages. She selected the first aid items she'd need to doctor Matthew's blister, and placed them on the table. "Let's prop your foot up on this chair," she said, pulling out the one beside his.

Bontrager pretended to busy himself at the sink. Washing his hands. Drying them. Folding the blue-and-white checked towel and hanging it neatly on the swing-arm holder. Then he went back to inspecting the inside of the offending boot. He wasn't fooling Beth. Peripheral vision told her that he was watching and intended to stay put while she tended to his little boy.

If he'd invested as much time in finding out why Matthew had chosen silence as a way to cope with his mother's death . . .

*Father, forgive me for the unfair, unkind thought.* He'd talked to the community's doctor about the situation. What more could he have done?

Beth chattered nonstop, doing her best to sound upbeat and confident as she dressed Matthew's foot. Once finished, she gave Matthew's toes a gentle squeeze.

"Aha! So you are ticklish, are you!"

His smile faded, but only a bit.

She grinned. "Do Sam and Molly know about this?"

Matthew's shoulders lifted in a shrug. Then his eyes widened with alarm as he looked left and right.

"Do not worry, sweet boy. Hear the hammering? They are still outside, adding boards to the tree house."

Relief flooded his features.

"You have my word: I will never tell them."

"Too late," Bontrager said.

His teasing grin reminded her of the Cheshire Cat from *Alice's Adventures in Wonderland.*

"I cannot count the number of times I've had to break up a three-way tickling match."

His gaze linked with Matthew's just long enough for Beth to read the love that bonded them. And words, she realized, had nothing to do with the connection. She envied them, for nothing like it had ever transpired between her and her father, between her father and her brother. Bontrager might never love her as a husband loves a wife, but that didn't stop her from hoping that in time, he'd consider her family, and deserving of such affection.

A sob ached in her throat, and to squelch it, Beth said, "You stay put, Matthew, while I fetch a clean sock from your bureau drawer. I know it is warm outside, but it will help hold the gauze in place."

Those moments alone upstairs gave her time to regain control of her emotions. If feelings like that rose up again, how would she temper them? *With God's help,* she thought, heading back downstairs.

"I chose one of your father's socks," she said, slipping it over the boy's foot, "because it will keep things in place without pressing too hard on your blister." She rambled on for another minute, explaining how airflow to the injury would encourage faster healing, that she'd change the bandage again at bedtime, and again in the morning. "By then," she concluded, as she gathered up the supplies, "we should see a big improvement!"

"How long before supper?" Bontrager wanted to know.

The clock above the sink said four-fifteen. "Thirty, forty-five minutes. No more than an hour." She was about to ask why he wanted to know when he stood beside Matthew's chair.

"Would you like to sit on the porch, watch your brother and sister work on the tree house?"

Matthew nodded, and without another word, Bontrager scooped him up and shouldered his way out the door.

"I will bring him milk," Beth said as he sat the boy in the nearest chair. "And sliced apples."

"Good idea." He tousled his son's hair. "Maybe I will join you."

There was something telling in the way he'd said *maybe*, and Beth had a feeling it had less to do with the clock than his desire to talk to her.

*So here you are,* she thought, taking the paring knife from the cutlery drawer, *alone with him in his big kitchen.* Would he solve the "what does he want?" mystery now, or make her wait until nightfall?

She made quick work of removing the apple's peel, and on second thought, decided to peel two more—one for Sam, one for Molly. She'd spread a blanket under the big oak tree, take Matthew to join them. An impromptu picnic, she'd tell them.

Bontrager, seated at the head of the table, used his pocketknife to scrape the offending threads from Matthew's boot. Wasn't he worried that the—what had he called the parts?—that the upper would separate from the shank?

"You were great with him," Bontrager said, breaking the comfortable silence.

The suddenness of his voice startled Beth, and the blade she was using to peel the apple nicked her fingertip. *"Oh, guck emol do!"* she complained.

"What do you mean, 'Oh, would you look at that?'"

She popped the fingertip into her mouth. "Nothing," she said around it. "Just a tiny scratch."

He was beside her in an instant. "Let me see."

Before she knew what was happening, he'd cradled her hand in his big, warm palm.

"It is fine. See? It has stopped bleeding already."

"Yes. It appears so."

"I should get back to the apples. The children will not like them if I allow them to turn brown."

"Yes, that is true." He turned her loose and went back to scraping Matthew's shoe lining. "It was good hearing 'the Dutch.' People use it still, but not enough. Feel free to use more of it. Lots more. I will enjoy it, and the children really should learn the old ways."

There was a certain permanence about his statement, and it all but alleviated her fears that Bontrager might have decided the wedding wasn't such a good idea, after all. It felt good. Reassuring. Beth washed her hands and cored the next apple. "*Als je dat volhoudt,*" she said, "*draag je dat leer uit.*"

"Oh, you think so, do you?" Bontrager went back to scraping. "Not to worry. Even if I do keep it up," he said, translating perfectly, "I will not wear out the leather."

"From your lips to God's ears . . ."

He met her eyes, and laughed, a rich, robust sound that filled the room . . . and her heart. She didn't believe for an instant that he'd hurt her, not intentionally, anyway. But just to be safe, Beth decided to guard her heart . . .

. . . even if doing so sent her right back to Nappanee, Indiana.

\* \* \*

An hour later, Aaron stared at the June page of his desk calendar. In less than two weeks, he'd turn to the July page. He shook his head. Another year half gone already.

Karl rapped on the open office door. "What are you doing here, boss?"

How many times had he asked his brother-in-law not to refer to him that way? A hundred? More? One day, he'd ask why Karl refused to address him by his given name. Today was not that day.

"Thought I would have a look at the materials list for the new job." Aaron opened the file folder and pretended to read the top page of the detailed contract between Bontrager Lumber and Michaels Construction. "Has Joe delivered the deposit yet?"

"Nope." Karl dropped onto the seat of the chair facing Aaron's desk. "And I'm not holding my breath."

Michaels had been coasting for years, in part because the owner spent entirely too much time and money entertaining the ladies, in part because it wasn't smart business to pay one line of credit with another.

"What a shame. This would have kept us busy well into the winter."

"Yeah, but it's just as well. The men are overworked as it is," Karl pointed out. "And so are you. Now seriously, what are you doing here? Hofstrom said you went home early to help the kids build a tree house."

"To make sure there were enough materials for the build," Aaron corrected.

"And . . . ?"

"And what?"

"They have what they need to get started?"

"They do. They have. Started, I mean. And unless they bend more nails than they sink, they're all set."

"You aren't tempted to supervise?"

Actually, Aaron had considered standing by, in case Sam or Molly had a question or ran into a snag. But then the whole blister-on-the-foot thing had happened, and . . .

In all honesty, the problem caused by the ill-fitting boot had little to do with his decision to head back to the office. Bethel. *Bethel* had been the reason. He'd watched Marta remove splinters, bandage skinned knees, inspect bumps and bruises. She'd done it the way she did everything . . . just another chore to get out of the way, with*out* tender words, comforting smiles, soothing gestures. Aaron had witnessed Matthew's calm, positive reaction to Bethel's gentle ministrations, but had no idea what to make of the feelings that had stirred in *him*.

Fisher had warned him about this. "You think it will be easy," the bishop had said, "running your marriage the way you manage your business, with cool, professional detachment. But as God is my witness, you are *wrong*."

He'd now spent not quite two weeks with Bethel. In that short time, Aaron had come to admire many things about her. Her drive and determination. Her organizational skills and knack for making even the most ordinary furnishings look decorative. He couldn't speak for the children, but her cheerful disposition all but made him forget that sometimes, usually at the end of a long day, she walked with a bit of a limp. He never would have asked her to, and yet she rose long before him every morning, and somehow, without making a sound, prepared him a hearty bagged lunch and a belly-filling breakfast. Her mindset was contagious, and he carried it to the office. It helped him face his own mundane office tasks with a more positive attitude.

By contrast, not once in his nearly eleven years with Marta had she packed him a lunch. On the rare occasions when she made breakfast, she'd done it grudgingly.

*Stop it,* he told himself. *Stop it!* Marta and Bethel were different in every imaginable way, and the comparisons weren't making it easier to keep that coolly detached distance the bishop had referred to!

"Thinking about the wedding tomorrow, boss?"

"No." And it was the truth. But now that Karl had mentioned it. . . .

"Stella told me that Bethel isn't the least bit worried, and that worries *her*."

"Why?"

"She says it isn't normal. That all brides are jumpy."

"And what does my sister think that means?"

"That Bethel is hiding her real emotions."

"Nothing wrong with that. People these days tend to talk too much about what ought to be private feelings."

Karl shook his head. "The girl barely knows a soul here. We're New Order, and Bethel lived her entire life Old Order. She's had to adjust to electricity. Plumbing. Telephones. Cars and trucks. You and the kids. The house—which even you'll admit was a *mess*. It's all brand new to her. So why *isn't* she behaving like a nervous Nellie?"

"Because," Aaron said slowly, "Bethel is an adult and, as such, has accepted her lot."

"Her lot," Karl echoed.

"You say that like God has cast her straight into the bowels of hell. Pleasant Valley isn't Paradise, but it's a good place."

Karl got to his feet. "We feel that way about it because we have nothing to compare it to." He stood in the open doorway to add, "What if, after *she* compares it to Nappanee, Bethel decides her old life was better, way better?"

"You're from Nappanee. Is that how you feel?"

"Not now, but . . ." He raised his arms, let them slap against his sides. "But I've been here for years. Built a life. Started a family. I have friends. Good, honest work. Bethel has none of that. And . . ." His arms lifted, fell again. "And she knows—because you *told* her—that she'll never be more than hired help. Think about it, Aaron. *Think* about it, then ask yourself why she isn't scared out of her little black boots." With that, he turned and left the office.

Aaron leaned back in his chair, laced his fingers behind his neck. One of the reasons he'd always liked his brother-in-law was because, like himself, Karl had always been a man of few words. *Not today!* he thought.

He closed the Michaels job file, and for the second time in as many hours, left the office. All during the short drive home, Aaron could think of little else but Bethel. He couldn't argue with anything Karl had said. One of these days, he'd admit it, but for now, a verse from Exodus dominated his thoughts: "I have been a stranger in a strange land." Although scripture referred to Gershom, it perfectly described Bethel's situation.

He'd been kind. Fair. Honest. But that wasn't good enough. Things were about to change for her . . . for the better. Because even a marriage that didn't include intimacy could be friendly, couldn't it?

* * *

Beth smoothed Matthew's shirt on the ironing board. She'd just finished pressing Sam's shirt, and before it, Bontrager's. What a difference in sleeve length, she thought, sliding the iron across the crisp white fabric. Would the boys someday be as tall as their father?

The question made her wonder what the original Mrs. Bontrager had looked like. It wasn't as if she'd come across a picture while organizing boxes and bins in the basement, because not even New Order Amish posed for photographs. Molly must favor her, Beth decided, because unlike her father and brothers, the girl had green eyes and almost brown hair. Based on the few things Stella had said, Marta had often been curt and standoffish. Neither trait described her daughter.

"You're nothing like your father," she whispered, placing the other sleeve on the board. So maybe Molly's disposition was unique to her, like her ability to draw and her talent for knowing what to say, and just when to say it.

That morning, while Beth gathered eggs, she'd peered through the henhouse door and seen Molly and Sam in the goat pen, pouring buckets of fresh water into the trough that serviced Willy, Lilly, and Clyde. The lively animals walked figure eights between the children's feet and hopped over one another, inviting hearty giggles that put the youngsters on their knees in the hay. Memory of their merriment brought a smile on her own face.

It faded, though, as she recalled what Sam had said when she'd headed into the small barn to milk Henrietta. "How many eggs?" he'd asked. "Nine," she'd told him. "Enough to make French toast?" he had wanted to know. She'd said yes, more than enough, and promised to make some for breakfast tomorrow.

"On your wedding day?" Molly had asked.

Sam pointed out that they had to eat, no matter what day it was, and followed up with, "Last time we went to a stupid wedding, they did not feed us until nearly supper-time. Remember?"

Stupid wedding. "At least you know he dislikes them all, and not just *yours*."

"Sorry? What did you say?"

Bontrager, at the top of the stairs, had heard her. Was she blushing? She must be. Why else would her cheeks and neck feel so hot in the always cool basement? She could only imagine what he must think of her. If she wasn't jumping with fright at the least little thing, she was talking to herself!

"Brought you some lemonade," he said, placing a glass on the closed lid of the washing machine.

"Thank you."

"Your cheeks are all flushed. Looks like you could use a break." He held up his glass, as if to toast the trousers, shirts, and Molly's dress, hanging on the clothesline she'd strung between two support posts. "Have you finished the ironing?"

"All but my own dress." She pointed to where she'd draped it over the back of a folding chair.

"Pale blue." Using the toe of his boot, he slid a wooden stool closer. "Very nice," he said, and rested an ankle on a knee. "Do you have a minute to talk now?"

"There is no clock down here, and I have never owned a watch."

"Last time I checked, it was a little after ten."

In twelve short hours, they'd stand side by side in the community's church to exchange vows. And by this time tomorrow night, she'd begin life as his wife . . . in his room, and in his bed. A chill rippled up her spine, which made no sense, no sense at all on this sticky June night.

"If you want to keep ironing, it won't bother me."

Something in his tone, in the way his brows had drawn together, made her knees weak. Beth moved her dress from the chairback to the ironing board and turned off the iron. "It can wait," she said, sitting across from him.

"I, ah . . ." He rattled the ice cubes in his glass. "There is something I need to tell you, Bethel, and if, after hearing it, you want to go home, I will understand."

"I have been home since I stepped off the train." *I can't imagine a kindhearted, generous man like you could have done anything so terrible that it would make me want to leave you and the children.*

"A man like me . . ."

Until he echoed her words, she hadn't realized she'd spoken them aloud. "I did not mean to interrupt, Mr. Bontrager."

He took a long, slow swig of his lemonade. Planted both feet flat on the floor. Balanced his elbows on his knees. And hung his head.

"Before my wife died," he began in a slow, quiet voice, "long before, I said some things. Ugly, hateful things."

"All couples say things they do not mean from time to time." She sent him a nervous smile, a feeble attempt at lightening the heaviness within him. "My married girl-friends in Nappanee complained about such things from time to time."

He glared at her. "And you listened? To sinful *gossip*?"

In their days together, she'd seen him angry. When Sam hadn't done his chores. When Molly spilled milk.

When Matthew stiffened from head to toe, making it next to impossible to carry him upstairs to bed. This, *this,* was a deeper, darker kind of anger, the kind she'd so often seen on her father's face.

"They knew the information was safe with me."

For a long time, he sat, stiff and silent, staring at some unknown spot on the concrete between his boots, but now he lifted his head, just enough to meet her eyes. "I apologize if I sounded judgmental."

*But not for* being *judgmental*?

"She wanted to leave me, leave Pleasant Valley."

Marta had wanted to leave the Plain life . . . or just Bontrager? The "street angel, house devil" phrase came to mind again. Was this his way of warning her, giving her an out, before his temper made her want to leave him, too?

No, that couldn't be it. Because yes, he'd been stern with the children, but they didn't fear him. Quite the opposite, in fact. At the sound of his truck grinding up the driveway, they stopped whatever they were doing and ran to greet him, and the way they looked at him, why, it bordered on adulation!

His lips formed a thin, grim line, and he went back to staring at the floor. There must be more to his story. Much more.

"Why do you think I need to know this, Mr. Bontrager, on the night before we are to be wed?"

"Your question shouldn't surprise me," he said, his voice barely more than a whisper. "Stella told me that you spoke highly of me, that when she gave you the perfect opening to talk about our . . . the specifics of our marriage, you refused to discuss it."

"I mean no disrespect. She is your sister, after all. But our private discussions were none of her concern. You must have good reason to keep the details—" But wait. He'd just said that Stella had given her a chance to reveal those details. "Do you mean to say she *does* know . . . everything?"

"No, she does not. Stella has always been a bit sneaky. She probably thought I'd tell her . . . everything . . . if she could convince me that she'd figured things out on her own."

If he hadn't shared the particulars with his sister, he probably hadn't shared them with anyone else, either. The relief was followed by disappointment, because if Stella was the type who'd try to trick her own brother, how could they ever be friends?

It had been a long day, and in addition to routine chores, she'd worked hours in the hot sun, making the front flower garden presentable, in case his family and friends wanted to visit after the ceremony. She blamed exhaustion and the late hour for the confusion that clouded her mind.

"I am sorry that you have carried those harsh words for so long, but I fail to see what that has to do with what the bishop said."

"What did he say?"

"That I needed to ask you to—how did he put it?—to come clean with me."

His frown deepened. "I see." Bontrager sipped the lemonade, then continued with, "A moment ago, you called me kindhearted and generous. If you're to spend the rest of your life with me, you need to know what you're getting into."

On his feet now, Bontrager began to pace. The back-and-forth motion caused lemonade to slosh onto the back of his hand, so he placed the glass on the washer, beside hers, and used one of the cleaning rags nearby to dry it.

"I told Marta she could go, though she'd given me no reason for her decision. But she'd have to leave the children, because I would see to it that she was shunned."

For a long time, Beth sat in silence, mulling over his words. They still didn't make sense. What had happened between Bontrager and his wife?

"Did Bishop Fisher threaten you?" she asked.

Confusion replaced the anguish on his face. "Threaten me? With what?"

She got to her feet, moved closer to where he stood. "With telling your secret. The things you said to Marta, did you confess them to the bishop?"

"I did," he ground out. "But not at first."

"Please help me understand why Bishop Fisher felt I needed to know about a trivial argument between a husband and wife!"

"It was hardly trivial."

*Then what* was *it, Mr. Bontrager,* what?

"On the day she died, Fisher came to me, to offer consolation. I sent him packing. Told him that I despised her, that I was glad she'd died."

And now, finally, it all made sense. Bontrager had been harboring the secret of his wife's infidelity.

"When you hear what I am about to say, Mr. Bontrager, you will think I am a horrible person."

"I cannot imagine you doing anything that would make me think such a thing, Bethel."

He was hurting, deeply. It was written on his handsome face and echoing in his ragged voice. So she said, "You say Marta did not tell you why she wanted to leave. But surely you know. In your heart, you know." Perhaps that would explain his wife's desire to leave him.

"There was another man." He aimed a thick forefinger in Beth's direction. "And if you think I intend to say more, you have another think coming."

From the moment Karl had called to explain his "come to Pleasant Valley to help my poor brother-in-law" scheme, she'd wondered why a man like Bontrager—successful, well liked, good looking—would settle for a mousy, limping thing like herself. She had her answer now: He'd never have to worry that another man would lure her away from him.

The realization stung, like the back of her father's hand connecting with her jaw.

She shook off the painful recollection. "Then your anger was . . . *is* justified."

"But Bethel, don't you get it? I wished her dead. The mother of my children! I wished him dead, too, and I barely knew him."

"She committed adultery. What man can forgive a transgression like that?"

"An Amish man. We are called to have faith. To believe that everything is God's will. Even hurtful, humiliating things."

He seemed determined to punish himself, and Beth searched her mind for a word, a phrase, a sentence that would loosen the cloak of guilt he'd wrapped so tightly around himself.

"Do you remember several years ago," she began, "when a deranged man burst into the Amish school in Pennsylvania, and for no reason anyone could explain, kidnapped, then killed five little girls . . . before killing himself . . . in front of the rest of the children?"

A look of horror replaced the anger and the guilt that had darkened his face. "None of us will ever forget that day."

"Look me in the eye, Aaron Bontrager, and tell me that *any* of that was God's will."

He stood, still and quiet, and slapped a hand to the back of his neck.

"When we heard the news in Nappanee, we gathered in the church to pray. I said the words, because it was expected of me, of all of us. 'We forgive him, Lord,' everyone said, because there must have been a reason God allowed the tragedy to take place, and that reason is His will." She took a step closer to Bontrager. "But I lied. I did not forgive that man. I will *never* forgive him. Do you know why?"

"No . . ."

"Because I cannot believe that He expects us to forgive such calculated evil."

"Jesus did."

"Jesus was perfect. I am far from it." *There,* she thought, *a little truth about* me *to consider!*

He shook his head. Nodded. Shrugged.

"Does Stella know?"

"About Marta?" A bitter laugh passed his lips. "No. No

one knows. Only the man she loved, and after I found out, he left town."

She couldn't have been more than ten when, while shopping with her mother in Oakland, the sight of glittering diamonds at Helbig's Jewelry Store drew her close, so close that she'd pressed her nose against the big window to get a better look. "Oh, Maem," she'd said on a sigh, "what makes them sparkle so?" The shop's owner stopped sweeping his front walk long enough to say, "When we get the stones, they are murky and dull, but we cut into them with sharp little tools. Fifty-two slices that go this way and that, and then we sand and polish until each facet catches the light and turns it multiple colors."

Like rainbows . . . *I have set my bow in the clouds, and it will be the sign of the covenant between me and the earth.* The truth, Beth thought now, must be a bit like a diamond, reflecting facts in multiple ways.

"Nothing you have said changes anything," she told Bontrager. "We must be practical. You still need someone to mind the children, take care of the house and grounds, tend the animals." *And I still need an escape from every bitter memory in Nappanee.*

"Well then . . ."

"And you have my promise: Not a word of what you told me will ever leave this house."

He inhaled a deep, shaky breath, let go of it slowly. "I believe you."

It seemed he had more to say, so she asked, "Is there anything else you need to tell me?"

A dry chuckle escaped his lips. "No. No, I think I've said quite enough. Except . . ."

She tensed, wondering what new facet of the truth he'd expose.

". . . except it is getting late, and I interrupted your ironing."

She followed his gaze to where her blue dress lay on the ironing board. "Yes. Yes, it is late." Beth returned to it as he made his way upstairs.

Halfway up, he stopped. "Good night, Bethel."

"Sleep well, Mr. Bontrager."

"You know, I think for the first time in a long time, I *will*." He moved up one step more. "I'm surer of it now than ever. I was right to bring you here."

Once he was out of sight, she turned on the iron. *Bethel Mast, you are a silly, simpleminded fool.*

Because in less than two weeks, despite everything she'd warned herself against, despite everything he'd just said, she was falling in love with Aaron Bontrager.

# Chapter Six

Beth whisked six eggs into a big bowl, added sugar, vanilla, and milk, and sprinkled the mixture with cinnamon. As soon as she heard movement upstairs, she'd butter the griddle and whisk it again.

While waiting for the Bontragers to wake up, she set the table, using dishes found the day before yesterday, while sweeping behind the furnace. *What a shame*, she'd thought, digging through the straw-and-newspaper-lined wooden box, *to hide them away, especially when every stoneware cup, bowl, and plate in the kitchen cupboard was chipped or cracked*. Now, a shaft of morning sun slanted through the kitchen window, accenting the white-on-white floral design that graced each scallop-edged piece.

Last night, after pressing her dress, Beth had washed and ironed the plain linen tablecloth and matching napkins stored with the dinnerware. Before starting the French toast batter, she'd slipped outside to cut flowers from the garden. Now, while placing the artful arrangement of black-eyed Susans in the table's center, she whispered, "There. Just the right touch of color."

She placed milk and juice glasses at the one o'clock position above each plate. Plain glass salt and pepper shakers sat to the left of the big flower-filled water pitcher, a matching butter dish to its right. She glanced around, from the bright white café curtains at the window and door to the muted blues of the braided rug under the table, from the perfectly positioned place settings to the syrup-filled gravy boat and serving platters that would soon hold French toast and crispy link sausages. She wanted everything to look perfect. Was it prideful to admit that the room looked lovely?

"If so, forgive me, Lord . . ."

Now the sunshine drew her attention to the calendar, where someone—Molly, if Beth had to guess—had circled today's date: Wednesday the seventeenth. The bouquet of yellow roses at the top of the page brought back memories of articles she'd read about Englisher weddings, featuring full-color photos of brides in gossamer gowns and tuxedoed grooms, reception halls packed with well-dressed guests, and tables stacked high with white and silver wrapped gifts. In a matter of hours, Beth, in a simple bonnet and plain blue dress, would become a married woman. Only a few would gather for the humble ceremony. If one or two wondered about the suddenness and secrecy of the nontraditional union between the all-business bereaved father and the limping stranger he'd summoned from Nappanee, they'd keep their questions to themselves. *Why should you be the only one wondering!*

Not that she was complaining. A wedding of any sort was more than she'd ever dreamed possible. Besides, with marriage came the unexpected promise that she'd never again feel alone, and thanks to the platonic nature of the pact, it also guaranteed she'd never again need to recoil from a man's touch. Bontrager's confession last night was proof that he'd go to great lengths to protect her, just as he'd protected his wife. By hiding the woman's transgressions, he'd guarded her reputation. Beth wasn't so naïve as to believe he'd done it purely for altruistic reasons: Keeping the humiliating secret had sheltered the children from the ugly truth about their mother . . . and protected his own standing in the community, as well.

The floorboards above her squeaked and creaked, and the soft beat of bare feet meant that the children were up. Slightly heavier footsteps told her that Bontrager was moving about, too. At most, she'd have fifteen minutes to prepare breakfast.

"Good thing you precooked the sausages," she said, and turned on the burners.

While the frying pan and griddle heated up, Beth poured milk and orange juice into the glasses and wondered who'd show up first. Matthew, more than likely. Those first few days, the boy had made a point of not being alone with her. Three days ago, though, he'd carried a book to the table and pretended to read while she cooked. He'd kicked a ball through the grass as she weeded the flower beds, watching intently as she pinched dead blooms from the petunias. It hadn't been easy, filling those quiet moments with topics of conversation that didn't require a reply—the prickly nature of scouring pads, the soothing calls of mourning doves, the rough handrail that impaled her palm with a splinter, gentle winds that helped diffuse the hot, humid June air—but Beth managed. With every lift of an eyebrow and each faint grin, she knew that he'd heard her rambling comments. And oh, how seeing that pleased her!

Sam walked into the room, wearing the pale blue pajamas she'd washed just yesterday.

"Good morning, Samuel. I trust you slept well?"

He stood several feet away from the stove. "Well enough, I expect. Had a dream that woke me, but not a bad one, so I went right back to sleep."

An invitation to ask for details? Or a test of her ability to mind her own business?

She dipped a slice of bread into the French toast batter. "I hardly slept at all."

"Because Molly snores?"

Beth laughed. "No, she barely makes a sound during the night."

"The floor, then."

Her pallet wasn't the most comfortable of beds, but most nights, she climbed onto it too tired to notice the hard wood beneath the stack of folded quilts.

"No, there is plenty of padding between it and me."

"Yeah, but even if that was a problem, it ends tonight."

Beth was glad to have something other than his inquisitive young face to focus on. She flipped the first slice of toast, and while it sizzled quietly, she soaked another. Thoughts of sharing Bontrager's bed had definitely crossed her mind. So had the notion that soon, she needed to find space for her few possessions in his room. For now—

"Are you scared?"

"Of what?"

"Of getting married, of course."

Though he didn't say it, Beth heard ". . . you numskull . . ." at the end of his sentence.

"I am trying not to think about it."

"Hmpf," he said. "You can't solve problems by avoiding them."

"Did your father teach you that?"

"He did. And he's right."

"Yes, it is good solid advice. I will take it to heart."

"Do you ever get tired of talking that way?"

By now, she'd stacked four slices of toast on the platter. "What way?"

"Like . . . like Bishop Fisher. He doesn't like the New Order ways. That's why, when he talks, he makes a point of using what Daed calls 'the Dutch.' I kinda think he's right, that the bishop would be happier if we *all* lived by the old rules."

"But you would not?"

"Nuh-uh! One of my school friends, David, is Old Order. No electricity. No telephone. No plumbing. So even in the middle of winter, when it's freezing cold and the snow is piled this high . . ." He held a hand at shoulder height. ". . . they have to use the outhouse. Which is way, *way* in the back of their yard. Even in the middle of the night. Once, he saw a bear on the walk back to the house." Sam shivered. "A bear!"

"A bear. Oh my!" She pretended to shiver, too. "That must have terrified David."

"I'll say. He told me he never drinks anything after supper." Sam leaned a little closer and lowered his voice. "His mother doesn't know it, but he keeps a bucket under his bed, for . . . emergencies."

Laughing, Beth said, "I wish I had thought of that. It would have spared me jumping out of my slippers when foxes or deer crossed my path."

It was the most he'd said to her, all at one time, since her arrival. Soon, Matthew and Molly would come downstairs, and much as she looked forward to wishing them a good morning, Beth hated for this pleasant conversation to end.

"So do you?"

Using one corner of the spatula, she nudged the sausage links. "Do I what?"

"Get tired of never using contractions."

"No, but . . . it is all I know."

"Think you'll start using them, like the rest of us? Once you've been here a while longer, I mean? 'Cause people tend to do that, y'know. Copy what others close to them do, I mean."

*The way you stand exactly as your father does, you mean?* "Anything is possible, I suppose."

One shoulder rose, then fell. "Okay if I grab a sausage?"

"May I do it for you? They are sizzling hot, and I would hate to see you burn your fingers."

He thought about it for a moment. "Sure. I guess. Okay."

Still smiling, Beth stabbed a fork tine into one link and carried it to the table. "It will cool more quickly if you cut it. Like this." Using the side of the fork, she chopped off one end.

Sam licked his lips, then sat down.

"What were Matthew and Molly doing when you left them?"

The shoulder rose and fell again. "Dunno what Molly is up to. Her door is closed." He popped the sausage piece into his mouth. "But Matthew was brushing his teeth," he said around it.

"And your father?"

"Polishing his boots. I could hear him." He pretended to move a shoe brush from side to side.

"But . . . the boots are brand new!"

"Daed is . . ." Sam's eyes narrowed as he searched for the right term. "He is particular. Don't worry. You'll figure that out soon enough."

*Particular? Not if the former condition of this house and yard are indicators!*

The boy jumped up, half-ran toward the staircase. "Matthew. You're finally up. Come and sit. Beth will get you a sausage."

Matthew met her eyes, as if seeking verification. "You may have one," she told him, "but just one. We do not want to gobble them all up before Molly and your *daed* join us, right?"

The boys sat side by side, and in seconds, both sausages were gone.

Now Molly skipped into the room. "Everything smells delicious!" Sitting across from her brothers, she said, "Did you iron my new dress, Beth?"

"I did. As soon as we have finished breakfast, I will carry everything upstairs for you, so that—"

"Why not let us do it?" Bontrager said. "You washed, dried, and pressed the clothes. Seems to me that's the least we can do." One by one, he met the children's eyes. "Right?"

"If it is all the same to you, Mr. Bontrager, I would rather do it myself, eliminate the possibility that those nice new things will get soiled."

"Good point," he said, and took his seat. The same one

she'd assigned to him on her first night in Pleasant Valley. Odd, she thought, how quickly and easily the family had adapted to the arrangement. It told her that, in some respects, they wanted—even needed—her guidance.

Sam ran a fingertip around the rim of his juice glass. "Why do you always call Daed Mr. Bontrager?"

"My own mother called my father Mr. Mast, right up until the day she died. I suppose it was . . . is . . . a sign of respect."

"Well, *my* mother called him Aaron."

Bontrager's eyes met hers, but only for an instant. It reminded her of how he'd looked last night. Angry. Hurt. And something else. She'd thought about it long into the night. Prayed about it, too. The something else, she'd decided, had been guilt. For a reason she didn't understand, Bontrager felt to blame for Marta's betrayal, as if he thought if he'd been a better, more attentive husband—

"Tomorrow, after you two are married, then will you call him Aaron?" Molly inserted.

No, not even then, though Beth had no idea *why*.

"'Husband' then?"

She busied herself by carrying the French toast and sausage platters to the table, then sat and, eyes closed, folded her hands. *Lord,* began her silent prayer, *thank You for putting a stop to the questions I cannot answer. Thank You, too, for my many gifts. Food to sustain me. Honest work to occupy my hands. The hope of family.*

Beth picked up the sausage platter and handed it to Molly. "Help yourself, sweet girl," she said. "We should eat up before everything gets cold!"

As the food disappeared, Bontrager fielded the children's questions: How long did it take to "get married"?

Who'd join them in the church? Would there be cake? His answers placated them, but it was clear from their still curious expressions that he hadn't fully satisfied them. The carefree back-and-forth exchange made it seem almost amusing that, for a minute last night, she'd thought him capable of any type of abuse.

"Help Bethel with the dishes, Molly, and afterward, take a bath. In the meantime, Sam, you help Matthew take his. And when you're finished, you take one, too."

"Let's get this over with, li'l brother," Sam shouted. He raced toward the stairs with Matthew close on his heels.

"But Daed," the girl whimpered, "they always leave a nasty ring around the tub. I hate having to scrub it off. That's why I like to take my bath *first*!"

"How about this?" Beth said. "You clear the table, and I will scrub the tub."

"But I hear the water running. The boys are up there, making a mess already."

"Hmm . . . that does present a bit of a dilemma. How about if I wash the dishes and you dry. By the time we have put everything away, Samuel and Matthew will have finished."

"And then will you braid my hair, Beth?"

"Of course."

"You're perfectly capable of doing it, yourself, Molly. Bethel needs time to get ready, too, you know."

Beth spared him from Molly's next protestation with, "It is early yet, so there will be plenty of time for both of us to bathe and dress. But while we are upstairs, Mr. Bontrager, would you mind looking after the boys, to make sure they stay neat and clean?"

"Of course." And then he smiled, a warm, wide smile that involved every inch of his handsome, well-rested face.

She was happy for him, and a bit envious, too. Since childhood, Beth had relied on several get-to-sleep tricks on nights when her father's behavior was most frightening. But last night, nothing had worked. Not prayer or deep breathing or even picturing writing "Go to sleep" over and over on an imaginary chalkboard. Her thoughts had been stuck on the dialog between Bishop Fisher and Bishop Lantz that had led to Bontrager's payment to her father. A tidy sum must have changed hands, or she'd still be a virtual slave to the Mast and Son Market . . . and her father. Did Bontrager now see her as property, like a horse or cow he'd purchased? Or did he pity her, the way Stella had when she'd learned none of the Masts would attend the wedding? Once she'd dozed off, she'd dreamed: The two of them had faced forward with the congregants behind them, men on the left, women on the right. The door had opened, silencing Fisher's prayer and causing everyone to face the back of the church . . . where her father and brother had stood in bib overalls that stretched tight over ponderous bellies. The image had roused her, and heart hammering, Beth had tiptoed downstairs, where she'd paced the dew-dampened lawn until the deep purple light of dawn touched the mountaintops.

Molly leaned closer to her father. "What's wrong with her?"

Beth realized her thoughts had distracted her.

"A little nervous, I expect," he whispered back.

"About the wedding?"

"I suppose. . . ."

*Pull yourself together,* dummkopf! "Well," Beth said,

smoothing her apron, "these dishes are not going to wash themselves, are they!" And with that, she began stacking plates.

Molly followed, collecting forks and butter knives, and behind her, Bontrager gathered the juice glasses, pinching the rims together, four in each big hand. A moment later, the three of them stood shoulder to shoulder at the sink.

Molly giggled. "Look, Daed, we're clustering!"

Chuckling, he said, "Yes, we are."

"Clustering?" Beth asked.

"It's what Daed says when we all stand really close together, like we're doing now." Another giggle. "I remember the very first time, on the back porch during a thunderstorm. We were all scared of the lightning until you said . . ."

"Why are we all crowded together like chicks under a hen!" they said together.

Picturing it, she laughed with them.

"I guess this is just one of the things that makes us Bontragers, right, Daed?"

He met Beth's eyes and said, "It's a family thing, all right."

It took a concerted effort to bring her attention back to cleaning up, and as she squirted liquid soap into the dishpan, Bontrager and Molly stepped back. He dipped the dishrag into the basin, wrung it out, and proceeded to wipe the table while his daughter put the salt and pepper shakers on the hutch, in precisely the same way Beth had, days earlier.

*It's a family thing, all right.* . . . Just words, spoken in haste because his little girl needed his agreement? Or God's answer to her prayer at breakfast, when she'd thanked Him for her many blessings, and for giving her hope that here, she'd found a safe haven, and family?

When he returned the dishrag, she said, "I appreciate your help. It means I will not have to rush."

"No need to thank us."

Molly stepped between them, slid one arm around his waist, the other around Beth's. "Yup, we're all in this together now, right, Daed?"

"Right."

Beth didn't know how to read his now serious expression and straightforward, one-syllable reply. Was it agreement? Or yet another facet of his truth, slicing through his cooperative façade?

"Thanks, Micah, for everything you did to make Bethel feel comfortable."

"Her request for a small, private ceremony was reasonable. I saw no reason to deny it."

"Are you coming to my mother's for a bite to eat?"

"Yes, yes, I'll just stop at home to pick up the missus and we will be there."

"I'm happy to drive you. . . ."

"No, no, no. The short walk and fresh air will be good for us." He started walking toward the house adjacent to the church. "See you soon, Aaron Bontrager, bridegroom."

He could still hear the bishop's chuckling as he followed the rest of his family. Aaron lagged behind a bit, soaking up the harmony of their interactions. Matthew, close by his side, kicked a rock, and up ahead, Sam and Molly exchanged good-natured barbs. When the two caught up to Stella and Karl, each grabbed a hand. A few yards farther down the road, Aaron's brother walked with Bethel. Seth must be in rare form today, for every now and then she laughed at something he said. As the melodic sound filtered back to him, Aaron counted his blessings, all seven of them.

A hot June gust nearly stole Bethel's cap, and when she reached up to catch it, the material of her apron-covered dress pressed to her body. It was the first time Aaron had noticed her trim waist and slender hips. He had to shake his head to get his mind back on track. *Think about her character*, he told himself, *and how quickly she'd whipped the house into shape*. His mother's front walk came into view. Tidy, he thought, but not nearly as colorful as his own, thanks to Bethel's hard work. Just the other day, he'd come home to find her on her knees in the lawn, wielding a hammer like a skilled carpenter as she banged nail holes into the bottoms of four dented buckets found in the shed. Drainage holes, she'd called them, to prevent rot as the transplanted flowers took root. The very next day, the plant-filled pails sat on the top porch steps, two on the left, two on the right.

God had blessed her with many talents, among them a gift for telling it like it is without sounding argumentative or accusatory. The pre-marriage interview at the church, for example, when Bethel asked permission to keep the number of guests as low as possible. While they put their heads together to discuss it, she'd turned to him. "Mr. Bontrager, may I . . . might we host a reception in the upcoming weeks?" A nighttime get-together, she'd described, with hot dogs and hamburgers and marshmallows toasted over the fire pit. What could he say but yes? As for the men, Aaron would never know if it was the honest simplicity of her requests or the idea itself that made them say yes, too.

So this morning, after a rib-sticking breakfast, he'd donned the new white shirt she laundered and pressed, topped it with his best straw hat, and stood beside her at the front of the church, where only his immediate family had gathered. Fisher kept his sermon blessedly short, citing the pairings of Isaac and Rebecca, Boaz and Ruth, Rachel and Jacob as examples of holy unions. He followed the stories with "Do you believe, brother, that the Lord has provided Bethel as a partner for you?" His tentative "Yes" shamed him. And must have unnerved Bethel, because from the corner of his eye, he saw her lower her head, as if praying for the strength to endure life with a man like him. He'd never forget that moment, or the way she'd answered Fisher's question of *her* with an immediate, resounding "Of course!" Her certainty seeped into him, and when they were asked, "Do you both promise to live in love, forbearance, and patience, until God separates you by your death?" *he* didn't hesitate to join her unwavering "Yes." Fisher concluded with a short prayer, sandwiched their hands between his own, and said, "May the God of Abraham, and the God of Isaac, and the God of Jacob be with you, and bless you richly, through Jesus Christ, Amen."

*And just like that, you have yourself a wife.*

"Hey, brother," Seth said over one shoulder, "stop woolgathering and get up here. I have something important to ask you."

If not for Matthew, he would have jogged forward. "How's the foot today, son?"

He answered with a tiny smile. No surprise, really, because in the midst of everything else she'd accomplished already today, Bethel had taken the boy aside, daubed antiseptic and ointment onto the blister, and applied a fresh bandage. And, just as she had at bedtime, she'd chattered reassuringly the entire time.

"Want to hustle up there with me, or should I carry you?"

A playful grin lit Matthew's face, and he raced ahead, stopping after a few yards to see if his father had followed. In no time, they joined Seth . . . and Aaron's wife.

At six-three, Seth stood nearly four inches taller than Aaron and outweighed him by a good twenty pounds of raw muscle, yet he was a tender-hearted, gentle soul.

"So? What's so important?"

A familiar, teasing smirk preceded Seth's answer. "Oh, I was just wondering . . . how it feels to be a bridegroom at your advanced age?"

Aaron gave him a brotherly shoulder nudge. "You make it sound like I'm a grizzled old man."

"Just kidding, big brother. And although I'll have to ask God's forgiveness for admitting it, the truth is, I envy you." He peered around Aaron. "No matter what anyone tells you," he said, winking at Bethel, "your husband is a good and decent man."

She continued walking and, looking straight ahead, said, "Who would say otherwise?"

The silence that followed lasted all of a second, but seemed far, far longer.

"No one," Seth said. "I was kidding, just kidding."

"Again," Aaron said. "When you get to know him better, Bethel, you'll find that he does that a lot."

She nodded, and Seth said, "May I call you Beth, or do you prefer Bethel?"

"Beth is fine."

"One day soon, Beth, I hope to ask you all about your long-distance courtship with my big brother." He elbowed Aaron. "Because until you got to town, I had no idea he'd been corresponding with you. Karl, the master secret-keeper, never let on that you were involved in a relation-ship with his cousin."

Because until a month ago, Karl hadn't known himself. Would she tell Seth that two long-distance phone calls hardly qualified as a relationship? Or acknowledge that her father had insisted on a cash payment before granting permission for Beth to leave Nappanee? From the moment Mast had suggested it, the exchange of money had left Aaron with a bad feeling, but by then, both bishops had been involved, and the pressure had been on.

"I hope you will feel free to visit us any time, Seth."

It didn't escape his notice that she'd put extra emphasis on *us*, sending the subtle message that such conversations would only take place with Aaron present. More proof that Stella was right: Bethel was protective—

"It is about time the bunch of you got here," Esther called from the front porch. "If that ham stays in my oven any longer, it will turn black as the night!"

He noticed that while everyone else filed into the house, Bethel hung back. Not that he blamed her. It couldn't be easy, becoming a wife without having met her husband's own mother. He should have introduced them sooner. But between work and the kids, and meeting with

Fisher, there just hadn't been time. *There* was *time,* he admitted, *but you chose to spend it by—*

This time, it was Bethel's soft voice that broke into his thoughts. "It is good of you to do this for us, Mrs. Bontrager. Thank you so much."

"It is I who should be thanking *you*! I am happy for a good excuse to get everyone here for a family meal. And a chance to meet my lovely daughter-in-law. What woman could ask for more!"

"How can I help?"

His mother pointed. "Go into the yard, find a chair, and sit down. This is your wedding day." She grabbed Aaron's wrist. "And you," she said, "you go with her. She does not know everyone well. What better opportunity to remedy that?"

"Esther," Karl said, "you're tasking this hermit with making introductions?" He dropped a brotherly hand on Aaron's shoulder. "Your poor wife!"

Wife. Officially. And permanently. *It must be ninety degrees in here,* Aaron thought. He ran a finger around his collar. "Speaking of wives, where is yours?"

"Home, picking up the twins." He lowered his voice. "Let me show Bethel around. If I look busy when Stella gets here, I might escape feeding-and-diapering duty."

"Go," Esther said, giving him a playful push. "Let their grandmother do it." She waved Bethel closer. "And their brand-new aunt will help, yes?"

"I would like that. It will give us a chance to get better acquainted."

"Aaron, son, I see you have married an optimist. Your wife actually thinks we will be able to talk while caring for two active babies!"

"While they nap, then," he said.

"Ach! God has designed this union. We have here two optimists. What a blessing!"

God designed. Married. Union. Wife. Blessing? At the moment, Aaron wasn't sure about any of it.

And then Bethel went into the kitchen, filled two glasses with lemonade, and, smiling, made her way back to him. He returned the smile and extended a hand to accept one.

But she gave it to his mother, instead.

"Why thank you, dear Bethel." Esther took a sip, and Aaron did his best to suppress laughter.

"I really wish you would let me help with something, Mrs. Bontrager. Standing around doing nothing always leaves me feeling . . . odd."

"Then go outside and sit. You will feel much odder if your blue dress absorbs the stink of ham and egg salad!"

Bethel, Aaron realized, was built to serve. And so was his mother. Without intervention, the affable "let me help"–"no thanks" dickering could go on indefinitely. He placed a hand at the small of Bethel's back and urged her ahead. And instead of balking, as he'd expected, she walked beside him.

"Oh look," she said. "How sweet."

Aaron followed her gaze to where all three of his kids had plopped, bellies down, on the thick quilt Stella had spread out for the babies.

Aaron guided her to the picnic table. The wind had mussed the red and white checkered tablecloth, and immediately, she smoothed the wrinkles.

"It is good that your sister is so energetic."

Her comment drew his attention to Stella, giggling like

a girl as she chased Karl and tried to douse him with a cup of lemonade.

"She will need every ounce of that energy once the twins are both on their feet."

"Mmm-hmm," Aaron said, though he didn't think it likely that they'd walk at the same time. Huge blue eyes were the only feature they had in common. The bigger, chubbier Micah had an abundance of shining auburn curls, whereas Mark's nearly white, fine strands made him appear bald. Micah had mastered the art of rolling over and sitting up, and when he smiled—which was often— he revealed two gleaming teeth. By contrast, the always-quiet Mark seemed perfectly content to coo at his own fists.

"How soon do you think we should reach out, invite people to our reception?"

"What are your thoughts?" she asked.

Aaron snorted. "If it was up to me, I'd say let's hope the bishop and elders forget about it."

Bethel turned slightly on the bench, and when she did, her thigh pressed lightly against his. "Do you think it is possible? That they will forget, I mean?"

Hope rang loud in her voice, widened her eyes, too. Not more than an hour ago, he'd promised to behave like a proper Christian husband. *Might as well start right now. . . .*

"We'll trust God to tell us what to do."

The light in her eyes dimmed a little, and she faced forward. Instantly, he felt a faint chill where their legs had touched.

"Yes. Of course." She met his eyes. "One of many things we will pray about."

*Starting when?* he wondered. *Tonight, perhaps, when she began sharing his room . . . and his bed?*

There were so many things Aaron wanted to discuss with her, things they ought to have talked about days ago. Not knowing how to introduce the potentially prickly topics, he'd avoided them. *Maybe you should've been praying about* that, *instead of pouring all your time into newly signed contracts, old contracts, and ongoing jobs.*

"Daed," Sam called, "how soon before we eat? My belly's growling."

"Ask your grandmother." *Her house*, Aaron thought, *her rules*.

"Come with me," Seth said. "We'll ask together."

His son and his brother disappeared into the kitchen.

"I should go with them." Bethel got to her feet. "Your mother will need help carrying the food outside."

"Wouldn't need to, if we ate indoors."

Bethel was standing directly in front of him when she said, "It is unusually hot and humid, but at least there is a breeze. She must have decided we would be more comfortable out here than crowded around the table."

He grinned up at her. "Oh. Fine. Take her side, why don't you."

She grinned back. "I took a vow this morning, Mr. Bontrager, to be on your side, always."

A bee buzzed his head, and when he waved to shoo it away, she winced, holding up a hand in self-defense.

It wasn't the first time Aaron had wondered what she'd survived back in Nappanee. Answers to that would have to wait. This could not: "I took vows this morning, too, and you have my word . . . I will never deliberately harm you."

Her fear diminished, but not much. He blamed the word "deliberately," for it hinted that if by chance he caused her pain, it wouldn't count.

She faced the back porch. "Your mother went to a lot of trouble today, all because I insisted on a small reception. Even missed the ceremony itself to do this for me. The least I can do is see how I might help her."

If he grasped her wrist to keep her from walking away, he'd only make things worse. So Aaron said, "Wait, Bethel. Look at me. Please."

Slowly, she met his eyes. "I want you to know," he said, "that I will not harm you. Ever. For any reason. Period."

Her gaze flicked over his face, searching, he supposed, for proof of sincerity. He waited until her eyes locked on to his. "Let me prove it to you," he said, "one day at a time."

She answered with a single nod. "A fresh glass of lemonade," she said, picking up his glass, "is the perfect excuse to go back inside."

He tensed when the screen door closed behind her, but at the sound of animated voices, he relaxed. A little. When he'd told his mother how he'd solved his child care problems, she'd blasted him with objections, starting with, "Marriage is hard enough when you love each other," and ending with, "You are *gek* if you think hiring a wife makes a lick of sense." He couldn't very well deny it. . . . The idea *was* crazy. And her opinion had remained firm, even after his reminder that both of his grandparents' marriages had started in much the same way, as arranged matches.

Matthew plopped down on the bench and leaned his head on Aaron's arm.

"All tuckered out already, eh, son?"

The boy shook his head.

"Then what? Cat got your tongue?"

Another head shake. But it didn't take a genius to figure out what was bothering his youngest child. He enjoyed the clean house, the tidy yard, the delicious meals, and even the tender way Bethel had nursed his blister. Matthew had accepted Aaron's explanation of the decision that would impact them all, but hearing the exchange of vows had changed *idea* to *reality*. Even at his tender age, the boy understood that in the space of fifteen minutes, their lives had been forever changed.

He'd said it before, but felt the need to repeat it. "She will be good for us."

Matthew sighed.

"You like her, right?"

He answered with a slight nod.

"You aren't afraid of her, are you?"

He shook his head.

"I have to work so I can buy food and clothes and shoes for you and your brother and sister, and that leaves no time for healthy meals or clean laundry." He glanced at the boy's foot. "Or to fix you up when you hurt yourself." He'd said all that before, too, numerous times. The last time they'd had this conversation, Aaron had wondered whom he was trying to convince . . . the children, or himself?

"Bethel will take good care of you. Of Molly and Sam." He paused, thinking of the supportive things she'd said about *him*. "She'll take good care of all of us." Another pause, and then, "Do you trust me, son?"

The boy met his eyes, and Aaron read the answer: Yes.

"Then stop worrying. Just have faith. We're gonna be all right now."

"Thanks to Bethel?"

"Molly, you move like a cat. How long have you been standing there?"

"I came to find out why Matthew looks sad. And now I know." She looked at her little brother, brushed blond bangs from his forehead. "Daed is right. We're gonna be all right. We're already better than before, thanks to Bethel."

Aaron scanned the yard, saw the twins sprawled on the quilt, fast asleep. Stella sat behind them, leaning on a tree; whether she was napping or resting her eyes, he couldn't tell. Half an acre away, Sam played catch with Karl and Seth. *He has a good arm,* Aaron thought, grinning when the ball smacked into his brother's palm. Was Sam worried, too, and hiding it behind his usual tough-guy façade? Or had he, like Molly, come to believe that the positive changes Bethel had brought to their home proved that she truly would be good for them?

"Yup, kids, we're gonna be fine. And I'll prove it, one day at a time."

# Chapter Seven

Three weeks had passed since the wedding, and every day of it, at least one neighbor had stopped by to extend hearty congratulations, and to welcome Beth to Pleasant Valley. The pantry shelves were lined with jams, jellies, apple butter, and pickles. Dr. Emily Baker brought an apple pie. Her mother-in-law, Sarah, brought a crocheted afghan, and her daughter Hannah had sewed a quilted table runner and matching napkins. Her favorite gift so far—though she'd never admit it aloud—was Willa's rich and creamy fudge. In every case, Beth served coffee, iced tea, and lemonade, and while the neighbors sipped, she wrote their recipes on three-by-five cards. By the end of that third week, she joked at supper that she'd developed writer's cramp.

The days were long, the work hard but fulfilling. Most satisfying of all was the way the family had settled into a comfortable routine. Bontrager rose at six every day and headed to the office immediately after breakfast. The children padded into the kitchen by seven-thirty, eager to find out what she'd prepared for their morning meal. Once they'd cleaned their plates, Beth sent them upstairs to dress, brush their teeth, and make their beds. And while they took advantage of the less humid morning air to play out back, she tidied the kitchen and started the laundry.

Today, as they collected eggs, milked the cow, and watered and fed all of the animals, storm clouds darkened the sky. The wind whistled through the yard, slamming gates and agitating the animals. If this kept up, one of them—or worse, one of the children—could be hurt.

"Help me move them all into the barn," Beth said. "They will be safer in there." *And so will you.*

Molly led Willy, Lilly, and Clyde from their outdoor enclosure. "Good thing Dacd built these walls high."

Beth hadn't been around during construction of the big outbuilding, but she could picture him estimating how high the goats could leap and adding three feet to that.

"Do you think Daed is in the yard?" the girl asked.

She was referring to the acreage behind the shop. It had taken an entire afternoon for Karl to show her around it. Like a small town, it boasted roads, some to accommodate the big rigs that hauled forested trees, others that led to stacks of massive logs, railroad ties, and telephone poles ready for shipment to buyers. Down one road, pallets of rough lumber were piled twenty feet high. Down another were two three-sided structures, one that held wood chips, a second for bark and mulch. Yet another road led to metal outbuildings used for sorting the hardwood by species and potential use, and whether the boards would be kiln- or air-dried. The office sat closest to the road, and behind it, the mill itself, which housed the largest, most powerful saws she'd ever seen.

"In the office, probably, 'specially if he saw that sky."

Sam had no sooner answered when rib-racking thunder roared above them. Next, fat raindrops hit the metal roof.

"Let's get inside," Beth instructed, "before the rain starts."

Sam helped check the stall gates and latch the double entry doors, and as they raced toward the house, the rain fell harder and the dark clouds churned and rolled above them. Just as they reached the porch, another crack of lightning put Matthew into her arms.

"Smell that?" Sam sniffed the air. "It's ozone. I read about it in a weather book."

"Oh, you and your books." Molly's teasing was short lived. "Goodness," she said, "it's raining so hard I can barely see across the yard to the barn."

"I bought a few art supplies last time your *daed* drove me to Oakland for groceries. We can bring them to the basement and make presents for his birthday."

"The basement? But this is the kind of storm that knocks out the power, and there's barely any light down there as it is."

"Sam's right," Molly agreed. "We need light to make cards."

"I found an old oil lantern while I was cleaning. A couple of flashlights, too." Extending a hand, she invited them to join her downstairs. Matthew held on tight, and within minutes, Sam and Molly followed, too. She'd set up the folding table in the middle of the laundry area, and Molly thought it would make a perfect workspace for their birthday projects.

"His birthday is tomorrow. Will you bake him a cake?"

"Of course." She placed the oil lamp on the washing

machine, then struck a match. "Which is his favorite? Chocolate? Angel food? Yellow?"

"Whoa, why are you lighting that thing now?" Sam wanted to know. "The power isn't even out yet."

"Like Daed says, it's just in case. Right, Beth?"

"Exactly." She blew out the match and, after replacing the chimney and adjusting the flame, said, "The bag of art supplies is upstairs. While I am gone, you can find chairs. And whatever you do, stay away from that lantern."

She heard the clatter of aluminum as they opened the folding chairs and decided to surprise them with a snack. Tossing apples and a sleeve of saltines into a bag, she grabbed a knife from the drainboard and returned to the basement.

"Crackers," Sam said, "with apples?"

"It was one of my mother's favorites." She spread a linen napkin on the table and proceeded to slice the first apple.

"Are you sad?" Molly asked. "That she died, I mean?"

"I miss her. I suppose I always will. But I believe she is in a better place, so I am happy for her."

The girl took inventory of the art supplies. "Construction paper. Colored markers. Plastic scissors. Glue sticks . . ." she recited. Then, "Our mother is in heaven, too."

In Nappanee, the bishop often lectured against followers' certainty of heaven and hell, saying it was arrogant to expect that faith alone guaranteed one's place in Paradise. Salvation, he insisted, was a God-given gift, one that could be opened only if the Almighty determined that believers had lived according to the Ordnung.

Molly rested both elbows on the table. "Do you think they have met?"

Her own mother's life had been one of servitude and piety. If anyone had earned a place in Paradise, she had. Beth had no idea where Marta would spend eternity. She trusted with all her heart that God forgives all sin, even sins as grievous as those committed by her father. If Marta had confessed her transgressions … But the children drew comfort from the notion that their mother now communed with the angels, and at the moment, nothing else mattered. "I suppose it is possible."

"She caught a cold," Sam said, "and it turned into pneumonia. And that's what killed her."

Matthew, who'd been eagerly watching the apple slices multiply, grew suddenly pale. Tears puddled in his eyes, and he hid them behind his hands. The boy cried often and easily, making him the butt of his brother's mockery. To protect him from another bout of teasing, Beth changed the subject. "Have you any idea what to make for your father?"

"A card," Molly said, "all covered with flowers."

"Mine will have trees on the front," Sam said. "Trees are his business. He'll like that."

"I have an idea for a gift to go with the cards," Beth said, "something you can make yourselves."

"What?" Sam and Molly said together.

"They are called silhouettes." She explained the process of aiming a light at their profiles and outlining the shadows they cast on paper. Beth demonstrated by holding her hand between the lantern's glow and a sheet of construction paper behind it.

"Clever way to get around the no photographs rule," Sam said, smirking.

Molly squealed happily. "Oooh! Can we start right now?"

According to the radio's weather forecast, the rain would last long into the night, and Beth wanted to save a few activities that would keep them busy throughout the day.

"We will have our snack first," she said, "and while we eat, you can tell me what you might write inside your *daed's* cards."

"I love you," Molly said.

"Best father ever," Sam added.

Matthew came out of hiding, and she held her breath, for it looked as if he might contribute, verbally, to the conversation. Molly and Sam sat, faces glowing with wide-eyed hope that their little brother had finally found a reason to speak. When it became apparent that he wouldn't, disappointment replaced expectation. Sam broke the sad silence with, "How did your mother die?"

When Bishop Lantz had come to arrange the funeral, he'd asked the same question, and Beth, too afraid to tell the truth, had said, "She fell and hit her head on the woodstove." She repeated the lie now and hoped the answer would avert additional questions.

"So you know how it is then," Molly said, "growing up without a mother."

It had been hard, enduring her brother's constant bullying and meeting her father's selfish demands, but prayer and bullheaded grit had helped her survive.

"But you had your father, like we do, to love you."

They were young, far too young to hear the ugly truth,

and so she said, "The Father's protection is vital." None of them needed to know to which father she referred.

Sam nodded, and so did Molly. Matthew, it seemed, had read between the lines, and Beth sensed that if he could speak, he'd pepper her with many questions.

She placed an apple slice atop a cracker and said, "This is how my mother ate them." Beth crunched into the snack. "Messy," she said, looking at the crumbs, "but just the right blend of salty and sweet."

Molly copied her, and Sam copied Molly. Matthew watched.

Beth fixed him a treat, and just as he gobbled it up, the bulb above the table flickered, then went out. She half expected him to panic, but instead, the boy calmly squinted into the lantern's light.

"See there? It's like Daed says. 'Just in case.'"

Beth lit a second lantern, this one powered by two C batteries, and placed it in the middle of the table, then spread the art supplies around it.

"Are you gonna make Daed a card, Beth?"

The only time she'd prepared fried chicken, Bontrager had told her it was his favorite meal, so she'd planned to make it, along with other preferences like mashed potatoes and gravy, buttery biscuits, corn on the cob, and for dessert, a chocolate layer cake. She'd secretly invited Esther and Seth, as well as Stella and her family, to join them, but hadn't given a thought to making him a card.

"I . . . well . . . Do you think I should?"

"Well, of course," Molly said. "He's your *husband* now." She slid a sheet of bright green paper from its package.

"You wouldn't want Grootmoeder to think you're not taking proper care of her little boy—"

"Yeah," Sam interrupted, laughing, "her big, muscly thirty-eight-year-old little boy."

"I heard her scold Maem once for letting Daed go to work in a wrinkly shirt," she continued as if Sam hadn't interfered.

"I remember that," Sam said, selecting blue paper and handing a yellow sheet to Matthew. "Do you think she ever told Daed about it?"

"Yes, I think she did. Because, after that, she taught Daed how to use the steam iron."

Sam met Beth's eyes. "Has he thanked you?"

"For what?"

"Ironing his trousers and shirts. He hasn't had to do it since you moved in."

"Not in so many words, but I know he appreciates it."

"If he hasn't said so, how do you know?"

"Well, Samuel, I know because he smiles as he snaps his suspenders into place."

"I've seen him do that." Sam smiled, too. "You can call me Sam . . . if you want to."

Beth remembered that first day on the train platform, when she'd worried that he aimed to make her so miserable, she'd beg to go home. She'd made up her mind, right then and there, never to let him see her fear. It gave her great pleasure—and relief—to say, "Thank you . . . Sam."

"What color card will you make, Beth?"

She examined the stack, which contained sheets of black, blue, brown, green, orange, pink, purple, red, yellow, and white. First, she folded a white paper in half, longways. Next, she grasped the scissors and cut shapes— a black hat, suspenders, and boots—and glued them to the card's front, in the order they'd appear on her new husband's tall, muscular body. As an afterthought, she snipped a short brown beard. It would have to do since the package didn't contain a color to match his facial hair. She put it into place, a thumb's width from the hat.

"Hey, that's pretty good," Sam said.

His sister agreed, adding, "What will you write inside?"

*Good question,* she thought. "What will you write?"

"Best *daed* ever," Sam said.

"No fair, copycat, that's what I was gonna write!" Molly objected.

"Not to worry, sweet girl. Just think of another way to say the same thing."

"Like . . .?"

"Like . . ." Beth thought about it for a minute. "Like 'Of all the fathers in the world, I am blessed that you are mine.'"

Molly grabbed the black marker, removed its cap.

"May I make a suggestion?"

The marker's tip hovered near the green paper.

"Write it in pencil first, so that if you make a mistake, you will not need to start all over again."

Sam grabbed a pencil and, twisting it in the tiny sharpener, said, "Great idea." He hunched over the table and, tongue poking out of the corner of his mouth, began sketching.

Beth turned to Matthew, who sat staring at the blank yellow page in front of him.

"Do you know what you might like to make?"

Slouching, he shrugged. Beth put a red marker into

his hand and, uncapping it, said, "Can you draw a circle for me?"

Instead, he traded the marker for a brown one, and drew a tree trunk. Thick limbs and thin branches. Soon, he'd added leaves. Blue sky. Flower-strewn grass. And a gigantic bird, soaring over it all.

"He will love it," she told him. And looking at what Sam and Molly had created, she added, "He will love all of these."

"Think he will hang them on the bulletin board behind his desk?"

"No, Molly," Sam answered, "and you know why."

She sighed, and in a bored monotone said, "Because these are not Plain." She frowned. "I don't get it. Why can Daed drive his truck and talk on the phone, but he can't hang some pictures in his office?"

"Because the truck and his phone help him make money, and since he tithes, like he's supposed to, the church is okay with it."

For one so young, Sam's cynicism was surprising. What had the boy seen or heard to explain it?

The bulb overhead flickered again, then flooded the basement with light.

"Great. Now that we're finished, the power comes back!"

"Oh, Sam, you can be such a sourpuss. Can't you just be happy that the lights are back on?"

He shot his sister a dirty look. "Beth, okay if I go upstairs, see if the rain has stopped?"

"It hasn't." Molly expelled a groan of frustration. "If you'd just stop complaining for a minute, maybe you'd hear it pecking the windows."

A spark of anger gleamed in his blue eyes, and before he had a chance to deliver a stinging reply, Beth said, "We can all move to the kitchen." She gathered up the supplies and made her way to the stairs. "You can keep me company while I start supper."

"What's wrong with your foot?" Sam asked from behind her.

"Nothing. Why?"

"Your limp. Most days, it's hardly noticeable."

In the kitchen now, Beth arranged the artwork on the table and searched her mind for something, anything, that would distract him from the subject. Her wish was granted when he stood at the door and peered outside.

"The rain coming out of the downspout dug a stream right into the middle of the yard." Nose pressed to the dusty screen, he said, "How long after Daed gets home do you think he'll say it's my job to fill it in?"

"The minute he walks in the door, I hope. Maybe then you'll be too busy working to gripe and groan about every little thing," Molly said.

He spun around, and the first thing everyone noticed was the gray splotch on the top of his nose. Laughing, Molly pointed. "Pinocchio's nose grew because he lied. Maybe Sam's nose is turning black because he can't stop griping!"

This time, Beth headed off a confrontation with, "Molly, that was not very nice."

She folded her arms, stuck out her lower lip. "It isn't easy being nice to someone who *isn't*."

Beth pulled out three kitchen chairs, and once they'd taken their seats, she stood behind Bontrager's place.

"Someday, I pray you will realize how blessed you both are, having siblings who care about you."

"She doesn't care about me." Now, Sam was moping, too.

"Why should I? You're *mean.*"

"Why should *I?* You're even meaner."

"Am not."

"Are too."

"Neither of you are mean. And you might not admit it right this minute, but you do care about one another. I can tell."

Matthew watched the exchange like a fan in the stands at a tennis match.

Sam was interested, and it showed in his voice. "How can you tell?"

"By the way you help one another and look out for one another." She cited examples, like the way Sam swatted the wasp that had landed on Molly's shoulder, and how she had handed him nails, the hammer, and boards, then held them in place while he worked on their tree house. "If you had seen the way my brother treated me when we were growing up . . ."

*Growing up, indeed*, Beth thought. On the day she'd left for Pleasant Valley, he had literally shoved her out the door. "Good riddance to bad rubbish," he'd snarled, tossing her bag onto the porch. "Do me a favor and be a good wife, will you, so that I never have to worry you will come back, ever."

"What is his name?" Molly asked.

"Vernon."

"Did Vernon hit you?"

"Often."

"And call you names?"

"All the time."

"I will pray for forgiveness, then, because that makes me angry!"

"Is Vernon younger or older than you?" Sam wanted to know.

"Younger, but he was always big for his age." She could almost feel the ache of kicks and punches Vernon had inflicted over the years.

"Then I will also pray for forgiveness, because I'm angry, too."

She hadn't shared that snippet from her past to make them angry, although it felt good, knowing they cared enough to feel protective of her.

"The reason I told you about Vernon was to give you something to think about. You two might squabble from time to time, but you know in your hearts that you love each other."

Matthew got up, wrapped his arms around Beth's waist. Tears of joy and gratitude stung her eyes, and she pulled him closer. Seeing her tears, Molly and Sam joined in the hug.

"Are we hurting you?"

"No, Molly. Quite the opposite."

"Then . . . why are you crying?"

"Because for the first time in a long time, I am happy."

"Look at us," Sam said, beaming. "We're clustering!"

Only one thing could make the moment more perfect. . . .

If Mr. Bontrager had been a part of it.


Even with the windshield wipers going full blast, it had been difficult to see. Aaron leaned over the steering wheel, squinting through the rain that sheeted down the glass, thanking God that traffic was light and his drive home, short.

Once there, he ran full-out from the pickup to the porch and still got soaked. He was shaking rainwater from his hat when he heard voices just inside the kitchen door. Beth, talking about her life in Nappanee. Specifically, life with her *brother*. He agreed with Molly and Sam: Hearing about the abuse she'd suffered at Vernon's hands was infuriating. He'd lived with her long enough now to believe that nothing she'd done had warranted it.

"Look at us," he heard Sam say, "we're clustering."

Normally, when they heard his truck rumbling up the drive, the children raced outside to greet him. Today, rain pounding the metal roof must have drowned out the noise of the big tires crunching over the gravel. He stomped his feet to alert them and so he wouldn't startle Beth. When she turned at the sound, he saw the tears in her eyes, tears she'd explained with, "For the first time in a long time, I am happy."

Aaron was happy, too, especially when she said, "Look, children, your father is home!"

They separated from her and clung to him, retreating the instant they pressed against his sodden shirt.

"You must be freezing, standing there in that puddle," she said. "I will go upstairs and bring back dry clothes." Halfway up, she leaned over the railing to add, "Hang your wet things in the mud room, and after supper, I will add them to the rest of the laundry."

If it had been wintertime, he'd have worn long johns. If he peeled off what he'd worn today . . . *What is she thinking?*

"Daed is blushing," Molly said into Sam's ear. "Because he doesn't want us to see him in his underwear."

"Doesn't want *Beth* to see that, y'mean," he whispered back.

They giggled, until Molly's brows drew together. "But wait. They share a bedroom and a bathroom now. Surely Beth has seen—"

"Will one of you get me a glass of water?" he interrupted. "I don't want to track grass clippings all over the clean floor."

Molly complied, but it was clear that she understood why he'd so abruptly changed the subject. Thankfully, neither she nor Sam said any more about it.

"We had to spend a couple of hours in the basement," his daughter said.

"Power was out again," Sam explained. "Was it out at the mill, too?"

"Yes, but only for a short while." Thanks to the gas-powered equipment, production wasn't slowed, even though the big fans that cooled the crew had stopped functioning.

"I wish I didn't have to wait until I was fourteen to work with you. I can't wait to run the big saws!"

It was rough, dangerous work that required physical strength and mental dexterity. Distraction, even a second of it, could cost a man fingers, limbs . . . or worse. And until Aaron was sure Sam could focus on a task for more than a few moments, the boy wouldn't be allowed near the powerful equipment.

"Soon enough, son. Soon enough."

Beth returned carrying a complete outfit, right down to clean white socks, over one arm. "My apologies, Mr. Bontrager. I should have known you would prefer to change in a more private place than the mud room."

"If it's all the same to you, I think I'll shower and change afterward."

"But you will—"

He held up a hand to silence her. "Not to worry. Just as soon as I finish, I promise to mop up every puddle I leave behind."

Beth waved the offer away. "If you think a clean floor concerns me more than the possibility that you might slip in one of those puddles, you are a hundred percent wrong."

As usual, she'd spoken with down-to-earth practicality, but the added note of care and concern woke an unfamiliar emotion in him. When he failed to find a name for it, he said, "Thank you. I won't be long," and made his way upstairs.

He noticed instantly that Beth had made a change in his six-by-six-foot bathroom. *Correction: our bathroom.* Even at first glance, he could tell it was a good change. . . .

On their wedding night, he'd crashed into the low, round table that had sat under the window since move-in day, and hearing his quiet grumbling, she'd knocked on the door, asked if everything was all right. "Ridiculous thing takes up too much floor space," he'd complained, "but since there's no other place to store my shampoo and shaving gear . . ." Without a word, she'd picked up every item, and returned to his bedroom. *Correction,* he thought again, *our bedroom. And she probably started planning, right then, how to improve things.* The round table was gone and, in its place, stood a tall, narrow oval table—one of the pieces his parents had brought over soon after he'd finished the house—that boasted a low shelf. "Why buy new things to fill the empty spaces," his mother had said, "when your father and I have more than we need!" Within minutes of their departure that day, Marta had instructed him to take it to the attic. Eventually, he'd put the set-to out of his mind, and the gift had been forgotten.

Until now.

Without saying a word, Beth had scrubbed and sanded it, and given it a coat of flat white paint. Neatly folded towels and washcloths were now within easy reach on its shelf, and on top, a blue-and-white cloth napkin had been laid on the diagonal beneath a box of store-brand tissues and a handleless white wicker basket. The shampoo, his razor, and his shaving cream were within easy reach inside it. He smiled, seeing the way her hairbrush nestled against his comb.

He climbed into the tub and adjusted the shower head. She'd changed the stiff, mildew-spotted shower curtain, too, using a sheet of clear plastic—the kind he used to wrap lumber for transport—sewn to an old bed sheet. Here, as in the kitchen, the parlor, the kids' bedrooms and even the front and back porches, her alterations had been simple, practical, and for the most part, free. When he'd designed the house, Aaron had pictured the way it might look with curtains on the windows and rugs on the floors. Admittedly, he and Marta had had all of that, and yet, he'd always felt the place was missing something.

*Turns out it was missing some*one, *not some*thing, he thought.

After carrying the sodden clothes to the basement, Aaron heard the children on the back porch swing, making a contest of reciting nursery rhymes. Sam topped Molly's "A-Tisket, A-Tasket" with his animated version of "Donkey, Donkey, Old and Gray." Back and forth they went, with Matthew in the middle, grinning and tapping fingertips on his knees. Aaron couldn't remember when they'd been as content. Couldn't remember when *he'd* felt more content!

Beth was outside, too, rocking and sewing buttons on one of his shirts. When she noticed him, she smiled. "You look refreshed."

The screen door squealed as he joined them outside. "Soon as the rain stops," he said, sitting in the rocker beside hers, "I'll oil those hinges."

"I rather like the noise." She wrapped thread round and round her forefinger's tip, rubbed until it formed a knot, and positioned another button where the lost one had been. "The squeak is like a doorbell, only less jarring."

He settled back into the faded floral cushions she'd made by covering old bed pillows with another old sheet. "I brought the sodden clothes to the basement," he said, "wrung them out and hung them over the clothesline."

"Thank you," she said without looking up.

"No, thank *you,* for . . ." Aaron didn't know where to begin. With the flowers that crowded those old metal buckets? The alphabetized spice rack and pantry shelves? Dust-free floors and furnishings, even now with the open windows inviting pollen inside? Those things, *all* of the things she'd done, were wonderful, to be sure. But it was the sense of calm her presence brought to the house, to the children, to him. "Thank you for everything," he said, meaning every word.

"Just doin' my job."

There wasn't a trace of sarcasm in her voice. *She's just stating a fact,* he decided. And the thought compelled him to say, "That would imply you're an employee. And you are so much more."

That got her attention, and when she looked up, Beth pricked her finger. She popped it into her mouth, to keep the blood droplet from staining the white shirt. He'd started seeing her as a friend, thanks to the many times he'd come home, dog-tired after a grueling day, and unloaded the day's problems in the office or the mill, with malfunctioning equipment or complaining customers. She had a knack for helping him put things into perspective, so that by the time they gathered at suppertime, he enjoyed every forkful.

"Something smells good," he said.

Sam stopped mid-rhyme to say, "Spaghetti and meatballs."

"Ah, Matthew's favorite."

His youngest son's wide smile exposed a gap where a front tooth used to be.

"What's this? You've lost your first tooth?"

The boy patted his chest, where a minuscule drawstring sack hung from the safety pin attached to his shirt. Englishers' children believed in the Tooth Fairy, who traded coins for shiny little teeth, but the Amish did not. Surely Beth hadn't encouraged the belief . . .

"What are you saving it for?"

"He wants to bury it," Molly said, "to see if anything will grow from it."

Aaron laughed. "Like a seed? But why?"

"Because," Sam answered, "you told him if he didn't do a better job brushing his teeth, crops would grow in his mouth."

Beth laughed, too. And then she winked at him, a sign of some sort, and he got the distinct impression that she thought he could decipher it. *Not without a lesson or two in signal reading!*

The oven timer dinged, and Beth packed up her sewing.

"What's that for?" Sam asked.

"Time to make the salad and put the garlic bread onto the griddle."

"Supper will be soon, then?" Aaron asked.

"Ten minutes," she said in the open door, "fifteen at most."

"Need any help?"

"No, but thank you."

When the door bumped closed behind her, he waved Molly close. "What did you kids do while the lights were out?"

"We made cards for your birthday."

"Did you now!"

"When you took Beth grocery shopping, she bought all the supplies. We made presents for you, too."

"Blabbermouth," Sam grunted. "Beth asked you not to tell. Now you've gone and spoiled the surprise!"

She slapped both hands over her mouth. "Oh, that's right. I forgot!"

"Don't look so worried. You didn't describe anything, so I'll still be surprised."

He got to his feet, walked to the edge of the porch and stretched. "Looks like the weatherman was right. The rain is finally letting up."

"Enough so we could go into the yard and play?"

"Better not. For one thing, I still see lightning over there, above the mountains. And supper will be on the table any minute."

"After supper, then?"

Aaron grasped the door handle. "We'll see."

He found Beth stirring spaghetti noodles in a big steaming pot. He stepped up to the stove, lifted the kettle's lid and inhaled the robust aroma of thick, red sauce. She handed him a spoon, invited him to taste it.

"Thanks!" He filled the spoon's bowl and carried it to the sink.

"Blow on it. You do not want to burn yourself."

"I won't." If an outsider overheard the conversation, they'd never guess the mystery of their atypical union. He'd been telling himself that keeping up appearances would be easy, since the only difference between their marriage and others was the lack of physical intimacy. And that since he barely knew her, keeping a safe distance should be fairly easy.

But it hadn't been.

Already, she'd endeared herself to the kids. To him, too. Only a man with a heart of stone could watch the effort she put into every little task and not appreciate it. And already, Aaron had begun to feel protective of her, so that each time she lurched at the sudden sight of him, his first impulse was to pull her close, apologize, assure her there was nothing to fear, especially not from him. It was also what he'd wanted to do as he'd watched her lovingly bandage Matthew's foot, gently braid Molly's hair, stitch up Sam's favorite shirt. And what about that first night, when he'd gone to bed before her? If he hadn't left the light on to help her find her way around the bed, Aaron wouldn't have noticed three hairline cracks in the ceiling. While he'd tried to figure out how he'd find time to fix them, Bethel had come into the room, her limp more noticeable without the thick-soled shoe. More noticeable than the

limp . . . she'd let down her hair. He swallowed now,
remembering that he'd wanted to fill his hands with it,
find out if it felt as soft as it looked. And this minute,
watching as she bent over that big pot, squinting into the
steam, the feeling returned yet again.

*Ignore it.* He stared out the window, hoping to spot
something that might quiet the desire. *It's just biology,
and nothing more.*

"Do you like it?"

*Oh, I like it, all right. I like it a lot.* But he knew she
was referring to the sauce. Aaron licked the spoon, held
it out. "Delicious. What brand is it?"

A tiny crease formed between her eyebrows. "Brand?"

"Ragu? Prego? Hunt's?"

The crease disappeared and the eyebrows rose higher.
"This is not sauce from a *jar,*" was what she said. But what
he heard was, "*I'd* never *serve the vile stuff!*"

"Sorry. I just . . . I thought, maybe, maybe you added
spices. Like my mother. And Stella."

"For your information, it is my own recipe."

For the first time since they'd met—probably for the
first time in her life—Beth looked a bit haughty. It made
him chuckle, because he had a feeling that if she was
aware of it, she'd ask God to forgive her sin of pride.

She relieved him of the spoon, dropped it into the sink.
"I used canned tomato paste and stewed tomatoes this
time, but only because I have not had a chance to plant
and put up my own."

If Matthew hadn't plowed through the door just then,
Aaron might have given in to this latest urge to wrap his
arms around her, because she looked utterly kissable standing there, taking offense.

She seemed relieved to see the boy, too, although he didn't know what her reason might be.

"Have you come inside to wash up?"

He held out his hands, palms up, as if to say, "Aren't they already clean enough?"

"Soap and water washes away the dirt we cannot see."

Matthew bobbed his head and grinned all the way to the stairs.

"You're wonderful with him. Just the medicine he needs, I think."

Her cheeks flushed slightly at the compliment. "He is a wonderful boy." The pleasure that had brightened her face dimmed as she raised a forefinger. "One day—God willing, soon—I will figure out how to get him to *talk*."

Since Marta's death, they'd all been trying to make that happen, but why admit it and dampen her buoyant mood?

Beth put the colander into the sink and, grabbing two oven mitts, said, "Do you mind telling Molly and Sam to wash up?" She grasped the pot handles. "Because just as soon as I drain these noodles—"

"Happy to do it, but first, let me lift that for you." He winked. "You do not want to burn yourself."

Half a second passed before she handed over the oven mitts. *What's going on in that pretty head of yours?* he wondered.

"Thank you, Mr. Bontrager."

While he dumped the pot's contents into the colander, he heard the telltale squeal of the screen door. "Children," she called, "time to come wash up for supper."

Sam, the first to enter the kitchen, stepped up to the sink just as Aaron placed the now-empty pot on the counter.

"She has you cooking now? What's next? Mopping floors and scrubbing the toilets?"

One glance was all it took to see the disappointment his son's wisecrack had painted on her face. "I wouldn't mind performing those jobs. Frankly, I don't know anyone who would." God willing, he had put Sam in his place and given her a reason to smile again, too.

And it had worked, judging by the grateful little smile that crinkled the corners of her eyes.

"Why is everyone standing around, looking . . . *weird*?" Molly wanted to know.

Without breaking eye contact with him, Beth said, "Because we are . . . weird."

The girl glanced at the ceiling, then continued on her way to the stairs. Sam followed and, as he climbed, said, "This whole 'going upstairs to wash up' thing is for the birds."

"Birds don't wash up, silly."

"Sure they do. In puddles and birdbaths. Why, just the other day, I saw a robin splashing around in Beth's wheelbarrow," Sam retorted.

"First of all, no one carries water in a wheelbarrow. And second of all, it isn't *Beth's* wheelbarrow. . . ."

Aaron tensed, hoping she wouldn't finish with "It's *Maem's* wheelbarrow, not Beth's." He'd told Beth time and again that the house and yard and everything in them belonged as much to her as the rest of them. Hearing anything to the contrary would make his claim sound less than honest.

"*Daed* paid for it, so technically," she said, rounding the last corner, "the wheelbarrow is *his*."

"Goodness." Beth returned to the sink. "Those two can bicker about anything!"

"Can't deny that. Couple months back, I halted a debate over whose laugh was loudest, of all things!"

She dumped the noodles into the sauce pot. "Well, at least their squabbling is friendly," she said, stirring. "And never physical."

"If it ever came to that, I'd put a stop to it, straight away." How Edward Mast could have allowed his son to abuse her was beyond Aaron. "What did your father do when your brother mistreated you?"

"He did nothing." She placed the big wooden spoon onto a saucer. "Why would he, when he so clearly enjoyed it?"

Enjoyed it? What sort of man liked seeing his only daughter mistreated!

Still, there hadn't been a trace of malice in her matter-of-fact answer. Maybe he'd misinterpreted what Beth had said earlier. Maybe the abuse hadn't been abuse after all, but just normal sparring between siblings.

But if that was true, why did she wince and flinch at his every move?

"Do you feel safe here, Bethel?"

She stopped rummaging in the serving spoons drawer to meet his eyes. "Yes. Of course."

Then why did he hear uncertainty in her voice?

"I have never raised my hand, in anger or for any other reason, against anyone. Not once."

"Good to know." Beth inserted something that looked like a cross between a claw and a ladle into the pot. "Children," she called out, "supper is ready!"

"Be right down!" they called back.

Beth placed the big pot in the center of the table and proceeded to fill the kids' plates. Standing behind Matthew's chair, she chopped the noodles into inch-long pieces. Cut the meatball, too.

"He will learn how to twirl the spaghetti," she explained, "but for now, why frustrate the boy?"

"Is there Parmesan cheese?" Molly asked, pulling out her chair.

"I almost forgot!" Beth went to the fridge, found and delivered it, and said, "There you go, sweet girl."

"Thank you, Beth!"

Sam snorted. "Would you like some spaghetti with your cheese?" All eyes were on him when he added, "Don't look at me. *I'm* not the one hogging it all!"

Giggling, Molly lifted both shoulders. "Sorry." And then she passed the container to Aaron. "Don't use too much or *someone* will bite your head off!"

"Are you looking forward to your birthday tomorrow, Mr. Bontrager?"

Beth sat and folded her hands in preparation for her silent, private blessing. Aaron followed suit, but not before saying, "Yes, I am. Especially now that I know there are cards and presents in the mix."

Sam sat up straighter, no doubt ready to light into Molly again for spoiling the surprise.

"Time to give thanks," he said and nodded as each child complied. He looked at Beth, whose playful smile told him she'd picked up on his truce-inducing move and approved. Oh, to have been blessed with mind-reading powers, because that smile said more, so much more!

"Beth, will you put candles on Daed's cake?"

She turned to him. "Would you like candles on your cake?"

"Do we even have a hundred candles?"

Laughing, Beth said, "As a matter of fact, I found a box of twenty-four. Half of them are only about an inch tall, though." She paused. "I have an idea. What if we put one candle right in the middle of the cake? I read, long ago, that it represents the light of life."

"Oooh," Molly squealed. "I like that. I like it a lot!"

"Much as I hate to agree with the blabbermouth, I like it, too," Sam put in.

"Matthew?" Beth said, "what do you think?"

He thought about it for a minute, shrugged, then held up one finger and nodded.

"It's settled then," Aaron said. "One candle."

The phone rang, and he got up to answer.

"Bad news?" Beth asked when he returned.

"'Fraid so. Karl says we need to deliver a truckload of wood to one of our best customers tomorrow. I told him I'd do it." He shrugged. "Seems the twins are teething and giving Stella a fit."

"Nice of you to go in his place. This customer . . . is he an Englisher?"

"He is."

"Strange."

"Why?"

"Because I heard they rarely work on July Fourth."

"Too busy going to parades," Molly said around a mouthful of meatball, "and watching fireworks."

Sam used the back of his hand to blot sauce from the corner of his mouth. "And huge backyard barbecues."

"Mr. McCartney told Karl that he and his family are up

here, using this as a working weekend. Between the festivities, they're adding an extra room to their cabin at Deep Creek Lake."

"Aw, but Daed, we had a whole *thing* planned for your birthday!"

"Sorry, kids, but Mack is one of our best customers. I can't disappoint him."

"What time will you make the delivery?" Beth asked.

"Nine. Why?"

"I have another idea. We'll go with you, and after you've dropped off the lumber, we can have a picnic at the lake."

"That's a two-hour drive . . ."

"We don't mind, Daed. It'll be fun," Molly said.

"Yeah," Sam agreed. "We'll play the punch buggy game."

"Punch buggy?"

Sam, concentrating on wrapping noodles around his fork, said, "Every time you see a Volkswagen Beetle, you punch somebody in the shoulder and say—"

"You say, 'punch buggy,' and that is *all* you do," Aaron said.

"Can we, Daed? Please?"

"It's a long way to go in that big old truck."

"It's okay." Sam dipped garlic bread into his sauce. "What is it you're always saying? 'You're children . . . flexible, inexhaustible, tough. . . .' We can do it. We can do it!"

"Bethel?"

"Fried chicken is perfect for a picnic."

"With mashed potatoes and gravy? Sounds messy," Sam said.

"I will make potato salad instead. It travels much better."

"What about the cake?" Molly wanted to know.

"Not to worry, sweet girl. We will save the cake for when we get back tomorrow night."

"And the cards and presents?"

"We will give them with the cake."

Aaron could see that her words had encouraged the children. Even Matthew wore an enthusiastic smile. Until she'd suggested the family outing, he hadn't realized how much *he'd* needed reassurance.

"I'll have to go to the mill early, load the truck. Could take a while."

Molly stood beside him, wrapping her arms around his neck. "If you're trying to talk us out of spending the whole day with you, *on your birthday*, you can't!"

She pressed a kiss to his cheek as Sam stood on his other side. "She's right. It'll be fun." He looked at Matthew. "Right, li'l brother?"

The smallest Bontrager nodded excitedly.

"Well then," Beth said, "it seems our plans are set. I will get up extra early to make the food."

"If I help, you won't have to get up so early," Molly offered, moving back to Beth's side.

Aaron might not be able to read Beth's mind, but he could read her face. She loved his little girl, almost as much as he did. And Molly felt the same way about Beth. He looked across at Sam, whose formerly wary expression had softened . . . at afraid-of-everything Matthew, whose gentle smile said the same thing: He trusted her. The children had loved their mother, but . . . but not like this.

If he had a mirror, Aaron wondered, would he look the same way?

# Chapter Eight

The following day found Aaron and Mack surrounded by their children at the front of Mack's catamaran on Deep Creek Lake. As the vessel motored through the water, Sam said, "I knew Deep Creek was big, but wow, I had no idea it was this big!"

"Last time I checked," Mack told him, "Deep Creek was still the country's biggest freshwater lake."

"You talk like it's yours," his wife, Peggy, said, laughing.

"Well, it is. A couple gallons of it, anyway."

"How big is this boat?"

"It's a catamaran," Molly corrected. "Isn't that right, Mr. McCartney?"

"Yup."

"Whatever." Sam rolled his eyes at his sister, then said, "It's almost as big as your cabin!"

And it was true, Beth thought. With its fully equipped kitchen, bathroom, comfortable living area, and two bedrooms, she wondered why they needed the cabin at all.

"What's that?" Sam asked, pointing to the back of the cruiser.

"A slide. If you go up top," Brenden said, "you can slide right down into the water."

McCartney's son, a few years older than Sam, had inherited his parents' gracious nature.

"Okay if I show the kids how it works, Dad?"

"If it's all right with their folks, it's all right with me."

Their folks. The term sent a little tremor through Beth, because it felt good, hearing that these friendly people saw them as a family.

"We did not pack swimsuits or towels," Beth said, "but it is good of you to offer."

"I always keep extra shorts for Brenden, down in the cabin. Elastic waistbands, so they should fit just fine. They could borrow Mack's T-shirts, too." Peggy squeezed Beth's forearm. "We've lived near the Amish for a long time, so we know about the Plain clothing rule. Trust me. The shirts are more than long enough to cover them up, right down to their knees."

Everyone was looking at her, waiting for her answer. But they were Bontrager's children, and she didn't feel right making such a decision. She looked to him for guidance. And while he considered the idea, McCartney said, "If it makes you feel any better, I'll loan you trunks and a T-shirt, and the two of us can take the plunge, too."

Beth pictured it . . . Bontrager, with his pale, blond-haired legs exposed. She'd caught glimpses of them as he climbed in and out of bed. And from time to time, felt them, too, as he repositioned himself during the night. But this? Grinning, she hoped he'd say yes.

"It is a blistering hot day. . . ."

"Follow me, guys," Peggy said, "and I'll get you all set up."

Everyone followed, except for Beth and Matthew, who remained in the cruiser's living area.

"Can you swim, sweet boy?"

He shook his head.

"Ahh, something else we have in common then. I never learned, either."

He looked slightly relieved, despite an undercurrent of regret that darkened his eyes.

"Just between you and me?" She shivered. "I am afraid of any water deeper than this." Beth held up her hand, made a C of her thumb and forefinger, and shivered again.

The boy nodded and stared across the lake, where a motorboat cut a path in the dark blue water, and thick evergreens formed a verdant backdrop to the sandy beach. The scene rivaled any of the picture postcards that filled the spinning rack in her father's store. It was enough to conjure a memory of his face, twisted with greed as he waved the bank deposit slip under her nose. "Your generous husband will never know that I would have taken half this much."

Beth blinked, hoping to erase the painful picture. *One day, Lord, I pray You will wipe it from my mind forever.*

In that moment, however, it was Matthew who blocked the image. He'd been watching her. Watching closely. He put his hand into hers, and Beth recognized his little-boy attempt to offer consolation. "You are a sweet, big-hearted boy, Matthew Bontrager," she said, drawing him near. As his arms tightened around her waist, she whispered, "I love you, too."

Together, they walked to the rail. She followed the

boy's gaze to the opposite shore, where sunlight crowned the white clouds and mountain peaks, glowed from the backs of snow geese and trumpeter swans, and sparkled on every undulating wave. To the left, gulls circled the water; to the right could be heard the yodeling tremolo of a loon. "God is quite the artist, isn't He, Matthew?"

"That He is."

Turning, she smiled. "How long have you been standing there?"

"Exactly long enough." Bontrager took a step closer. "I didn't startle you this time."

"And I appreciate that." Beth assessed his outfit, a long orange T-shirt, decorated with the smiling cartoon face of the Orioles bird. Beneath it, the hem of his black shorts fell just below his knees. A pair of bright blue goggles hung from a bent forefinger. "Seems you are ready to— how did Mr. McCartney put it?—take the plunge."

Sam and Molly and the McCartneys stepped up behind him. Like Bontrager, his children wore long T-shirts and carried protective eyewear.

"Well, time's a-wastin'," McCartney said and motioned toward the stairs that led to the upper deck.

No one wasted any time following him, and within minutes, Molly's gleeful squeals blended with Sam and Brenden's happy shouts. Their fathers splashed down too, and Matthew, clinging tight to the rail, smiled.

"Are you sure you don't want to join them?" Peggy asked Beth. "I'm sure I can find something for you to wear, too."

"Oh, no. Thank you, Mrs. McCartney, but I cannot swim."

"Please. Call me Peggy. Mrs. McCartney is my mother-in-law's name." Smirking, she added, "I hope you get along well with yours."

"Esther? I have not had time to get to know her well, but she is a good, caring woman."

"So Mack was right, then, about your whirlwind romance."

Without knowing how much Bontrager had told his customer, Beth didn't know how to reply.

"It's okay," Peggy said. "Family bonds take time, but when you're in love, like you two are, well, as long as you have each other, there's no rush, right?"

What had she done to make Mrs. McCartney believe they were in love!

"You'd have to wear a bag over your head to hide it. I don't mind admitting, I'm a little envious. It's been a while since Mack looked at me the way Aaron looks at you."

How could a complete stranger have noticed something that she hadn't?

"Hey, Beth!" Sam shouted from below. "Watch this!" He performed a forward roll, disappearing underwater for a moment. When he surfaced again, he waved.

Beside him, Molly emitted a tiny shriek. "Something touched my leg! Daed! Help me! There's something in the water!"

He swam up, slid an arm around her, treading water with his free hand. "It's just a fish, sweetie."

"What kind of fish?"

"The resort stocks the lake," Brenden said, "with bass, catfish, trout, even pumpkinseed sunfish . . . easiest fish to catch, because they'll eat just about anything."

"Hey Daed," Sam said, "can Matthew and I go fishing later?"

"Why wait?" McCartney said. "We have gear onboard. Plenty to go around."

For the next hour, both families stood, quietly chatting and waiting for their rod tips to bend. When it became clear that the fish weren't biting, Peggy said, "You guys churned up the water and scared all the fish away! Let's go into the cabin and dig into that basket of great-smelling fried chicken Beth brought."

They crowded around the small table, chatting and laughing like old friends as the food disappeared.

Brenden helped himself to a drumstick. "Where do you fish, Sam?"

"Trout Run, mostly."

"Sounds familiar," Mack said. "Near the abandoned coal mines, right?"

Aaron nodded as Brenden said, "So awesome! Have you been in 'em, Sam? The mines, I mean?"

"No," Aaron answered in his stead. "Grown men have gone into those shafts and were never seen again."

"If they're so dangerous, why'd those men go in?"

"Because, Brenden, they believed the rumors that a bank robber hid his loot in one of the tunnels."

"Was the story about the robber real, though?"

"Some say yes, some say no. But if the men who vanished hadn't been on the hunt for quick riches, they'd be alive today."

"How do you know they aren't?"

"They were found, buried under tons of rubble, two weeks after they went missing."

"You're scaring him, Daed," Sam said, and took a second helping of potato salad.

"I'm not scared," Brenden said, sitting up taller. "Just never heard that story before, that's all." He grabbed another drumstick. "Is Trout Run near your house?"

"Takes fifteen, twenty minutes to walk there, but it's worth it. We always catch our limit."

"So do you live on a farm?"

"Not exactly. But we have a couple acres. And some critters."

"No foolin'? How many? What kind?"

Sam provided a list, describing the chickens; the goats, Willy, Lillie, and Clyde; Henrietta the milk cow's floppy ears; and Caramel, the Belgian draft horse and his long blond mane and tail.

"You have a favorite?"

"Caramel, I guess. He's really gentle."

"What about your brother?" Brenden nodded at Matthew. "Does he ride, too?"

"Nah. But he likes all the animals, and they like him."

"Yeah, that makes sense. Most kids his age are noisy. Guess they like that he doesn't say anything at all."

The simple statement made Matthew the center of attention, and he buried his face in Beth's side.

"Sorry, Matt. Didn't mean to embarrass ya." He looked at Sam. "Is he shy? Is that why he isn't talkin'?"

"No. He just . . ." Sam shot a sympathetic look toward his little brother. "He hasn't talked since our mother's funeral."

The seriousness of the subject, combined with Sam's somber tone, must have compelled Brenden to say, "Man. How cool is that, Dad? The Bontragers have, like, a dozen critters, and Mom won't even let us have a dog!"

"Your mother and I don't have time to take care of a pet," McCartney said.

In other words, Beth thought, they weren't willing to

ensure that their son learned how to be responsible for one—

"If you guys aren't in a hurry to get back to Pleasant Valley," McCartney said, "why don't you join us top-deck to watch the fireworks. They put on one heckuva display over the mountains."

Bontrager didn't answer right away, so Peggy said, "Maybe they'd rather you just take us back to shore, Mack."

Molly and Sam looked so hopeful, Matthew, too, that Beth hoped he'd say yes.

"Yeah, okay." Aaron smiled at them each in turn, then looked at her. "Do you mind, Bethel? It'll be pretty late when we get home."

He'd asked her opinion, as if it mattered, and that touched her. "You are right, the children would like to stay, I think. And so would I."

McCartney motored into the middle of McHenry Cove, along with dozens of other boats, and dropped anchor. Peggy waved Beth into the galley, and together they prepared a platter of cheese and crackers, sliced apples, and grapes, and arranged tall, frosty glasses of iced tea on a tray. It was nearly dark when they delivered the snack, and they were greeted with a round of hearty applause.

Sam and Brenden wolfed down their share, then pulled two chairs up to the rail and kicked back to stare into the sky.

"Daed?"

"Molly . . ."

"Do you think . . . maybe Brenden can come to the

house one day, so he can see all the animals, maybe ride Caramel?"

"I think . . . maybe that's a fine idea. If it's all right with Mr. and Mrs. McCartney."

"Sounds good," McCartney said. And Peggy agreed.

"They're starting!" Brenden yelled, pointing toward Marsh Mountain.

Everyone got to their feet, made their way to the rail in time to see the faint trail of smoke drifting across the charcoal sky, then vanishing into nothingness. Another flare sped upward, a wriggling, squiggling red streak that hung, silent and motionless, then unfurled like a massive umbrella before sprinkling the earth with crimson sparks.

A blue stripe followed, and like the red one, it, too, swelled into a hypnotic canopy. Next, green, then gold, white, orange, each as dazzling as the one before. Aaron moved to Beth's side, placed his hand next to hers on the railing. She'd tilted her head to the heavens, mesmerized, it seemed, by the luminescent colors. He was spellbound, too . . . by the bright colors that shimmered across her face. He heard the soft *oohs* and *ahhs* of his children, of the McCartneys, but had no desire to find out what had inspired them.

"Bethel," he said softly, "is this your first fireworks display?"

She seemed reluctant to look away. "Yes. And you?"

"Not on purpose, like this, but yes, I've seen them before. Six, maybe eight times."

Beth held his gaze to say, "If I never see another, I will remember this one."

He stood nearly a foot taller than Beth, outweighed her by no fewer than forty pounds. And yet, suddenly, he felt small and insignificant. What he had ever done to deserve a woman like this, Aaron couldn't say. For a reason he'd never understand, the Almighty had chosen to make them man and wife, for all time. He prayed, right on that spot, for enlightenment, for guidance in earning this gift, every day for the rest of his life.

A gut-wrenching pang of guilt shook him, just as surely as if he'd been standing on the raft during the firing of each powerful rocket.

Aaron took a step back, then two, to examine the feeling. He'd never been harsh with Marta. In fact, he'd always made a point of treating her gently, even when, as a new bride, she'd rejected his advances. Yes, he'd been lonely, but it hadn't taken long to learn that hard work and long hours diminished his yearning. And yes, she'd grown up dirt poor, and that's why, when some shiny new thing caught her eye, he always found a way to give it to her, even if it meant overtime hours and finding other, innovative ways to balance the household budget. He hadn't complained, not once, when he had come home to a disorderly house, disheveled children, untended animals. He hadn't complained, but admittedly, her behavior had carved a chasm between them, one that grew deeper with each passing year. If he'd been more loving, more attentive, would she still have sought affection from another man?

Peggy sighed. "Wasn't that just gorgeous!"

"It was," Beth agreed.

"But it never lasts long enough, does it?"

"Twenty minutes," said Mack, firing up the catamaran's engine. "Five more than last year."

Matthew yawned, Sam stretched, and Molly looked almost asleep on her feet.

"Well, we'd better be on our way." Aaron extended a hand to Mack. "We appreciate your hospitality. It was a good day."

Stepping away from the helm, Mack accepted the handshake. "And I appreciate the way you dropped everything to deliver the wood. Thanks for your help assembling those walls, too. That's sure to take hours off my work tomorrow."

It was a short trip back to shore, and a short walk from the dock to Aaron's pickup. The families said their good-byes and made promises to stay in touch, and they were on their way.

Five minutes into the drive, Beth said, "I think your cake and presents will have to wait for tomorrow. The children are fast asleep already."

"That's what a long day on the water will do."

"A long, good day." She looked over at him. "I enjoyed it. Did you?"

"I did." *Right up until my conscience grabbed me by the throat.*

"They are very nice. . . ."

He heard a certain reservation in her voice. "For Englishers, you mean?"

"Not at all. They were very accommodating, and I never got the impression they think the Plain life is . . ."

"Weird?" he finished, grinning.

"Something like that," she said around a yawn. "But what I meant was, I wonder what they will think, if they visit. We might seem backward to them."

"Why would they think that?"

"They have so many modern conveniences. Cell phones. Tablets. There was a television in every room at the cabin.

I saw them when Peggy showed me around. Even the boat had three of them. And a computer in the galley."

"Mack is a successful businessman and needs to stay on top of things when he isn't in the office. Those things are like . . . like a carpenter's tools, saws at the mill, or . . . or the pots and pans in a cook's kitchen."

"You manage without those things, and you are the most successful businessman in all of Pleasant Valley!"

She sounded . . . *proud* of him. The headlights of an oncoming car lit the pickup's cab, and he saw that she didn't just sound proud. Beth looked proud, too. Aaron could only shake his head. Did she have any idea what she was doing to him! Every day, in every way, just by being Beth, she made it harder to live by his self-imposed rule: Treat her well, but keep your distance.

A single question hammered in his mind, one he'd never asked himself before. . . . *Why?*

Why did he have to keep his distance? They were husband and wife, united by a church-sanctioned marriage . . .

"I heard the boys talking," she said, breaking into his thoughts. "About going fishing tomorrow. What about Molly? She looked so hurt when you gave them permission to go without her."

He still hadn't recovered from his self-interrogation when he said, "Molly can spend the day with my mother so she has a special treat too. It'll be good for all of them. Boys need to get off by themselves from time to time."

Even to his own ears, he'd sounded as though he was hinting that he needed time, too, time away from *her.* He hadn't meant it that way, and that's what he would have told her if she hadn't said, "You will go with them, then?"

"No. I have to work. One of the men wrenched his

shoulder, torqueing a bolt on the debarking machine. We're on a tight deadline, so I'll have to take his place."

"They will be safe? Fishing, all by themselves?"

"Sure. They'll be fine. They've made the trip there plenty of times, and always came back with a creel stuffed with trout."

"That is too bad."

He chanced a peek at her. "Too bad? Why?"

"I do not know how to cook fish."

"But I thought Karl said there are a dozen rivers near Nappanee. And that people come from all over to fish in them."

"Yes, that is true. But my father and brother did not like fishing. Or fish."

"Ahh. I see."

"Do you know how to prepare trout?"

"Matter of fact, I do."

"You can teach me, then. No need to worry. I am a quick learner. You will only need to show me once." She paused. "Do the trout taste . . . fishy?"

He laughed. "Not if you know how to cook them. And I know how to cook them."

And there it was again. The look that was a mix of admiration and respect.

The dashboard clock said eleven-twenty-three, and if he hoped to run that machine without shaving his skin instead of tree bark, he'd need a good night's sleep. But how was that supposed to happen with a woman like this sharing his bed? No, not *a* woman like this, Aaron thought. *This woman.*

# Chapter Nine

"Are you sure you have everything you need?"

"Fishing poles, creel, tackle box . . . Yup, that's everything," Sam said.

"First aid kit?" Beth asked.

"Last time we went fishing, Daed made me put a couple of bandages and some alcohol wipes into the box." *Top-right compartment,* Sam thought.

"What about this?" Beth held a paper grocery bag by its neat fold. "Sandwiches, apple slices, cookies, and a thermos of iced tea. Sweet with no lemon. Just the way you like it."

"Matthew, can you carry it? I've got everything else."

His brother nodded. *Boy, it would be cool if you'd just say yes.*

"Do you have something to sit on? A blanket? A towel for each of you?"

That would've been nice . . . if they didn't have to walk a mile and a half to get to their favorite spot. Sam already felt overloaded by gear.

"They're sturdy young boys, Bethel. They'll be fine."

*Thanks, Daed!* It had taken some getting used to, but

now he liked the way she fussed over him, over Molly and Matthew. But sometimes it really took some patience not to shout, *"Enough!"*

Daed was smiling that smile again. The one that he and his siblings usually aimed at chocolate cake. The one Sam hadn't seen since before Matthew was born. Since Beth got here, Daed smiled a lot. Laughed a lot, too. Well, not at first, because until Beth, there hadn't been a lot to smile or laugh about. It gave Sam a good feeling. Good enough that he'd started thanking God for Daed's happier mood during his bedtime prayers.

"Keep an eye on the sun in the sky—but remember not to look directly at it—and be home by two."

"Okay, Daed." *Man. Beth is rubbing off on him.* "Let's go, Matthew. We're burnin' daylight."

They walked a while and, looking for something to say to drown out mourning doves, crickets, and noisy crows, Sam observed, "Funny saying, isn't it . . . burnin' daylight."

Matthew shook his head.

"You don't need to stare at the ground all the time, you know. I know why you do it—I did it, too, until I was about four—but *dunner uns gewidder,* Matthew, you're not gonna step in a hole if you look up once in a while, but you *will* miss the sunrise . . . again!"

His brother looked at him, eyes wide, mouth forming an O.

"I know, I know, I shouldn't have said *confound it.* But sometimes you just . . ."

Sam stopped talking. *Why waste your breath?* His brother would keep right on walking with his head down, missing the sunrise and a whole lot of other cool things.

Like the white tails of deer they'd startled, flicking left and right as they ran for safety. And eagles floating overhead. *Pretty weird,* Sam thought, *that a bird that big makes sound that small.*

Now, Sam stopped walking, too, and pointed. "Matthew! A dog just ran into that mine shaft!"

His brother came to a full halt, looked toward the mine.

"It was limping and bloody." He dropped the fishing gear. "We've gotta help it."

Matthew grabbed his arm, forced Sam to meet his eyes.

He'd gotten pretty good at reading his brother's moods, just by studying his face. He could see that Matthew was worried. Scared, too. Of what their father would say? Or of going into the mine?

His brother's lips parted and he mouthed a word: "Coyote."

"No, it was a *dog*. Mostly white. With blood on its hind leg. Probably got hit by a car."

But Matthew still wasn't satisfied. This time, he mouthed "Dangerous."

"It'll be okay. We won't go in too far. Just far enough to check on the dog. I swear."

Sam left the trail and ran into the woods, straight toward the rotting timbers and crumbling stone walls of the mine's entrance. A quick glance over his shoulder told him Matthew had followed. But he wouldn't have needed to look. The paper bag rattled enough to scare away every creature in a ten-mile radius.

"Put that thing down," Sam scolded. "The dog is already scared enough."

This time when he stopped, Sam stood mere feet from the opening. The scents of mildew and dust and rotting wood blended into a foul smell, foul enough to make Matthew crook an elbow over his nose and mouth.

"Fine. You stay here." *Big baby.* "But I'm gonna check on that dog."

It felt like a hundred thoughts were whirling in his head: *It might bite. It could have rabies. But what if it doesn't? What if it's somebody's pet that got lost during a camping trip? Or . . . it might be mean enough that some family decided to shove it out of a moving car.* He'd seen that happen once, driving into town with his father. That dog had been smaller. Black and fuzzy. Until it rolled under the wheels of the eighteen-wheeler up ahead. The memory was enough to make Sam swallow. Hard. *This one might just be a regular dog. A family dog . . .*

"I can see him," he told Matthew, taking another step inside. "He's just sitting there, looking sad and hurt. I think he's friendly." Sam bent at the waist, extended a hand, palm up. "It's okay, boy," he said softly, calmly. "Nobody's gonna hurt you."

It didn't move, not even when he took another step.

The dog blinked. Licked its lips.

"We just want to help you."

Another step, and this time, the dog got up, limped deeper into the cave.

"Aw, c'mon now, I thought dogs had some special instinct that tells them the difference between good humans and bad ones."

Now the dog stood, head down and trembling.

"Yeah, it's cold in here. It's warm outside though, really, really warm. Don't you remember? Before you ran in here?"

It backed away, ten or twelve feet. The farther it went,

the darker it got. Light, a skinny beam of it, filtered through an overhead crack, just enough that Sam could see the strange, creepy glow of the dog's eyeshine. "Stay, boy. I just want to help you."

He peeked over his shoulder again and wasn't surprised to see that Matthew had not followed. Just as well. If the dog was this terrified of one person, he'd be twice as frightened if his brother was here, too. Besides, then he'd have two 'fraidy cats to look after.

When Sam inched forward, he saw that the dog had moved back another foot or two. Saw, too, that, just behind it, the faint light hit a tilting, off-center post. But what was it supporting? His gaze followed its line to where it connected, barely, to a cross beam that, long ago, had probably formed the top of a doorway. His father had taught him enough about construction to know it was a header, and it didn't take a carpenter to know that over time, it had fractured under the weight above it. Dust—probably the only thing holding it in place—sprinkled from the jagged crack. If the dog took just one step back, it would bump into that tilting post.

Now no more than three feet separated him from the dog. If he moved quickly enough, he could rush the wounded animal, grab it, and get out before that beam collapsed. "I'm doing this for your own good, so don't bite me, okay?"

Sam put every muscle into it, and hurtled forward, arms extended and a hundred percent prepared to scoop the dog up and run like his life depended on it.

Because it might.

The sudden move startled the dog, and it whirled around, slamming its injured right rear into the post.

Gray grit poured down, completely covering the dog. It did what any dog would do, and shook, from nose to tail, scattering dust around it. He could still grab it . . . if he hurried. Ignoring the sound of wood groaning overhead, he lunged again, filled both fists with the dog's blood-sticky fur, and pulled it to him. It yelped, but he ignored that, too. *You'll forgive me once you're safe. . . .*

The tiny slice of light went out, as if he'd flipped a switch. The terrifying groaning noise became a deafening roar as the ceiling caved in. It seemed like an hour passed before things were quiet again.

Sam felt the dog trembling in his arms. He opened his eyes, and saw that thankfully, blessedly, the cave-in had opened a new place for light to sneak in. He tried to sit up, but couldn't budge, thanks to the mound of grit, dirt, big rocks, and boards that covered them.

"Matthew? Matthew! Can you hear me?" *Well, that was pretty stupid. Even if he* can *hear you, he won't say so.*

It made him mad. Madder than he'd ever been. Because there was no reason for Matthew not to talk. None. Until this minute, the only one he was hurting was himself. *If I get out of this, that's what I'm gonna tell him!*

The dog whimpered. "Don't be scared, boy. My brother is out there. He'll go home. I just know he will. And bring back help. You'll see. It's gonna be all right. I promise."

He was thirsty. So thirsty. Sam licked his lips, tasted blood, felt the swelling that had already started in the corner of his mouth. He ran his tongue across his teeth. *Great. Just great,* he thought, *a loose tooth.*

Everything hurt, and he took inventory. His head. His right arm. Left leg. Even his fingers, and the toes of his left foot ached.

*You have to get out of here!*

Again he tried to sit up.

Again he failed.

A sob ached in his throat. A tear slid into his ear. And a wave of dizziness swirled in his head. He remembered the stories his father and Mr. McCartney had told last night, about men who'd ventured into abandoned mines in search of buried treasure. And he was scared. More afraid than he'd ever been in all of his ten years.

"No fair," he mumbled. "I wasn't being greedy, like those guys. I just wanted to help this poor, injured dog."

It licked his cheek, whimpered again.

"We'll be okay," he choked out. "We'll be okay. We'll be okay. We'll be okay. . . ."

And then he passed out.

In all his six years, Matthew had never heard a noise like that. Had never felt a jolt like that either, not even when the thick cloud of dust belched from the shaft's mouth. He sat up, rubbed grit from his eyes, then scrambled to his feet.

Sam was in there, behind the huge mess, calling his name.

*Answer him. Tell him you want him to come out!*

Matthew opened his mouth, tried to answer his brother, but nothing happened.

*Should have practiced once in a while, to make sure your voice still worked.*

A couple of times, he'd almost tested it. When they'd walked away from the graveyard behind the church, after burying his mother. The day one of the chickens had pecked the back of his hand as he'd gathered eggs, nearly drawing blood. During the ride home from the train station, after picking up Beth. She'd looked so scared, and he'd wanted to tell her not to be. The day she'd put a bandage on his blister, when he should have at least said thank you. But this? Matthew had never wished he'd tested his voice more than right now.

He listened for a long time, hoping Sam would call out to him again. That would mean he was okay. Stuck behind the wall of dirt and boards and rocks, but all right. The silence was scarier, even, than the thunderous explosion, and he began to cry, something he hadn't done since Dr. Baker had told the family that his mother was very, very sick because her cold had turned into pneumonia . . . the cold she'd caught from *him*. He'd felt helpless that day, but it didn't compare to what he felt now.

Matthew started running, hard and fast, over the path that ran alongside Trout Run, through the low-hanging pine branches and prickly brush that grabbed at his trouser legs, and didn't stop until he was in the kitchen.

Beth had just filled a mug of coffee. His *daed* said thanks. They both stopped. Looked at him as if he'd grown a third eye.

"Matthew," Beth said, and put the coffeepot back on its warming plate. "What on earth have you gotten into? You are covered in dirt!"

"Where's Sam?" Daed asked, leaning left a little to look around him.

Beth laid one hand on his shoulder, used the other to pluck sticker burrs from his hair as his *daed*, now standing behind her, pulled another burr from his shirt. He got down on one knee, exactly as he had to tell him how sorry he was, but his mother had passed away. Only this time, he didn't look sad. Daed looked worried. Real worried.

"Where. Is. Sam?" he repeated.

Matthew opened his mouth to say, "The mine . . ." But nothing came out. Nothing but air. And a mountain of regret.

"Just look at him," Beth said. "His eyes are the only things not covered with dust. And that is only because he has been crying." She didn't wait for Daed to respond. Beth placed both hands on his shoulders, turned him to face her. "Answer your father, Matthew. Please."

He heard the panic in her voice. Yet again, he tried to say it. *Mine . . .*

Beth's grip tightened, and she shook him. Bending so that she could stare into his eyes, she echoed his father's words: "Where. Is. Sam?"

Matthew watched as she looked up at his father. Watched as her usually calm expression darkened. She was terrified and angry. Angry with him.

He looked up, saw that his father felt the same way. Sounded furious, too, when he said, "We can tell that something terrible has happened to Sam."

Nodding, he broke free of Beth's grasp and started for the door. But his father was quicker, and his big hand wrapped around Matthew's little one. "You want to help him, don't you?"

Another nod, more emphatic this time. Why wouldn't they just come with him? If they'd just follow him, he could show them right where the trouble was!

Beth pulled him close, hugged him tighter than he'd ever been hugged. She was crying, too, when she said, "Your father, your sister, everyone has been so patient

with you." She held him at arm's length. "But our patience
has ended. You have to talk to us. For Sam's sake." She
shook him again, harder than before. "Please, Matthew.
Talk to us, son!"

She'd called him son. *Son!*

*God above, help me. . . .*

"M-m-mine," he stammered.

All color drained from Beth's face. His father's, too.
But they had understood: There had been a cave-in, and
Sam was trapped inside.

His father stood, grabbed his keys from the hook near
the back door. "Call 911," he told Beth. "Have them meet
us there." He rattled off the name of the abandoned mine.
Mentioned Trout Run. A mile marker. The sign marking
the trail.

The receiver was in her hand, her fingertip in the dial's
nine hole when she said, "Wait for me. I want to come."

"Better if you stay here. Molly is at my mother's by
now. You'll be gentler, breaking it to them. Tell Stella, too,
ask her to call Karl at the mill. He'll know what to do."

"M-m-me?" Matthew squeaked out.

"No, son, you stay here with Beth."

And then he was gone.

Through his fog of tears and terror, Matthew heard
Beth repeating his father's instructions into the phone.
When she hung up, its bell echoed for a second or two.
Then she grabbed his hand. "Let's hurry, sweet boy. We
need to spread the word. See if we can get someone to
drive us to the mine, so we can help."

As they ran up the road, she gave his hand a light
squeeze. "I know it was not easy, telling us," she said, her
voice breathy from exertion, "and I am proud of you, son."

Son. Again. She must really care about him to say it twice.

If he hadn't talked soon enough to save Sam, would she feel that way, still?

Word traveled quickly, and in a very short time, nearly every man in Pleasant Valley had made his way to the mine. They formed a bucket brigade and spent the next two hours passing the dirt shoveled from the mine into a shifting heap at the head of the path.

Six burly first responders had helped, too, and by the time they found Sam, they were as grimy and sweaty as the rest of them. Now, in the ER cubicle where nurses gently scrubbed dust from his boy's face, he twisted his hat into a wrinkly tube, and gave thanks through his tears.

"Doctor said he's pretty banged up," Karl said, "but he'll be fine."

"How many times has he asked about that dog?"

His brother-in-law grinned. Not much, but it beat the worried frown that had preceded it.

"And how many times has he told the 'why I went into the mine' story?"

"I lost count. Somebody called a vet, though. When the doc picked the dog up, I heard him tell one of the nurses to make sure the kid knows that he saved its life."

Leave it to that boy of his to put his own life in danger trying to help an injured animal.

"Think he'll want to keep it?"

Yes, knowing Sam, that would be his first question . . .

once Aaron promised not to punish him for putting himself
at risk.

"Well?"

"He'll ask. No doubt in my mind."

"Will you let him?"

"Probably."

"How will Beth feel, having a dog in the house?"

Knowing her, she'd go along with anything that might
hurry Sam's recovery.

"She got used to living with four two-legged pigs. I
think she'll adjust."

Karl snickered at that. He soon grew serious, though,
and added, "So . . . how are things going for you two?"

Translation: Are you a bona fide married couple yet?

Without taking his eyes off Sam, Aaron said, "Things
are going well." He looked at Karl long enough to add,
"She's been a good addition to the family." Following a
teasing jab to Karl's ribs, he said, "So thanks."

Another snicker. "You're welcome." The grin faded
again, and this time Karl said, "Heard from her father?"

"Not a word."

"From what I gather, that's a blessing."

He met Karl's eyes again. "What do you mean?"

"Edward wasn't exactly a gentle daddy. Lots of vile
rumors about him . . . and things he did to Beth."

He said more, lots more, and every word confirmed
Aaron's worst suspicions. No wonder Mast had demanded
such a hefty price for his daughter. And no wonder she'd
always been skittish around him, no wonder she'd done
her best to steer clear of men. It had taken a lot of courage
to travel halfway across the country and agree to move in

with a complete stranger, not knowing whether or not that stranger would subject her to the same abuse. It gave him a whole new reason to admire her.

"What about Vernon? Has he written, at least?"

"Not a word," Aaron said through clenched teeth.

"No surprise there." Karl shook his head and repeated, "Rumors . . ."

"I hope she never hears from either of them again, but God help them if they ever show up here."

"I don't know what you have in mind, but . . ." Karl pounded a fist into a palm. "She was my favorite cousin back home, but she's more like a sister now." He scowled. "If they have the gall to show up," he said, shaking the fist, "I'll help you balance the scales of justice."

In Aaron's opinion, there was no punishment severe enough.

"Daed?" Sam lifted his head and, when he saw Aaron, smiled.

"Go back to sleep, son."

"Can't. These things hurt." He raised his right arm, not an easy feat considering the weight of the plaster cast on it, and wiggled the toes of his left foot, the only things showing thanks to the cast that started just above his knee.

*Small price to pay for your life,* Aaron thought.

"The doctor said they won't cut 'em off for six weeks."

*Eight,* Aaron corrected. But why add to the boy's worries?

"Where is Matthew?"

"Home, with Beth and Molly."

"Guess he was pretty scared, huh."

"Scared enough to tell us where to find you."

Sam lifted his head again. "What? Matthew *talked?*"

Lying back again, he smiled. "Well, ain't that somethin'. Guess he just needed a good reason."

Karl stepped out of the cubicle. "Think I'll head home, unless you need me for anything."

"No, we're good. His doctor said they want to keep an eye on him tonight, because of the concussion. Tell you what you could do, though. Stop by the house, let Beth and Molly know Sam's all right and we'll probably be home before suppertime tomorrow."

"You got it, brother." Waving to Sam, he said, "Sleep well, nephew. Stella and I will pray for you tonight." And, on the way out, "Looks like you're stuck in one of those uncomfortable pink recliners."

"It's only one night."

"Well, don't worry about anything at the mill. Those guys think the world of you, and they'll work like dogs to get things done."

When he was gone, Aaron stepped up to Sam's bed.

"Daed, have you heard anything about the dog?"

"Someone called a veterinarian, and I hear it's doing fine."

"Whew. I was worried. He was hurt pretty bad even before . . ."

A wise choice, Aaron thought, to stop before repeating "cave-in."

"Daed?"

"Hmm. . ."

"Are you mad?"

"Right now, the only thing I'm feeling is overwhelming relief that you're all right." The boy had already suffered enough—and would continue suffering for two months more—for disobeying strict instructions to stay away from the mines, no matter what.

"What about Beth?"

Not once in the time she'd been with them had Aaron seen her angry . . . until Matthew's refusal to talk had threatened Sam's rescue.

"She was worried, all of us were, but no, son, Beth isn't angry."

"Whew," he said again. Then: "I still can't believe Matthew actually talked."

"He had a serious choice to make. Remain silent, or speak up and save his favorite brother."

Sam laughed a little at that. "His only brother. I guess he kinda likes me after all, huh."

"Yeah, maybe just a little."

"How's Molly?"

"She was at your *grootmoeder's* when we got the news, and I haven't seen her yet."

"I'm sorry, Daed."

"For what?"

"For scaring everyone. I knew I shouldn't have gone in there, but . . ."

His eyelids drifted shut, a sign that the pain meds had finally taken hold. When Marta had been hospitalized, he'd nearly worn a path to the chapel. He considered returning, but thought better of it. He didn't want Sam to wake up and find himself alone. Designers had done their best to add color and cheer to the cubicle, but not even the colorful confetti-like material of the curtain around the bed could warm the chilly, antiseptic spacc.

He dropped heavily onto the Naugahyde chair cushion, and leaning forward, held his head in his hands. *Lord, thank You for sparing my son. Give me strength to help him heal. Thank You, too, for reviving Matthew's voice. Give* him *the will to continue talking!*

Pausing, Aaron drove both hands through his hair, held them there for a moment as tears stung his eyes. Grateful tears. Joyful tears. Long pent-up tears. How many times had he gone to the Almighty, pleading for the strength to act as mother and father to the children, begging for answers to hard, hurtful questions: Why had Marta cheated? And why, once she'd reluctantly decided to stay with him, had sickness ravaged her lungs until she could no longer breathe?

*If I played any part in her sin, forgive me now . . .*

Beth came to mind. Soft-spoken, big-hearted, hard-working Bethel Mast who, by taking his name, his children and his home, had put a stop to the dread that he'd felt upon rising each day, who'd given him reasons to *want* to come home, and not just show up because it was expected of him.

*Help me show her, Lord, that for the rest of her life, she'll be safe. Help me love her, too, as she deserves to be loved.*

He sat up, leaned back in the chair, and closed his eyes. *Help you love her.* Aaron huffed. *As if you don't already.*

The tears abated, and the sob that had ached in his throat, disappeared.

In their place came relief. Welcome, blessed relief.

He stretched out his legs and crossed one ankle over the other.

And despite the creaking, uncomfortable chair, Aaron slept.

# Chapter Ten

The following afternoon, the first thing Aaron saw when he peered through the front screen door was that Beth had rearranged things. A lot of things.

Molly, seeing them on the porch, held the door as he carried Sam inside.

"Sam! You're home at last! We've all been so worried about you!"

"It's good to be home," the boy said, and followed it up with, "Daed, I can walk, if you let me lean on you a little."

"Give it a few days," he said, "until you get used to hobbling around on those clunky things."

He looked around the room, then met Beth's eyes. "What's all this?"

"When Karl told me about the cast on his leg, I knew Sam would not be able to get up and down the stairs. At least not at first. He did not mention the cast on his other foot." Hands clasped at her waist, she said, "This arrangement will make it easier, I think, especially since this room is just steps away from the powder room."

That explained the bed over there under the windows,

but why had she dragged the kitchen table and chairs into the room?

"You did all this by yourself?"

"I had trouble falling asleep, and you know how I hate wasting time."

"She did it all while Matthew and I were sleeping," Molly said. "I can't believe we didn't hear a thing!"

"We've had a lot of excitement the past few days. You needed your rest."

The instant he eased Sam onto his bed, Beth was beside them, pulling back the quilt and sheet, fluffing pillows, stacking them against the wall. "There," she said, giving the top pillow a pat, "now you can sit up and see what everyone is doing."

Aaron nodded toward the table and chairs.

"Oh, that." Hands clasped under her chin, she explained. "I knew that none of us would feel right, eating in the kitchen while poor Sam was stuck here in the parlor all by himself."

"I see," he said. "Makes sense."

"It will be easy enough to put everything back where it was once Sam has healed."

With three rooms of furniture in one space, the parlor should have felt crowded and disorganized. Leave it to Beth, he thought, to make it seem that things should have been arranged this way all along.

"Since we were out very late night before last, and scattered in different places last night, I thought we might celebrate your birthday tonight."

"Chocolate cake," Molly said, "with ice cream?"

"Why not!"

She applauded. "And since Matthew is talking now, can he blow out the candle to celebrate, Daed?"

"Why not!" he said, echoing Beth's remark.

"Say something, Matthew," Sam put in. "Sounds like everyone has heard you talk except for me."

"Welcome home, Sam."

"Wow. Your voice is almost as deep as mine. Wow!"

The phone rang, and Aaron was still chuckling when he said hello. It was the vet, calling to let him know that the rescued dog was doing well. There was evidence that he'd been neutered, but not chipped; given his overall raggedy condition, it wasn't likely anyone was looking for him. He was now up to date on all shots, and tests for Lyme disease, heartworm, and kidney and thyroid disease had all come back negative. The injury to his hip had been x-rayed and stitched up, and the prognosis for a full recovery was good. Thanks to an enthusiastic vet assistant, his toenails had been clipped, his teeth had been polished, and he'd had a bath. And because of the extraordinary circumstances, there'd be no charge. After Aaron thanked the man and hung up, he seated himself on the edge of Sam's mattress, then waved Molly, Matthew, and Beth closer to repeat the doctor's report.

"Does this mean he's ours?" Molly asked.

"On one condition."

All three children listened closely.

"You are responsible for feeding him, for making sure he goes outside to do his business, and for cleaning up what he leaves in the yard." He wagged a finger to and fro. "I do not want to hear that you've let Beth do it in your place—because you know she will." Pausing, he inspected their eager faces. "The only one who gets a pass is Sam.

And just as soon as he's free of those casts, he'll do his share." Another pause, and then, "Got it?"

"Got it," Matthew said.

The hour between Sam's homecoming and suppertime passed quickly, with Molly and Matthew on either side of Sam, listening as he read from Jack London's *Burning Daylight*. Beth, in the rocking chair across from them, added stitches to the afghan she'd been crocheting, and Aaron, open Bible in his lap, wished, just for the moment, that photographs were permitted within the Plain life, because a scene like this would surely bring him comfort in his golden years.

Beth disappeared into the kitchen and returned carrying a tray piled high with plates, bowls, flatware, and tumblers. He half-rose from his chair to help, but she smiled and said, "I am fine."

Without being told to, Molly left her brothers to wash up, and proceeded to distribute the tray's items. And when they gathered around, nothing felt different, with the exception of having the dining table in the parlor while Sam precariously balanced a plate on his lap.

Also without being asked, Molly helped clear the table, and while Beth put the dishes in the sink to soak, his little girl raced into the basement, and came up holding a cardboard box.

"Should he close his eyes to choose his presents, Beth?"

"No, but that is something we can try on *your* birthday."

"Unwrap the square package first," Sam said.

Aaron took his time peeling the wrapping from the box and recognized the inside-out red and green holly paper Stella had folded up and tucked into a shirt box last

Christmas. Took his time, too, sliding off the lid while Sam impatiently rapped his knuckles on his leg cast.

"Ten-penny nails," Aaron said. "A box full of them."

"Pulled 'em out of the old barn floorboards. They were bent, and I hammered 'em straight."

Mostly straight, Aaron thought, grinning. "This must have taken hours."

"Yeah, but I remembered that you said the price of nails was getting ridiculous, so I didn't mind."

"A very thoughtful and practical gift, son." He replaced the lid, set the box aside. "Thank you."

"Mine next!" Molly said, clapping. "Mine next! It's the long, skinny one."

She so often talked and behaved as if she were much older than her years. It was a pleasure, seeing his little girl *behaving* like an eight-year-old for a change.

He tugged at the longest end of a cord of crocheted yellow yarn that held a sheet of green construction paper in place. She'd made the box herself, by carefully folding newspapers into a rectangle and gluing them into place. In it, she'd tucked a long black cord.

"It's a string tie," she said, in case there was any doubt. "Beth taught me how to knit, and I made it, myself."

He held it up, inspected it. Had Beth taught her how to prevent fraying by flattening thimbles on each end?

"You can wear it for special occasions, like the other men do," Molly said.

"I'll do that. And I have a feeling every man will want one just like it. Thank you, sweet girl. I love it!"

She blushed prettily as Matthew moved closer. "Just two left," Aaron told him. "Which one is yours?"

The boy pointed, and for a tense moment, Aaron worried

he'd retreated into his former silent world. It didn't matter what Matthew had rolled up in the red bandanna. His favorite gift came when his son said, "I think you'll like it."

Inside the bandanna, he found three plain white handkerchiefs, each with thick, wrinkled hems.

"Beth showed me how to thread a needle, and how to sew, and she let me cut up an old pillowcase to make them." He leaned in close, grabbed one, and demonstrated. "I folded the edges over, like this, and sewed 'em down, like this." His arm rose and fell, rose and fell, as he took imaginary stitches. Big, wide-spaced black stitches.

"My old ones were getting threadbare, so this is a perfectly timed gift."

"Just be careful," Matthew warned, "because a couple of the knots are pretty big. You could get a scratch, blowing your nose."

Laughing, Aaron gave him a quick, sideways hug. "I'll keep that in mind. Thank you."

There were four handmade birthday cards in the cardboard box. Four cards, and one more package.

"Read the cards first," Beth said. "I think the children are excited to see your reaction."

He picked up Molly's, the green one, first. She'd painstakingly cut a bouquet of white and yellow daisies and a red flower that almost resembled a rose and glued the petals and leaves atop a hand-drawn vase. Inside, she'd printed, *Of all the fathers in the world, I am blessed that you are mine.*

She'd drawn a heart and, inside it, signed her name.

"It's very pretty, and I can tell it took a long time to make. I love it, and I love you."

Matthew, still standing beside Aaron, chose his own

card next. The front boasted a brown beard. Above it, a black hat and below it, black suspenders and boots. Big black letters spelled out *DAED*. Inside, in shaky block letters, scattered haphazardly across the page, he'd written *HAPY BIRHDAY*. He had a feeling Beth had written the words on a separate page, and the boy had copied what he *thought* he'd seen. No signature here. *None needed,* Aaron thought, smiling. "It's wonderful, Matthew." And he thanked him again.

"Beth helped," the boy said. "There aren't many colors in a pack of construction paper. Black wouldn't work, and neither would yellow or orange." One shoulder lifted in a boyish shrug. "So brown it is."

"He's right," said Sam, pointing at the card he'd made . . . brown, with lines drawn on it to resemble a wooded board, sported black dots that spelled out *HAPPY BIRTHDAY DAED*.

"Nail holes!" his son said from the bed. "Get it?"

Laughing, Aaron said, "Yeah. I get it. Very imaginative." He opened the card and read inside: *TO THE BEST FATHER MADE BY GOD. LOVE, SAM.*

In past years, they'd celebrated his birthday at his mother's house, with supper and a cake. Cards and gifts had never been part of the festivities, and Aaron didn't quite know what to say, now that things were coming to a close.

"Beth's present next," Molly said, handing it to him. "The card is inside the box."

"After coordinating all of this, you wouldn't have needed to give me anything," he told her. "But thank you."

She just sat quietly, a light smile lifting the corners of her mouth, waiting . . .

She'd wrapped her long, narrow box with brown paper, the kind grocery bags are made of, and tied it with a crocheted cord. It was similar to the one that bound Molly's gift, but Beth's was blue.

"She used that color because it matches your eyes."

Had Beth shared that bit of information, or had his daughter made an educated guess?

"The metal things are from suspenders Uncle Karl was throwing away," Molly explained.

He held them up, examined inch-wide lengths of soft black material attached to shorter lengths of elastic. The suspenders he wore, and the spare pair in his closet, had been purchased at Walmart, but not even the machine-produced suspenders could compare with Beth's meticulous stitches.

"They're perfect," he said, looking at her. *Like everything else about you.* "With all that you do around here, when did you find the time?"

"On the nights I cannot sleep, I come here, to the parlor, where I can read or sew or knit until I get drowsy without disturbing anyone."

She said it as if it was no big deal, but based on the precision of every inch, she'd had a lot of sleepless nights. And he'd been the beneficiary.

"I measured them against your extra pair, but you might want to try them on later to make sure they are the right fit."

Elastic at the clips. Adjustable at the back. He didn't need to try them on to know they'd fit—probably better than the store-bought suspenders. But he'd do it if it made her happy.

"Time for cake," she said, and hurried into the kitchen.

She returned carrying clean forks and cake plates. When she came back the second time, Beth held a triple-layer chocolate cake with one fat candle burning in its center. "We wish you a happy birthday, Mr. Bontrager, and many, many more."

Aaron could think of few things he'd like better than spending many, many more years with Bethel. Because like it or not, and in spite of his ridiculous rule, he'd fallen in love with Mrs. Bontrager.

Having made her usual "I cannot sleep if there are dishes in the sink" excuse, Beth stayed up later than Aaron. And as usual, she'd barely made a sound, changing into her nightgown. Should he say something? Let her know that he wasn't asleep?

Except for the soft splash of rain against the window-panes, silence had fallen over the dark house.

"I feel bad, leaving Sam down there, all by himself."

"How did you know I was awake?"

"Your breathing is different when you sleep."

Aaron added that to the rest of the things she'd learned about him. Things that helped her make his life noticeably better.

"Sam's a big boy. Besides, if he needs anything, he knows we're close by." He pictured the table she'd pushed up to the bed, to assure that Sam's books were within easy reach. Beth had probably placed a glass of water on it, and beneath it, a small trash can for discarding candy wrappers and the occasional tissue. "Besides, you can't very well sleep upright in a chair."

"I suppose you are right. . . ."

"Thanks for everything you did to make him comfortable. For the birthday party, too."

"I thought the children—and you—needed something joyful to think about other than . . ."

"Other than how close we came to losing him?"

"Yes."

Upon hearing Matthew's sputtering proclamation, her face had drained of all color, and Aaron would never forget the fear and heartache that widened her eyes . . . the same fear and heartache that pulsed through him, because she loved the children, too.

"But I'm still torn between wanting to hug the stuffing out of Sam and wanting to wring his neck." He linked his fingers together, tucked them between the pillow and his head. "I mean, why would he take a chance like that!"

"Because he was thinking with his heart, not his head."

Sam had always been a deep thinker. Empathetic. Often, his mother had called him sensitive, in such a way that it sounded like a criticism. It was one of the reasons Sam worked so hard on his tough-guy façade.

"He puts so much effort into behaving older than his years."

"I was thinking the same thing."

"He is so good at it, in fact, that when he tests my patience, I have to remind myself he is only ten."

"I can't believe how close we came to losing him. If you hadn't put the fear of God into Matthew, made him talk . . ."

"While I was tucking Sam in tonight, he asked me to pray with him. He thanked God for saving his life because, in his words, 'Daed does not handle death very well.'"

Sam had been four when Aaron had lost his beloved grandparents, and barely six when they had buried his father, his best friend in all the world. And then . . . Marta . . . He thought he'd done a fair job of mourning privately after each funeral, but all three times, Sam had caught a glimpse of his sorrow. At his young age, he'd probably blamed *those* tears on grief, not fury and shame.

"He's right."

The simple admission was a stinging reminder of the worry and fear he'd saddled his children with. Bitter regret coursed through him, because his indefensible conduct had robbed them of two and a half years of childhood innocence. Two years they'd never get back.

Beth must have sensed the reason for his sudden silence, for she turned onto her side, placed a hand upon his shoulder.

His precarious hold on self-control cracked, and before he knew what was happening, Aaron found himself crying softly into the crook of her neck. He'd promised to protect her, and here he was, blubbering like a fragile child. How could he expect her to trust that he'd meant his vow?

She pulled him closer. So close that Aaron could feel her heart, beating against his chest. Gentle fingers alternately combed through his hair, stroked his back and shoulders as she kissed away his tears. He struggled to thank her for righting his gone-wrong world, to admit that he loved her for it, but the words stuck in his aching throat. *Is this what it was like for Matthew?*

The soothing touch of her hands, the soft breaths against

his cheek, calmed him. Now, as he listened to the ticking clock and the rain on the roof, he gave in to drowsiness.

When had he flung a leg over her hip and wrapped his arms around her? he wondered.

"You are a good and decent man, Aaron Bontrager, and you must never, *ever* forget that."

If someday he allowed himself to believe her words, it would be because God had blessed him . . . with Beth.

"Sleep well, Mrs. Bontrager," he said, and fell asleep.

# Chapter Eleven

"What a surprise, seeing you," Esther said.

"Oh now," he said, bussing his mother's cheek, "it hasn't been that long since I stopped by." He'd seen his mother and sister at the every-other-Sunday services, but thanks to his heavy work schedule, it had been nearly eight weeks since they'd spent time alone.

"You look tired, brother," Stella said as he sat. "Are you getting enough sleep?"

"More than enough." He reached into the playpen and hoisted Micah into the air. "Just look at you." He bent to tousle Mark's hair. "Every time I see you two, it seems you've grown an inch."

The baby sat on his knee and released a long string of baby talk as he played with Aaron's beard.

"Hot out of the oven?" he asked, pointing at the pie on the table.

Laughing, Esther cut him a piece.

"Take care not to let that little monkey get his fingers into it," Stella said, "or you will wear cherry filling in your beard!"

Esther, seated across from him, folded her hands on the table. "Were your ears ringing?"

He speared a cherry, cut it in half, and fed it to Micah. "What do you think, nephew? Seems the bees have been buzzing, and I've been the main subject in the hive."

"Yes, we have been talking."

"Not about you," Stella said. "About Bethel."

"You've been saying good things, I hope."

"We think it's time for her to come out of the house, start interacting with the rest of the community."

"She attends services," he said around a bite of crust. "And the socials afterward."

"But unless someone makes a point of speaking to her, she stays to herself. Why is she so shy?"

Esther agreed. "People are starting to talk."

"And what are *people* saying?"

"That she's standoffish," Esther said.

"Stuck-up," Stella added.

"And snooty."

He frowned at them. "This is the first I'm hearing of any of this. I thought you liked Beth."

"We *do* like her," Stella said. "We like her a lot. And we want others to feel as we do, so she'll feel more at home here in Pleasant Valley."

"Was she this way in Indiana?" Esther asked.

If so, Aaron thought, she'd had good reason. But it wasn't his place to tell his mother and sister what Beth had lived through in Nappanee. "A few people in her town were less than kind," he began, "because of her limp. I suppose Beth thinks if she keeps her distance, she's less likely to hear such things . . . if anyone here would be so thoughtless, that is."

Esther waved his opinion away. "People have visited. Welcomed her with jams and jellies, bread and pies, even pot holders and potted plants. It's up to you, son, to do something about it."

"About what?"

"Why, about her shyness, of course."

"I like Bethel just the way she is. And if you want the truth, I like the privacy her shyness affords me."

"Good grief," Stella said.

And Esther sighed. "At least encourage her to come visit with me when Stella is here." Pausing, she patted Aaron's hand. "You don't want people feeling unwelcome in your home, do you?"

*If they feel unwelcome,* Aaron thought, *it is as much their fault as Beth's. She is new to town and working hard to adapt to the New Order ways.*

"The road goes both ways," he said. "I know that Beth would welcome anyone who came to call."

"He's completely missing the point," Stella told Esther. Facing Aaron, she said, "You brought her here. Without discussing it with anyone, I might add. So it's up to you to help her blend in."

He could have reminded Stella that bringing Bethel here had been her husband's idea. But why drag poor unsuspecting Karl into this quagmire?

"Every time we get together," he said. "she's treated you well, and you seemed comfortable with her, too."

"I am the mother. She is supposed to come to me, not the other way around."

*What an outdated mindset,* he thought. Getting to his

feet, he handed Micah to Stella. "Thanks for the pie, Maem."

"But you only took a bite!"

"Enough to know it's delicious." *By the way,* he felt like saying, *Sam is doing well. Nice of you to ask about him.*

Aaron jammed the hat onto his head and shouldered his way out the door, uncertain why he was so upset. And then it hit him: Maybe Stella was right, and he hadn't done enough to help Beth adjust to her new home.


"You don't have a mop for that?"

Beth looked up, saw Stella and Esther peering through the back screen door, and scrambled to her feet. "Come in, please!" She used her apron to dry her hands.

"Aaron doesn't expect you to work from sunup to sundown." Esther placed a cherry pie on the table. "The missing piece . . . your husband ate it. Well, a bite of it, anyway."

Stella placed a pitcher of lemonade beside it. "He paid us a little visit this morning. This is a peace offering."

Esther stepped into the arched doorway between the kitchen and parlor. "How are you doing, grandson?"

Sam knocked on his cast. "Itchy."

Facing Beth, she said, "How much longer before they remove the awful things?"

"He will have x-rays day after tomorrow. If the bones have healed properly, Dr. Baker will remove them."

"My prayers have been answered."

Esther pulled out a chair and made herself comfortable while Stella helped herself to four plates and tumblers from the cupboard. "You have definitely worked your way into my brother's heart," she said, passing them out. She grabbed a knife, too, and cut into the pie.

Beth didn't know what to say. Ten, maybe fifteen minutes ago, Aaron had looked calm and happy, sipping the coffee she'd poured him, talking about his newest account. He hadn't mentioned a word about stopping at Esther's house first. If this was a peace offering for Bontrager, why was Stella slicing the pie now?

"Where are the twins?"

"Home, with Karl. Aaron gave him the day off." She delivered pie and lemonade to Sam.

"Yes. A Saturday off. How charitable of him," Esther put in.

"The mill is busier than ever. For weeks now, Mr. Bontrager has been working weekends, taking the place of family men on the crew."

"Hmpf," Stella said around a bite of crust. "My brother, the generous do-gooder. *He* is a family man and ought to spend more time at home himself."

Beth didn't know what was going on here, but she didn't like listening to Esther and Stella attack her husband. They'd known him all his life, so why were they behaving as though they weren't aware of his generous traits? She would have said so, but respect for his mother and sister kept her quiet.

Esther pointed at the pot simmering on the stove, and Beth said, "Chicken stew."

"Dumplings? Aaron loves dumplings."

"Yes, but it is too soon to add them." What on earth was going on here?

"And that?"

She followed her mother-in-law's gaze to where a casserole dish sat cooling on the counter. "Apple cobbler. I will put it into the oven to warm while I mix up the dumplings. Unless he prefers more of your pie."

"Hmpf," Esther said again. "Dessert? On a Saturday?" She shook her head. "*We* only have it for special occasions. No wonder you have no time to go out."

*Go out?* Beth repeated mentally. *Go where?* "Every day is a special occasion," Beth said. "Mr. Bontrager works hard and deserves to feel that this is his haven."

"His father worked hard all his life, and he was satisfied to eat dessert on holidays."

"But you baked this pie," Beth said, glancing at it, "and today is not a holiday."

"I baked it," Stella said. "Bought too many cherries and had to use them before they went bad." She looked into the parlor. "New curtains? I heard Walmart was having a sale."

"I made them from some old bed linens I found in the basement."

Smiling, Stella shook her head. "Is there anything you *can't* do well?"

"No wonder Aaron defended her so heartily," Esther said.

"Defended me? Against what?" Against *whom* was the better question!

"That was too strong a word, Maem." She looked at Beth to add, "He was defending him*self*, actually."

"But why?"

Stella and Esther exchanged a guilty glance. "Better get back," Esther said, "before the babies drive Karl mad."

Stella rose, too. "You're right." And to Beth, she said,

"Now that they're crawling, they're into everything. Why, Micah can climb out of his playpen faster than you can say 'Stop!'" She punctuated the information with a nervous laugh.

If something had happened during Bontrager's visit with his mother and sister, Beth felt duty bound to smooth any ruffled feathers. Especially since it seemed *she* was the cause of it.

"If Mr. Bontrager said or did something to offend either of you, I am sure it was unintended. As I mentioned, he has been working hard to meet all the new orders, much harder than usual, from dawn till dark most days. Like anyone under those circumstances, he gets a bit impatient from time to time."

"Oh?" Esther said from the doorway. "So you are saying he has been snappish with you and the children, too?"

"No, that is not what I said. He has been patient and kind, as always, despite his hectic schedule." Beth thought of the companionable conversation they'd shared shortly before his mother and sister had arrived.

"I am glad to hear it."

"Is there something I can do for you? Is that why you stopped by?"

"We stopped by," her mother-in-law said, "because we are family."

"And good members of the community," Stella added.

"We want to make sure you feel . . ." Esther's gaze darted to Stella's face, then back to Beth's. ". . . *welcome* in Pleasant Valley."

Their expressions, their voices, even their posture told Beth they were sincere.

"Thank you. And I thank you for the pie and lemonade."

She forced a smile. "I know Mr. Bontrager will enjoy both. And just as soon as I can, I will return the plate and pitcher." *Filled with one of* my *recipes,* she thought.

"You will tell my son that we stopped by?"

"For a friendly visit," Stella said.

"I will." And when she told him, if he wanted to share details about visiting them, she'd listen. If not, she'd respect that, too. He had enough on his mind without worrying about the women in his life.

The women called to Sam, wished him well, and made their way down the driveway, punctuating their animated discussion with emphatic gestures. "Talking about you, no doubt," Beth thought, grinning to herself.

On her hands and knees again, she went back to scrubbing the floor.

"Why did Grootmoeder come?"

"To bring us a cherry pie," she said.

The answer seemed to satisfy Sam, for he turned his attention back to his book.

Like it or not—and because of her shyness, Beth did *not*—she'd have to make a greater effort to get closer to her mother-in-law and sister-in-law, for Bontrager's sake. *And you need to ease up with this brush, or you will rub the varnish from the hardwood!*

Championing her spouse was harder than she'd thought.

# Chapter Twelve

A week later, she returned the pie plate filled with beef pot pie and the pitcher filled with slow-brewed iced tea. "This was not necessary," her mother-in-law had said, "but thank you." After fifteen minutes or so of casual conversation about the weather, the weeds, and the twins, Beth promised to stop by again, soon. "Give my best to Stella," she said, and hurried back home.

She could have used caring for Sam as her excuse for not staying longer, but from the third day on, the boy had been getting around wonderfully. Everyone was amazed and relieved when the casts came off a week ahead of schedule.

But Sam's recuperation hadn't been the reason Beth had been avoiding Stella and Esther. Despite their earlier visit, she was unsure of her place in Bontrager's family. And she didn't want anyone in Pleasant Valley to guess at the unusual nature of their marriage.

A glance at the kitchen clock told her to expect Bontrager any minute now. Because of his overloaded work schedule, they'd been eating an hour later than usual. He'd insisted on shutting down the mill on Sundays, though, and when she'd mentioned in passing this morning that it might be nice to have pot roast after services, his face had lit up, so she'd made it tonight, instead. Wouldn't he be pleasantly surprised!

Bontrager looked more haggard than usual when he hung up his jacket and hat and bent to pat the dog's head.

"Cold outside?"

"There's definitely a chill in the air." He stepped up to the sink to wash up. "But it's late August, so it's to be expected."

Beth knew he was tired, but the powder room was just around the corner, not all the way upstairs. Would he ever learn to use it instead of the kitchen sink?

*You sound like Esther and Stella!* she thought, and thanked God that she hadn't said it out loud.

"Coffee?" she asked.

"No, but if there's lemonade, I'd love some."

He took his seat as she poured a glassful. "Thanks, Bethel."

"Children," she called, "will you wash up, please, and set the table?"

The three had worked out setting the table quite well and all on their own: Sam distributed plates, Molly napkins and flatware, and Matthew positioned the glasses.

"That's what I like to see," Bontrager said. "Teamwork."

Beth slid out the oven rack and moved the roasting pan to the stove's front burner.

"Let me carry it to the table." He held out his hands and waited for her to take off the oven mitts.

Beth could have told him that he'd worked hard all day, that she was perfectly capable of doing it herself.

*An exercise in futility,* she thought, and handed over the pot holders.

During the meal, the children took turns telling him how they'd spent their day.

"I taught Traveler to fetch," Matthew said. "He's really good at it!"

At the mention of his name, the dog smiled and wagged its tail.

"Now you need to teach him not to drool all over the ball," Molly said, wrinkling her nose, "because . . . *ick.*" She sipped her milk, and added, "Beth taught me two new knitting stitches. One is called seed, and the other is the bamboo moss. I'm having a little trouble with the passing-over part of that one, but Beth says I'm a quick learner, and that if I practice, I'll be able to do it with my eyes closed." She stabbed one fork tine into a crisp roasted potato. "I'm making something for *you,* Daed, for Christmas!"

"Is that right?" he said around a yawn. "I've never been one to wish my life away, but I can hardly wait to see it." He turned to Sam. "And what were you up to today?"

"I finally, *finally* finished the tree house. Well, except for screwing some hinges into the door and windows. I want to close it up when we aren't up there, to keep the raccoons out, and to make sure birds can't build nests in it."

"It's August, silly. Birds don't make nests at this time of year."

"I know that, *silly.* I'm just looking ahead. Daed says good planning is important."

"And it's true," Bontrager said, and hid a yawn behind one hand. "How about passing the biscuits, son?"

While he buttered one, he met Beth's eyes. "I don't need to ask how you stayed busy all day." He held up the biscuit. "These are delicious. And you could cut that beef with the side of a spoon."

"She did more than that," Molly said. "She put up two dozen jars of pickles, too. I know exactly how many, because I helped her put them on the shelves in the root cellar."

Sam snorted. "I thought you were scared . . ." He wiggled his fingertips beside his face and deepened his voice to say ". . . to go down into the dungeon."

"I was, until Beth cleaned it up. A spider doesn't have a chance to build a web down there now."

Bontrager shook his head. "Amazing."

"What is?" Matthew asked.

"Not what. Who." He was looking directly at her when he said it. "I need to check it out."

"New shelves, clean floor, and every jar has been dusted and polished," Molly said.

Sam snorted again. "No way I'll believe you helped with all of that, too."

"If everyone has had enough, let's clear the table so I can serve dessert."

Bontrager perked up a little. "What's on the menu tonight?"

"Peach cobbler with ice cream," Matthew said, stacking plates.

Beth served Bontrager first, and as he spooned up his first bite, the phone rang.

"Please don't let it be one of the guys," he said to the ceiling.

Unfortunately, it was.

By the time he hung up, worry had drawn frown lines on his forehead. "Moses had an accident. I need to drive him to the ER."

"Why do you have to do it?" Molly wanted to know. "You just got home!"

"I'm the only one with a vehicle that can make it up the mountain." He shrugged into his jacket. "God willing, I'll be home before you go to bed." He dropped a kiss onto her forehead, and then he was gone.

"What kind of accident, I wonder," said Sam.

"Must be something pretty bad," Molly said. "Daed looked a little scared."

"Your father will update us as soon as he can," Beth told them. "Would it make you feel better if we said a prayer for Moses?"

All three children nodded, then bowed their heads as Beth said, "Father, we ask that You watch over Moses. Give the doctors and nurses at the hospital the wisdom to know how to help him, and protect his wife and children from worry and fear."

Satisfied that the man was in good hands, the children devoured the dessert with gusto. When they finished, Matthew asked, "Okay if we work on our puzzle until bed-time?"

"And can we wait up for Daed?" Molly asked.

"*May we,*" Sam said to his sister. "Don't you pay any attention in school at all?"

Beth said, "Yes, Matthew, you can work on your puzzle. As for staying up late, Molly, that will depend on how many other patients are at the ER." *And how severe Moses's injury is,* she thought.

An hour passed, then two, and the children had almost

completed the puzzle when the phone rang. They gathered close as Beth listened to Bontrager's report of how Moses had sawed off his thumb. When he finished, she said, "It is good you got him there so quickly. The children and I will pray that the operation is a complete success."

"Operation?" Molly echoed.

Beth held up a finger, asking for a moment of silence. "Is his wife there with him?"

"No way to get here. Soon as they take him to the OR, I'll come get her, bring her back here."

"Does she have someone to stay with the children?"

"Her mother lives with them."

"Well, please let her know that if she needs anything, anything at all, she need only ask."

His voice was soft and caring when he said, "Hearing that doesn't surprise me a bit. Kiss the children goodnight for me. Looks like I'll be here for quite some time."

Earlier this evening, he'd walked through the door looking worn-out. What would he look like when he felt that he could leave the hospital?

Beth let the children stay up an hour past their bedtime and, after tucking them in, decided to wait up for their father. She passed the time reading. Knitting. Praying. She must have dozed off shortly before dawn and woke with a crick in her neck when Matthew tapped her shoulder.

"Daed isn't upstairs. Is he at the mill?"

"No, sweet boy. He is still with Moses."

"He didn't call?"

She shook her head. "Sorry."

Sam and Molly, leaning over the railing, had heard the whole conversation.

"He didn't call because the phone would have woken us up," Molly said. "Daed is thoughtful that way."

"Must be pretty serious," her brother said, passing her on his way down the stairs, "for him to be at the hospital, still."

Matthew looked a little flushed, and she drew him closer, pressed her lips to his forehead. "My goodness, sweet boy. You have a fever."

She hurried to the kitchen and filled a glass with tap water. "Drink it down, Matthew."

After placing the empty glass in the sink, she dialed the clinic. Willa, the nurse there, answered, and Beth told her that the boy was warm, very warm.

"Can you get hold of Aaron, so he can drive you in?"

Beth explained that wasn't possible because of what had happened to Moses, but, with the children within earshot, left out the part about how he'd sawed off his thumb.

"Gimme a sec," the nurse said. And when she got on the line again, she added, "I'll be right there to pick you up."

Half an hour later, after a thorough exam, the doctor held up a pair of tweezers . . . and a fat black tick. "Here's the culprit," Dr. Emily Baker said. "Found this guy at the base of Matthew's skull, hidden deep in his hair." She dropped the arachnid into a small plastic bag and zipped it up. "I need to draw some blood to check for Lyme disease. I've found half a dozen ticks in the past week alone, and none have transmitted any diseases, but since he has a fever, I want to do the blood work."

Willa made quick work of preparing a tray, then changed gloves and thoroughly cleaned Matthew's bite. She and Emily spoke softly but firmly, explaining every step of the process, effectively keeping the boy so distracted that he barcly flinched when the needle went in. Emily drew three vials of blood, and Willa labeled each. And in the same calm voice, Emily told Beth how to care for Matthew until the test results came back. "Nothing to worry about, mind you. He probably just has a cold bug. I didn't see any swelling around the bite. Worst-case scenario, we'll put him on an antibiotic."

"You're one brave kid, Matt," Willa said, ruffling his bangs. She looked at Beth. "How 'bout if I call Aaron for ya?"

"The poor man hasn't had a decent night's sleep in weeks, and probably didn't get any last night. He's been at the hospital since dinnertime yesterday. There's no sense worrying him unnecessarily."

"Yer a peach, Bethel Bontrager, and I'm sure Aaron considers himself a lucky man."

Beth had heard that Willa and her little girl had moved to town just a few years ago, met and married Max, the local contractor, and never looked back at her Englisher life. She might dress like someone Plain, Beth thought, grinning, but she surely didn't talk like one!

Now, Willa held out a big bowl. "How 'bout a lollipop, guys?"

All three smiled, and all three helped themselves to one.

"Well, we're done here," she said, putting the bowl back onto the counter. "Let's get you home."

Willa agreed to come inside long enough for a cup of tea and took over in the kitchen while Beth turned the sofa into a makeshift bed. Once Matthew was settled in, she brought him water. He protested, but only until Willa said, "Remember what Dr. Baker said, kiddo. . . ."

He emptied the glass and, in minutes, fell asleep.

Willa must have anticipated the children's questions, because she made tea for them, too.

"Will he be all right?" Beth wanted to know.

Willa patted her hand. "He'll be fine."

"But . . . the doctor said he might need medicine."

"Only if the tick had a disease. She also said that isn't very likely."

"Then . . . why does he have a fever?"

"Kids get fevers for all kinds of crazy reasons. All you need to remember is, Beth, is that Emily knows her stuff. Soon as those blood tests come back, she'll know what to do."

Satisfied, the children drained their cups and asked permission to go outside.

"Jackets, please," Beth said.

When the door closed behind them, Willa said, "So how goes it, girl? You all settled here in Pleasant Valley?"

"It is a lovely town."

"All settled into married life? And don't tell me Aaron is a lovely man. He's a great guy, don't get me wrong, but he'd never win a warm-and-friendly award, if y'know what I mean."

If Willa had ever seen him with the children, she'd know without a doubt just how warm and friendly he truly was.

"Has he told you about Marta yet?"

"What about her?"

"You know . . . the boyfriend? It was all over town. Well, not *all* over, but we hear things at the clinic that some folks don't. If Aaron hadn't gone to bat for her with Bishop Fisher, she would've been shunned, for sure."

"My goodness . . ."

"For a while there, the way I heard it . . ." She moved closer, lowered her voice so Matthew couldn't hear. ". . . Aaron's mother told somebody, who told somebody else, that she thought you-know-who was the other guy's kid." She nodded in the direction of the parlor. "But then he was born, the spittin' image of his daddy, and nipped *that* rumor in the bud."

How awful for Bontrager, to learn that his wife had been unfaithful, to have forgiven her, then have to wonder for nine long months whether or not his youngest son was his!

"Don't take it personally if he's not all touchy-feely. A lot of Amish men are like that. He'll show affection in other ways, like being appreciative of the way you've turned this place around, and the way you pamper his kids."

Beth could only think about the night of his birthday party, when he hadn't just looked grateful, but had told her how much he appreciated what she'd done to make it happen. Sharing that story would have changed Willa's mind about him, but the woman already knew far too much—or thought she did, anyway—about Bontrager's private business.

"Well, I'd better get back to the clinic before Emily sends out the search dogs."

"Thank you for driving us to the clinic and back."

"Don't give it another thought. I love any excuse to drive Li'l Red."

Once Willa had steered the tiny pickup onto the road, Beth checked on Matthew. Still warm, but not nearly as warm as before. A good sign that when Dr. Baker called, she'd have good news to share.

She hadn't given a thought to dinner and decided to surprise them with breakfast for supper. Quick, easy, filling, and reasonably nutritious, it had become one of the kids' favorites. Especially if it involved bacon.

"Beth?"

She carried another glass of water to Matthew, and he drank it right down.

"Feeling any better?"

"My head hurts a little, but I'm okay. Can I go outside with Molly and Sam?"

"Not just yet. You still have a fever, and that means you still need to rest."

"Can I color, then?"

"Of course you can." She placed a serving tray across his lap, arranged construction paper and colored markers on it. "There you go. But if you feel sleepy, let me know. I will move this so you can take another nap."

There were clothes in the dryer and another load in the washing machine. Beth had just returned to the kitchen, carrying a basket of laundry, when Bontrager parked in his usual spot near the front porch.

"What's Matthew doing on the couch?"

Beth told him how they'd spent their day, and he went directly into the parlor.

"Hey, son. Feeling all right?"

Smiling, he showed his father the thick white gauze pad taped to the bend of his elbow. "Dr. Baker took blood. A *lot* of blood." He held up three fingers. "Put it into little glass bottles. She's testing them, to make sure I don't have tick fever."

Chuckling, Bontrager said, "Beth tells me you were really brave. I'm proud of you."

Matthew went back to coloring, and Bontrager returned to the kitchen.

"Don't know what I'd do without you," he said. "Thanks. Again."

"No thanks necessary. Are you hungry?"

"Matter of fact, I'd rather take a shower."

"And a nap."

"I might just take you up on that."

He slept through supper. Through the children's bedtime ritual. Nearly two hours after she had tucked them in, he padded into the kitchen on big white-socked feet, his hair askew, and his beard, too. "I can't believe I slept so long!"

"You must be hungry by now. Let me fix you something to eat."

As if on cue, his stomach growled, loudly enough that it made both of them laugh.

"We had breakfast for supper," she told him, opening the refrigerator door. "The children loved it. I saved some pancake batter for you. Bacon, too."

She'd just turned on the flame under the griddle when he said, "Right now, I'd eat a rock if you buttered it."

"That would guarantee a no-dirty-dishes meal, but it might be a little heard on your teeth."

"Yeah, I suppose." He inspected his fingernails. "Sorry that I left you alone so long, to handle . . . everything."

"You have absolutely nothing to apologize for. It was not all that long, and of course you had to help Moses. The children understand that as well as I do. How is he, by the way?"

Aaron poured himself a glass of milk, downed it, and refilled the glass. "The surgeon said he believes Moses will regain much of the use of his hand. It'll take time, of course, and he's facing a long rehabilitation, but God willing . . ."

"He has a wife and children," she said, flipping a pancake, "more than enough incentive to do whatever is required."

Bontrager sat at the table, leaned back in the chair. "I checked on Matthew before coming downstairs. No fever at all. So thanks for that, too. Did he fuss much about having to stay inside to rest?"

"Only at first. I suggested that he make thank-you cards for Dr. Baker and Willa. That kept him busy for all of fifteen minutes!" She laughed, used the spatula as a pointer. "I put them there on the counter and told him you would deliver them next time you were on that side of town."

"I'll make a special trip. Emily doesn't send bills like a regular doctor, so it's the least I can do. And while I'm there, I'll pay her."

"Two birds with one stone?"

"As long as you butter it."

Again, they shared a moment of companionable laughter.

"Matthew made a card for me, too. It made me cry."

"That bad, huh?"

Oh, how she loved that sweet, teasing grin! "No, that *good*. It is there, with the others. See for yourself."

He crossed the room in three long strides, glanced at the drawings intended for the doctor and her nurse, then picked up the white construction paper card Matthew had made for Beth. He read the front aloud:

"'Thake you,'" the boy had written, and surrounded the words with a big, crooked pink heart. Bontrager turned to the inside. "'You our good. I love you.'"

A slanting smile brightened his tired face. "Nearly made me cry, too." He put the card back where he'd found it. "Because I'm jealous."

Bontrager returned to his chair as Beth used the spatula to flip the bacon slices in one frying pan. She cracked two eggs into another.

"He's right, you know."

"About . . .?"

"You *are* good."

She held her breath, wondering if he'd add *I love you,* as Matthew had. When he didn't, Beth exhaled slowly. Bontrager cared about her, and it showed. In the way he talked to her. In the way he treated her. It wasn't exactly her dream-come-true scenario, but she could live with it. Easily.

Beth slid the bacon onto a saucer, carried it and the stack of pancakes to the table. Butter, syrup, salt and pepper, and last, the eggs. She moved to the sink with every intention of washing the griddle and frying pans while he ate.

"I'll help you with those later," he said. "Sit with me while I eat?"

Bontrager ate with enthusiasm and, between bites, told her what had happened during his hours at the hospital. He'd signed papers that authorized the hospital to send the bill to the sawmill, instead of to Moses, and done his best to help Moses's wife understand the surgery.

"Moses wasn't afraid of the operation. You won't believe what he *was* scared of."

"How he would support his family if he could not work?"

"Exactly." He washed down a bite of crispy bacon with a swallow of milk. "I told him not to worry about it. Said since he'd never taken a day off in fifteen years, I'd pay him a month's salary, and that after he got the go-ahead from his surgeon, we'd put him to work in the office."

"Kind and generous. Good and decent."

"What's that?" he said distractedly.

"Nothing. Just practicing my adjectives."

He looked puzzled. "Adjectives, huh." Bontrager pushed back from the table, patted his stomach. "Man, I'm stuffed. That was some breakfast. . . supper. . . meal. . ."

"All of the above." She got up, started clearing the table.

And he yawned.

"You should go back to bed, try to catch up on all the sleep you have lost in these past weeks. As busy as you are at the mill, it may be weeks more before you get another chance like this."

"Hey. I promised to help with the dishes if you kept me company." He stood and started carrying things to the sink. "I'm a man of my word."

"You need rest a lot more than I need help." Beth pointed toward the door.

Bontrager held up his hands like a man being robbed at gunpoint. "Okay. All right. Fine." He chuckled. "I can . . ." He yawned again. ". . . take a hint."

She watched him walk toward the stairs. A strong, steady gait that told anyone watching that this was a man who knew where he was going, and why.

Beth giggled into her fist. *Going to bed, because he is bone weary.*

With the dishes done, she scoured the sink. Movement outside caught her eye. There, backlit by the low-hanging moon, a doe was leisurely munching the petunias she'd planted along the walk. One by one, the purple blooms disappeared. Bontrager had warned her that what the deer didn't devour, they'd trample.

*Two days,* she thought. *Two days, wasted.* Hours in the hot sun, crawling around on her hands and knees, digging out every weed, every blade of grass. The work had left her with broken fingernails. Calluses. Knicks and cuts as her knuckles scraped the flagstones. How dare that animal just stand there, feasting, as if Beth had put the flowers into the ground just for her!

She rapped on the window, and the doe raised its head, stared for a minute, then went back to chomping until there was nothing left but bent stems and a few scraggly leaves.

Beth flung open the back door, tromped across the porch. "Go away, you greedy pig! I hope you get a belly-ache!"

That did the trick, and as the deer high-tailed it into the woods, Beth reveled in her success.

Her joy lasted only until stark reality hit: The deer would be back tomorrow. And the day after. She'd bring friends, and when they found the sidewalk flowerbeds barren . . .

Of all the words she could have chosen, why that awful one?

Beth turned out the kitchen lights, the ones over the sink and stove, and the hanging lamp above the table.

Moonlight glinted from the chrome toaster, the sheen of the hardwood, the white-painted cabinet doors. It was a beautiful, comfortable room for family to gather, a family that had welcomed her as one of their own. Through the wide arched doorway, a cozy parlor. The deer had destroyed her garden, but there were acres outside where she could start over . . . and build fences to protect her precious posies. Upstairs, she had a safe place to sleep, a place where she'd never again have to fight off *any* man's unwanted advances.

So much to be thankful for, so why couldn't she get past the knowledge that she'd never have a child of her own?

That same bright lunar light pooled on the card Matthew had made her. She smiled, remembering the misspellings, the uncertain pen strokes that said *You our good* and *I love you.*

She *had* a child of her own . . . three of them, in fact. No, she hadn't given birth to them, but Beth couldn't have loved them more if she had.

Above her, a soft thump told her that one of them had hopped out of bed. Matthew, probably, needing to use the bathroom. Beth said a little prayer that when he went back to his room, he'd fall quickly asleep, and settle into a happy dream.

She had a husband up there, too. That night when he had thought he'd lost Sam . . . He must trust her a lot to have let her see him at his most vulnerable. That openness had compelled her to say, "You are a good and decent man, and you must never forget it."

If it ever seemed that he'd forgotten it, she'd remind him what he'd done for Moses. How he treated the rest of his employees. His love for the children. The way he'd saved her.

Feeling more fulfilled and secure than she had in many years, Beth ascended the stairs and tiptoed into the boys' room. Sam, as usual, had kicked off his quilt, and she slowly, carefully slid it up to his chin. Leaning over Matthew's bed, she kissed his forehead. Just as Bontrager had said, cool to the touch. *Thank You, Lord,* she prayed, then peeked into Molly's room and heard the sounds of peaceful slumber. And then, their father's room. *No, our room.* Moonlight had found its way in here, too. He looked so young, so innocent, that all she wanted was to hold him again, the way she had on the night after the cave-in.

By the time she returned from changing into her night-gown, he'd sprawled spread eagle across the mattress. A phrase from one of the books she'd read to Matthew that afternoon came to mind. *All the better to hold you, my dear,* she thought, fitting herself into the small triangle between his arm, waist, and thigh.

Oh, how she loved this man. This good and decent man.

And Beth fell asleep, completely unaware of the width of her smile.

Aaron woke slowly, groggily. Every limb felt weighted down, his lips and eyes sandpaper dry.

Behind him, he heard Bethel's steady, quiet breaths. Felt the warmth of her body, pressed tight to his. He took stock, realized that not only had he hogged the bed, but the blankets, too, and she'd instinctively moved close for warmth. Slowly, so as not to wake her, he turned onto his side, facing her, and shared his covers.

Oh, but she was lovely. Perfectly arched eyebrows accentuated the long, thick lashes dusting her cheeks. Her lips, slightly parted, turned up at the corners, and he hoped it was because pleasant memories had filled her dreams.

One small hand rested on the pillow, fingers splayed . . . callused and chapped from hard work. Work performed on behalf of himself and the children. Aaron hadn't planned on resting his hand atop it, but before he realized what was happening, that's exactly what he did.

She stirred, ever so slightly, and inhaled, long and slow. Aaron didn't want her to wake up. Not yet. Because he liked having the freedom to explore every contour, every angle, every inch of her face.

If he had to choose a favorite time of day, it would be this . . . morning twilight . . . when the moon and sun, in a struggle for control of the sky, streaked the earth with shades of yellow and orange, and skimmed the clouds' bellies with pink and purple. That's what he saw on the other side of the window. To check the time, though, he'd need to roll onto his other side, and risk waking Bethel. He took a guess, instead. Five, five-fifteen . . .

He had a meeting at nine, but needed to get to the mill before seven, so that when the men arrived, he could bring them up to date on Moses's condition. If he left now, he might get in two or three hours' work before McCartney showed up for another load of lumber.

Aaron turned onto his back, and from there, onto his side. He eased one leg, then the other, from the bed, being sure not to make a sound when his feet hit the floor. If he'd ever felt more like a clumsy oaf, he didn't know when.

Sneaking across the room, he plucked up yesterday's clothes, haphazardly tossed across the chairback, and flung them over one arm. Near the door, he stooped to retrieve one boot, then the other, along with the balled-up socks he'd tossed into the corner.

Traveler was waiting for him in the hallway and treated Aaron to his best doggy grin. Normally, the mutt slept with Sam, but now and then, he wandered into Molly's room, bunked down with Matthew, or even slept on the braided rug beside their bed.

Their bed. He liked the sound of that. Liked it a lot.

"Shh," Aaron said, slinking past Traveler. "Bethel is sleeping."

The dog followed him to the powder room, where he used his spare comb and toothbrush, and donned his slightly wrinkled shirt and trousers. It followed him into the kitchen, too, and sat at his feet, hoping to catch any crumb that might fall while Aaron slapped together three cheese and mustard sandwiches—one for breakfast, two for lunch—and stuffed them into a paper bag. "If you tell anyone I did this," he said, squeezing a slice of bread into a doughy ball, "I'll deny it." He tossed it, and Traveler caught it. *Good thing the kids aren't up.* Because he'd made sure to explain why "people food isn't healthy for dogs."

"Outside, boy?"

Traveler trotted to the now-open door and darted outside while Aaron slipped into his jacket. He was about to pull the door closed behind him when he spotted the stack of construction paper on the counter beside Matthew's cards. He chose a yellow sheet, and using a fat blue marker, wrote: *Bethel—You were sleeping so soundly that*

*I didn't have the heart to wake you. See you tonight, Aaron.*
Grinning like a lovestruck schoolboy, he drew a tiny heart
beneath his name, colored it in, and leaned the note
against the salt and pepper shakers.

The grin became a wince when he fired up the truck.
He'd just spent twenty minutes sneaking around like a bur-
glar, and it would be a shame if the engine's rumble woke
her. God willing, she couldn't hear it from the back side
of the house. When he called later to see how her day was
going, would she mention the silly heart? Would she
figure out that it symbolized what he hadn't yet found the
courage to say?

He loved her.

The mill and parking lot were dark when Aaron rolled
in. A good thing, since he always got more done in the
hours before the phone started ringing and the equipment
began roaring. He settled in behind his desk and grabbed
the top file. Inside were his preliminary notes, followed
by the order sheet that specified the size and price of each
top plate, sole plate, trimmer, joist, and stud. The contract
spelled out loading, shipment, and payment dates. Rough
sketches of the small housing development, initialed by
the builder, preceded a hand-written note in which Albertson insisted on white oak—underlined three times—for
framing, hickory for flooring, and mahogany for cabi-
netry. He'd worked with guys like this before, sticklers for
detail who knew what they wanted and when they wanted
it. If Aaron came through, they got along fine, and established longstanding business relationships. One slip-up,
though, might be enough to send ripples of discontent

from the front office to the back lot, and snuff out any hope of future orders.

Aaron scribbled a few more notes onto the folder, then moved on to the day's jobs list. Moses would have run the debarker today, prepping hickory trees his loggers had harvested and delivered last week. A man needed two fully functioning hands to run any machine in the mill, and Moses wouldn't be ready for weeks, maybe months. Aaron looked forward to bringing his brother-in-law up to speed on his plans for their big, burly employee: Asking Moses to take care of most clerical work would free up Karl to meet with prospective customers. Aaron could have added those meetings to his schedule, but the challenge would be good for Karl . . . and give Aaron more time at home.

Flipping light switches as he made his way into the shop, he admired the way his employees policed their area. *You need to let them know you appreciate things like this,* he thought, because happy workers build successful companies.

Upon reaching Moses's section, he flipped another switch, fired up the drum debarker, and put on his safety gear—helmet with face shield, gloves, protective apron— and inspected the machine. It appeared to be in perfect working order. No surprise there. Moses had always fine-tuned things before, during, and after his shifts.

Before yesterday's accident, Moses had selected logs from storage and transported them to the conveyor. He'd adjusted the rifters and cut depths, too. Only a handful of men could run this operation alone, so Moses would be sorely missed. And when Aaron finished for the day, he'd be sore from shoving and pulling logs into the machine.

In a perfect world, he'd purchase a rosserhead debarker. Newer, more efficient technology allowed it to perform at any temperature, even on frozen wood. The disadvantages? It was pricy and could only debark one log at a time.

When Karl showed up, Aaron had been at it for more than an hour, a good two hundred and fifty tons' worth of work, by his estimation. At least he'd finished what Moses had started.

Aaron shut the machine down and removed his helmet. After the rest of the crew arrived, the men discussed Moses's prognosis and the day's schedule.

"No sleep again last night, huh?"

"Actually, I slept great." The memory of Bethel, cuddled up to him, kicked his heartbeat into overdrive. *I would've slept better facing the other way. . . .*

"After running Moses's wife back and forth and sticking with the big guy at the hospital? Yeah. Right. The guys and I can handle things here. Why don't you go home, catch a few winks?"

"I'm good. Really. But I have plenty to do in the office. Join me, so I can fill you in on a few things."

"Sure. Just let me check in the logging trucks. Ten minutes," Karl said, walking backward. "Fifteen at most."

*Just enough time to call home.*

The thought of hearing her voice was enough to rev his heart into high gear again. Had he ever felt this way about a woman before? No, hc hadn't.

The admission woke a sleeping monster: The now-familiar guilt, born of wondering if he'd been to blame for Marta's offenses.

When he got to his desk, he called Albertson, to let him know he could expect his delivery, right on time.

"Fine," the man said. "I'll clear my schedule."

Well, Aaron thought, if his conscience couldn't be clear, at least Albertson's schedule would be.

# Chapter Thirteen

"Matthew sure does love that dog," Molly said.

"He's supposed to be mine, but he spends all his time with *him*," Sam complained.

"Not all of his time. He sleeps with you. And anyway, if you did more things with him, he'd probably spend more time with *you*," Beth pointed out.

"I saved his life. What more does he want!"

"He's a dog, Sam. He only wants to be loved."

Beth understood, all too well.

"Plus, anyway," Molly continued, "Matthew does all the dirty work, like picking up poo in the yard, and washing his food and water bowls. And he doesn't even complain about it. So why are you complaining?" She paused, then said, "Oh. Wait. Complaining is what you *do.*"

"Be quiet. I'm trying to write," Sam said.

"What are you writing?"

"A book about Traveler."

"Really? What's it called?"

"*The Boy Who Saved a Dog*."

"That's a terrible title. No one will want to read a book like that."

Sam shrugged. "Says you."

"Beth, do you think that's a terrible title?"

"Actually, I like it." The pup trotted into the room and sat at Beth's side. She scratched his head. "What do you think, Traveler?"

The dog gave a one-woof reply and smiled.

"How many pages have you written?"

"Thirty-three," Sam said.

Molly giggled and looked up at Beth. "I'm guessing the words are *this big*." She held up both hands, leaving six inches between the palms. "That's the only way he could fill up that many pages."

Sam replied with a two-note, "You'll see. . . ."

"When?"

"When it's finished."

"When will that be?"

"When it's finished!" he said through clenched teeth. "Beth, will you please ask her to leave me alone? I can't concentrate with all her blabbing."

Beth extended a hand to the girl. "Why don't you and I take a walk?"

"Where?"

"Your grandmother's house. I baked banana bread, and I want to take a loaf to her."

"Can Traveler come?"

"He can walk with us, but he will have to wait outside. You know how she feels about animals in the house."

Molly sighed. "Yes." She giggled again. "If she doesn't like animals in the house, why does she let Sam inside? He eats like a pig!"

Matthew laughed. "That's funny, Molly!"

"Oh, hush, little brat. You eat like a pig, too," Sam retorted.

"That *isn't* funny." He turned to Beth. "Can I come too?"

"Will you ever learn? It's *may* I come," Sam said.

Beth held out her other hand. "We should go. I want to be back before your father gets home."

"The book will be done by then. *May* I read it after supper?"

"I think that would be wonderful!"

The phone rang, and Beth picked up. "Dr. Baker . . ."

"Emily, please. I'm just calling to let you know all is well. Matthew's tests came back negative."

"God is good."

"No more fever?"

"No, and he's up and about and behaving like his usual energetic self. But, do you know . . . what caused the fever, then?"

"Could have been any one of a dozen things. Some kids are more sensitive than others, and they can spike a low-grade fever because of allergies. A molar popping in. Matthew might have picked up a twenty-four-hour bug. If it had been any of those things, prescription meds wouldn't have helped anyway. We'll keep an eye on him. No reason to expect the fever will return, though, so I wouldn't worry if I were you."

She thanked the doctor and hung up.

"I passed the tests? My blood was good?"

"Yes, Matthew," she said, hugging him, "you passed the tests."

Molly hugged him, too. "See? I told you everything would be all right! Now let's deliver that banana bread!"

Beth considered calling the children's father, but thought

better of it. He'd been carrying a double load at the mill, and an interruption might slow production, which could mean additional hours at work.

"Shouldn't we call Daed first," Sam said, "and let him know Matthew is all right?"

Like an actor entering the stage on cue, Bontrager walked through the back door.

"Daed! What are you doing here!"

"I live here, Molly."

"Don't laugh at me, Daed. You know what I mean. You're usually at work at this time of day."

"He's at work at *all* times of the day lately."

"Sorry, Sam," he said, pointing at the snacks scattered around the boy's work space. "Just trying to keep the pantry and refrigerator full."

"We'd rather eat a little less and have you home a little more," Molly said.

He gave her a sideways hug. "I love you, too. And things will slow down soon. They always do during the winter."

"We were just on our way to bring Groosmammi some of Beth's banana bread. You should come. She'd like that."

There were dark circles under his eyes, and his lips had formed a thin line. It was how he always looked when he'd gone without sleep. She had no way of knowing how well he'd slept last night, if he'd slept at all. She'd tucked his sweet note into the handsewn, sleeveless shirt under her dress. Until today, its only purpose was to provide extra coverage. Now, it kept his thoughtful words close to her heart.

"Your father looks tired," she said. "I think maybe he came home to catch a quick nap."

He sent a grateful smile in her direction, then said, "It's okay. I'll go with you."

"We will not stay long. You can rest once we are home again."

"Sam? You're coming, right?"

"May I stay here and finish my book?"

"Save your place with a bookmark and pick up where you left off after we say hello to Groosmammi, to your aunt and cousins."

"I can't mark the page, because this isn't a regular book. It's the one I wrote. I only have a few more pages, and it'll be done."

Bontrager nodded slowly. "Ah, I see. That sounds like important work, so yes, I suppose you can stay here and finish up." He turned toward the door. "She will miss seeing you, though."

"No, she won't. She doesn't even like children. I heard her say so. More than once."

"She wasn't talking about *us*," Molly said, looking hurt. "We're her grandchildren. She *has* to like us!"

What a shame, Beth thought, that the woman had said things in the presence of her grandchildren, things that had led Sam to believe she preferred not to spend time with them. She pitied her mother-in-law because, given half a chance, they would shower her with affection. If they could make a total stranger feel like family . . .

"I know it is not far, but perhaps we should drive instead of walk? Conserve your energy?"

He laughed. "I'm tired, but I think I can manage a one-mile walk without fainting." He extended both hands, and each of the children took one.

As the foursome made their way down the path, Matthew pointed out the damage done by the deer.

She prepared herself for a teasing "I told you so." Instead, he said, "For the first time in my life, I wish I had a third hand."

"What?" Molly said. "Why?"

"So I could hold Beth's hand, too."

"She's carrying the bread," Matthew pointed out. "With both hands."

"Good point. I guess I'd feel pretty goofy, walking around with three hands."

But the caring look on his face said he wouldn't feel goofy at all.

The visit with Esther was pleasant enough, in part because Seth was there, teasing and cracking jokes, as usual. It was short, too, thanks to Bontrager's yawning.

"You're back too soon!" Sam grumbled. "I haven't finished yet!"

"What's left to do? Maybe I can help," Molly suggested.

Sam considered the offer. "You can be my illustrator. But," he said, finger in the air, "you have to draw what I tell you to."

"What about me?" Matthew asked. "What can I do?"

"Go into the barn and see if you can find a long wooden dowel. One half-inch thick."

Bontrager looked over the children's heads, told her with his eyes that he didn't get it, either.

"There is a bucket of dowels in the shed," he said. "Under my work bench, right beside the door. You'll find a yardstick in there, too. That'll help you make sure you find one that's a half-inch in diameter."

"See if there's any shellac while you're out there," Sam said. "It's spelled s-h-e-l-l-a-c."

Matthew scampered outside, excited about his assignment, and Traveler followed him.

"Shellac? Isn't that for floors and furniture?"

"After you finish the illustrations, I'll show you how I'll use it for the book."

In the kitchen, he stepped up close and lowered his voice. "Are you as fascinated as I am?"

"He told Molly the book will be ready when it is ready. So yes, very."

"I don't know about you, but I'm looking forward to Sunday."

"It will be nice, attending services with all of our children healthy at the same time."

His eyes widened when she called them *ours*.

"I agree." Then, "How would you feel about dinner in town after service? All of us. Except for Traveler, of course. We could go to Mom's Country Cookin'. Not too fancy, not too expensive, not too far away."

Sam fist-pumped the air as Beth said, "Seems the children will enjoy it."

He looked disappointed. "But not you?"

"Why . . . why yes. I will enjoy it, too. Very much!"

"Good. And you know what? I'm not just looking forward to Sunday, I'm looking forward to showing you kids off." He grinned at her. "You, and the best-looking Amish woman on the East Coast."

"Mr. Bontragcr!" She felt the heat of a blush in her cheeks.

"The truth is not sinful."

Beth was flattered. It was hard not to be when a man like him said things like that!

"I think your mother was pleasantly surprised by our visit."

He smirked. "Clever girl."

"Excuse me?"

"Neatly done . . . the change of subject. Or should I say the *attempt.*"

She pretended that a streak on the oven door had caught her attention and spritzed it with window cleaner. "She did not seem overly pleased about the bread, though," Beth said, polishing the glass. "She does not like bananas?"

"Even people who don't like bananas like banana bread. Unless they're weird."

"I hope you are right." It was her turn to smirk. "I will never live it down if she gets sick from eating it!"

Bontrager snickered. "I'd better get outside, see what's keeping Matthew."

"Good idea."

As he made his way to the shed, she said to herself, "I have been meaning to clean and organize things out there. We certainly do not need another son buried in a cave-in!"


The children had been antsy for days. Beth blamed it on their excitement about Sam's book. They'd planned a special presentation after church service, and if they'd said once that they wished Sunday would get here soon, they'd said it ten times.

They squirmed through the bishop's sermon, too. Molly presented quite a ladylike picture, there on Beth's right.

Hands folded in her lap, she looked straight ahead, moving only enough to adjust her cap. It had been particularly challenging for Matthew to sit still once he spotted his father on the other side of the church. "Why can't I sit over there with the men, like Sam?" The question hadn't been delivered in his usual boisterous voice, but it had been loud enough to invite hushed snickers and clucking tongues from the women seated nearby.

"Please, Matthew, no talking in church," Beth whispered.

"But—"

She laid a finger over his lips, and he got the message. Over dinner, Beth would help him understand why men and women were seated separately during the service, and why children were expected to sit quietly. Until then, she intended to hold on to his hand, so that she could give it a gentle squeeze if he talked out of turn again.

When she looked up, she saw Bontrager. It would be hard not to spot him, when he sat head and shoulders taller than the men seated around him. He smiled. Winked. Nodded, and she read it all to mean that he agreed with the way she'd handled their youngest son. Micah Fisher was smiling, too—not something the somber bishop did during sermons. A time or two in her adult life, she'd heard the phrase "If only the floor would open up and swallow me." Beth had considered it quite nonsensical, but now, when it felt as if every parishioner was judging her maternal skills, she didn't find it the least bit absurd.

The service seemed to go on forever, and despite the chill in the air, Matthew's small hand felt damp within her own. If that didn't teach him not to talk in church, she didn't know what would! Outside, in the bright sunshine, she turned him loose.

"Sorry, sweet boy, but if I had not held you that way, the ladies behind us would have scolded you for sure."

"I know. I'm sorry, too. I promise to be quiet next time."

"Uh-oh," Bontrager said, "looks like someone is in trouble."

Matthew, afraid of disappointing his father, rested his chin on his chest. Before Molly had a chance to tattle on him, Beth said, "Not at all. Matthew was wondering why men and women are separated in the church." She gave the boy's shoulder a light squeeze. "Something we can talk about in the restaurant?"

"Good idea. Should we go straight to the diner?"

"We'll miss the baseball game," Sam said.

"We go to church every two weeks, and unless the weather is horrible, there's a game after every service."

Beth hadn't expected to enjoy watching the boys play, but after just one game, she'd become a fan, and looked forward to standing on the sidelines, cheering both teams.

"We can miss one game. How often do we get to eat in a restaurant?"

Sam said, "That's true. And the sooner we leave, the sooner we'll get home and the sooner I can show you my book."

The only thing that had excited him more was hearing they could adopt Traveler.

"What about Traveler?" Matthew pouted. "He's already been alone for a long time."

"He'll be fine," Bontrager assured him. "He has plenty of space to run out back, and if he wants to, he can take a nap on his bed on the porch." He chucked the boy's cheek. "Besides, we'll be home again in a couple of hours."

During the drive to the restaurant, Sam explained how he'd strengthened the page edges by dipping the holes in shellac. Once they dried, he'd pushed the wood dowel in and out through them. "When I was writing," he said, "I left big margins, so it's easy to read the story even when the book is open."

"That's why he ended up with so many pages," Molly explained. "*Thirty-three pages*," she emphasized.

The trip to the restaurant was short, and as he parked in an empty slot, Sam asked how he knew about Mom's Country Cookin'. "The owner used to work for me. Had to quit, to help out his mother after his father had a stroke."

"Is the father better now?"

"No, Molly. I'm afraid he passed away."

"And the mother?"

"Homer lost her not long after. He and his wife own the diner now."

"I hope nothing like that ever happens to you, Daed. Because I don't know the first thing about running a sawmill."

Bontrager laughed, and Beth said, "Your father has many, *many* years to teach you."

One eyebrow rose slightly as he met her eyes. "Many, *many,* huh?"

"God willing." *Because I want to grow old with you, Aaron Bontrager!*

Inside, they seated themselves as a tall, black-haired woman approached the table.

"Well, as I live and breathe, if it ain't Aaron Bontrager! Where you been, handsome?"

"Working, mostly. And it's good to see you, too, Gladys."

"My, my, my," she said, arms folded over her ample chest as she inspected the children. "The three of you get bigger 'n' bigger, ever' time I see you." Gladys gave Beth a quick once-over. "An' who's this purty li'l thing?"

He slid an arm across her shoulders. "This is Bethel, my wife."

"Do tell! Well, as I live and breathe," she said again. "Finally decided to take my advice, did ya?"

Bontrager's crooked smile was hard to decipher. Shyness? Or embarrassment at the attention she'd called to them?

A young girl walked up to the table, carrying a stack of plastic-sleeved menus. Her nametag said ALLIE. "Should I come back, Gladys?"

"No, no. These young'uns look near starved." She laughed, and the hearty roar filled the diner. "Bet that bishop of yours kept you in the church all the livelong mornin', didn't he?"

The children's smiles mirrored their father's, and Beth decided *awe* defined the look. And who could blame them, with this big, loud woman towering over them?

Allie took their drink orders, and when she was gone, Gladys said, "Jus' look at the lot of you. Why, you Aye-mish is just as cute as cute can be." She gave Bontrager's beard a gentle tug. "I'll tell Homer you're here. He'll want to say hello."

Beth hoped that neither he nor the children had noticed the Englishers at the next table laughing and pointing.

Their unique accent, something between Canadian and Midwestern, identified them as locals. As such, they should be accustomed to seeing Plain people in town, shouldn't they? One middle-aged woman in particular seemed intent on making sure the family heard her crude comments. The children looked mortified, and although Bontrager pretended he hadn't heard the remarks, Beth knew that he had. The way he worked his jaw, the flash in his blue eyes were proof of it.

The woman huffed, slapped the tabletop, then snapped her fingers to summon Allie. "Can't you move these . . . these dirty weirdos to another table?"

Dirty? In clothing that still bore creases from her iron, with polished boots and not a hair out of place?

Poor Allie. The girl clearly had no idea how to react. "What did they do?" she asked.

"They're just *there,* looking all haughty, like they think they're better than everyone, because they live like, like . . . like . . ."

"Keep your voice down," her husband said. "You're making a spectacle of yourself."

She exhaled an angry, exasperated sigh. "*They're* the spectacle, sitting in their weird clothes." She pointed at Beth and Molly. "And those ridiculous hats." Now she jabbed a finger in Bontrager's direction. "I'll bet there are fleas in his beard." She shook her shoulders and cringed. "Get them away from us, or we're leaving!"

Bontrager stood, placed his napkin on the table, and calmly said, "Bethel, children, let's go."

The woman laughed, a wicked, grating sound. "Brothel?" She said it loudly enough for everyone to hear. "See? I told you . . . only a weirdo would give a child a name like that." She flicked her fingers, as if to shoo them away. "Go already, and be quick about it. Before one of your fleas jumps out of your beard and makes its way to us."

The family followed Bontrager toward the door, where he stopped at the front counter and handed the cashier a twenty-dollar bill.

"But sir, you didn't even order meals yet."

He stood, tall and straight-backed and wearing a stiff smile. "We had beverages, and you will need to re-set the table." Then he held open the door, glaring at the woman as the family filed past. "Apologize to Gladys for us," he said to the cashier, "and tell her we will see her and Homer another time."

No one said a word as he backed out of the parking lot, then maneuvered into traffic on Route 219. The drive to their next stop was short, and once they were seated at a chrome-trimmed red Formica table, Sam said, "Good choice, Daed. Why didn't we just come here first?"

This diner wasn't as large as the last, but already, Beth liked it better, for no reason other than the fact that other diners had politely nodded and smiled when the family walked in.

Bontrager stood aside while Beth slid into the booth, then reached across her to grab a stack of plastic-sleeved menus leaning against a chrome napkin holder and passed them out. "Molly, will you help Matthew choose something?"

The girl, seated near the windows, leaned over and quietly read from the children's selection. Sam, wrinkling his nose at those choices, said, "Daed? May I order off the grownup menu?"

"You always clean your plate, so why not."

"See anything you like, Beth?"

It was hard not to notice that he'd abbreviated her name. To save time? Or because the rude woman had raised the similarity between her full name and a house of ill repute?

"There was better food on the other menu," Molly pointed out. She peered over the top of the menu to meet her father's eyes. "Why did we leave there, anyway?"

"Because the woman was spoiling for a fight. And you know what the Ordnung teaches about that."

Beth could almost see the gears turning in Molly's head as she tried to remember specifics of the Amish teachings.

"I felt like punching her," Sam said without looking up. "Right in the throat."

"And what would that have accomplished?" his father asked.

"It would have made it harder for her to insult us." He went back to reading. "For starters."

"True enough. But then you would have proven to the other Englishers that what she said was true, that the Amish are weird."

"Well, it *is* kinda weird that we can't even defend ourselves against people like that."

Beth wished Bontrager was sitting across the table, instead of beside her, so that she could read his expression when he said, "There is nothing to defend. We live as we do because it is God's will for us. What Englishers—what anyone else thinks—is unimportant. *He* is the only being we need to impress."

The boy lifted one shoulder, and Bontrager added, "He knows it is hard, this living Plain, and I believe if we could ask which lifestyle He likes better, the Englishers' or ours,

He would choose ours. That," he said, rapping his knuckles on the table, "is good enough for me."

She covered his fist with her own, felt the tension that his calm voice had hidden. "I am so honored to be part of this family," she said, squeezing his hand, "and I am proud of the way each of you conducted yourself in that diner. It would have been easy to lash out at that woman, but that would have made us just like her."

Molly sniffed. "She deserved some sort of punishment for being so mean. She's a grownup. She should have known better."

"Think of it this way," Beth continued. "If we had given in to the temptation to put her in her place, she might have remembered our words for a day or two. But she will never, ever forget the peaceful, godly way we behaved. Maybe, just maybe, a little bit of us rubbed off on her, and next time she sees an Amish family out and about, she will not be so quick to judge."

All through the rest of the meal, they talked and laughed. About the snowstorm that was predicted in the coming days. Whether or not there would be enough to make snowballs and snowmen and snow forts. How good it would feel coming in out of the cold to warm themselves in front of the woodstove.

They discussed the chickens' tendency to lay fewer eggs when it was cold, and how the goats were the exact opposite, jumping around like acrobats when the temperatures turned cool. Matthew wondered what Traveler had been up to in their absence, and Sam couldn't wait to saddle Caramel and ride him through the snow.

Tears stung Beth's eyes as she watched the cheerful

faces and enthusiastic voices of the children . . . *her* children in every way that mattered.

"What's wrong, Beth?"

"N-nothing." She smiled. *Not a single, solitary thing!*

"Then why do you look like you're about to cry?" Molly asked.

Bontrager leaned forward to get a better look at her face, and upon seeing her damp eyes, he flipped his hand over, wrapped his fingers around hers.

She wiped moisture from her cheek. "Happy tears, because you bring me such joy, and I just love all of you so much!"

Wearing the charming grin that always produced a dimple in his left cheek, he turned slightly on the padded bench seat. Scooted closer, too. "And we love you," he said, then kissed her cheek.

Hours later, with the children asleep upstairs, he recounted the events of the day, starting with her deft management of Matthew's misbehavior in church and ending with Sam's book.

"I have a confession to make," he said.

"Oh?"

"Come with me."

She followed him to the hall closet, watched as he got onto his knees and shoved aside winter boots and the box of scarves, hats, and mittens she'd stored there, and pried up a wide floorboard. Beth stepped up and peered over his shoulder, into the dark compartment he'd exposed, then straightened as he removed a gray metal lockbox. He set it aside, leaned closer, stuck a hand into the hole, and after patting the floor beneath it, produced a small key.

Sitting back on his heels, he unlocked the box. Its lid

emitted a quiet squeal. So did Beth when she saw what he'd hidden inside:

A shiny black pistol.

"What is *that* for!"

"Protection."

"From *what?*"

"Anything that might threaten our safety."

She saw two small boxes. "Bullets?"

He nodded, then closed the lid and put everything back the way it had been. After closing the closet door, he said, "No one, and I do mean *no one,* knows about this. And I'd like to keep it that way."

"I have dusted and scrubbed that floor half a dozen times. I cannot believe I never noticed the . . . your vault."

Chuckling, he made his way back into the parlor. "That was the idea. I think my father would be proud. He's the one who taught me how to hide miters in sawn wood. In this case, though," he said, sitting on the middle cushion of the sofa, "it's a skill that safeguards against anyone ever detecting my hiding place."

"Your secret is safe with me." She sat beside him.

"I didn't want you finding it, accidentally." He winked. "You're a stickler for detail, and I was afraid that someday, while cleaning or stowing the kids' boots, you might find it. You're safer now, knowing it's there."

Beth supposed he was right, and yet . . . "But we do not believe in violence, so I do not understand."

He told her about the bear he'd encountered one night last spring, while gathering an armload of firewood. After the long winter's hibernation, it hadn't been at all pleased to see another living being between it and its search for food. It had reared up, exposing every huge, yellow tooth in its head as it bellowed a warning that it intended to clear the path by any means necessary.

Next, he shared the story about what had happened, weeks later, when four drunken Englisher boys had broken into his truck, in broad daylight. They'd consumed enough whiskey to bolster their courage and make them believe that stealing the truck would be easy, since the Amish considered fighting—even in self-defense—a sin. Sin or not, Bontrager told her, he'd stood his ground, using feet and fists and rocks scooped up from the gravel driveway. They'd landed a few solid blows that had left him swollen and bruised, but he'd given worse than he'd gotten, and sent them packing with a fierce threat of what would happen in case they ever returned.

Beth's heart pounded as she realized what might have happened to him if he hadn't fought back.

"Where were the children?"

"At Stella's, thank God. While I was washing up, I looked into the mirror and saw the damage they'd done. Asked myself how much worse it would have been if the kids had encountered them instead of me."

"So you bought a gun?"

"You bet I did."

"Could you . . . would you use it? If they came back, I mean?"

"I would."

Bontrager had answered so quickly that she believed it, and that frightened her. He must have seen her fear, because he said, "It isn't likely I'll ever need to use it, but it's comforting, knowing it's there in case I do."

"Would you know *how* to use it?"

"I would," he said, more firmly this time. "I drove to

the other side of the mountain, found a clearing in the woods, and emptied three boxes of ammunition, shooting pinecones out of the trees."

"The poor trees," she said, trying to lighten the mood.

"The cones would have fallen to the ground eventually, anyway."

She heard a *but* that he didn't say, and finished, silently: *But he left the woods knowing he could hit what he aimed at.*

"Does this upset you?"

She studied his serious face.

"No."

The answer seemed to surprise him. "Why not?"

"Because I trust you."

And it was true. Beth knew, deep in her soul, that he'd never take the pistol from its lockbox unless, deep in his soul, he believed it was the only way to protect his family.

She'd pray, from this moment forward, that God would make sure he'd never feel that need again.

# Chapter Fourteen

It had been weeks since Bontrager had shown her his secret hiding place, and ever since, she'd walked a wide path around the closet. Tonight, as she hung the children's jackets, Beth decided that had to stop, before one of them noticed and started looking for reasons *why*.

"Are we still having cocoa before bed?" Molly asked.

"Of course. Would you like to help?"

The girl smiled. "Sure! Then maybe I can make it myself sometimes!"

"What about popcorn? Can we have that, too?"

"Matthew, Matthew, Matthew," Sam said. "How many times do I have to tell you, it's—"

"It's *may I,*" Molly and Matthew said together, laughing.

They gathered around the stove, singsonging the ingredients as Beth added them to the sauce pan: "Butter. Sugar. Vanilla. Milk. Cocoa . . ." and completely forgot about the popcorn.

Now, they gathered around the table as Matthew said, "Sam, will you read your book to us again when we go to bed?"

"Sure, sure." He looked down the table. "You want to listen, Daed? And you, too, Beth?"

"Sounds good, son."

"Hey," Molly said, pouting. "What am I, chopped liver?"

The family laughed in reaction to her use of the words Esther uttered any time a plate was passed or an invitation issued.

Half an hour after the children quieted down for the night, Bontrager peered over his Bible at her. "It's a pretty good story, isn't it?"

"He has used his God-given gifts well. Molly, too. Her drawings are so good!" She stopped knitting. "They have inherited your artistic talents, I think."

"Artistic talents? No," he said, chuckling, "they didn't get those from me."

"No need to be modest. I have seen your doodles. On paper napkins. Envelope flaps. Matchbook covers. If there is a pencil and scrap of paper nearby, it will soon be decorated with landscapes, bowls of fruit, the children . . ." Traveler strutted by just then. ". . . the dog. Nothing is off limits. And everything is very realistic."

"Good thing the lights are low."

She went back to knitting. "Why?"

"Blushing isn't very manly."

"Everything about you is manly," she said, wrapping cream-colored yarn around her forefinger. "Everything."

Whatever he'd planned to say in response was interrupted by the trilling of the phone.

"Hold that thought," she said, setting her knitting aside again.

She was smiling when she said hello. Smiling when she recognized Karl's voice.

"It's your brother-in-law," Beth said, holding out the receiver.

Bontrager groaned as he took it from her. "The men are working an extra shift," he said, "to finish up Albertson's order."

He was smiling, too, when he said hello. But almost instantly, his expression changed. So did his voice.

"When?" Then: "The kids?" And: "I will meet you there."

"He is at the hospital. Stella, too. My mother had a stroke. At least, that's what the paramedics told Karl."

"How awful. I am so sorry. But it is a good hospital."

He grabbed his jacket and hat. "Soon as I know more, I'll call you."

"Who is with the twins?"

"Stella's cousin Rachel," he said, and hurried out the door.

Beth spent the rest of the night right there on the sofa, listening for the phone. But the only sound in the room was the *klick-klack* of her needles. By the time it rang shortly after dawn, she'd almost completed the cable knit sweater, intended as one of his Christmas gifts.

"She can't be alone," he said, his voice low and gruff with worry, "and refuses to go to a rehab center. Stella is beside herself, wondering how she'll manage the house and the twins and—"

"Bring her here," Beth interrupted.

"But, Beth, you already have so much to do. The house.

Three kids. A dog." A quiet chuckle sounded in her ear. "Me . . ."

"How soon can she leave the hospital?"

"The doctor says just as soon as her condition has stabilized, they'll send her home."

"What does that mean? A day? Two or three? A week?"

Bontrager laughed. "Knowing my mother, she'll demand to leave as soon as possible."

"You will stay with her, yes?"

"For the time being."

"That gives me plenty of time, then, to get things ready."

"What things? Wait. You can't haul a bed downstairs all by yourself, the way you did after Sam's accident."

"I will ask Karl to help. There are four beds upstairs in her house. Four empty beds. He can bring one here. He can help me rearrange the parlor, too, so that she will feel at home here." She paused. "May I ask a question?"

"Of course. Anything."

"Is she able to get around at all? Hold a spoon? Drink from a cup?"

"Yes and no. Her entire right side is paralyzed, so she can't walk very well. And she's not entirely rational."

"Everyone here is strong and capable. We will help her."

"If she'll let you." Impatience rang loud in his voice.

"What choice will she have?"

"Good point . . ."

She'd grown accustomed to hearing him say that.

". . . but I hope you know, this isn't going to be easy. Maem is angry at what's happened to her."

"And who can blame her? But everything will be all right, in God's time, so there is nothing for you to worry about."

If only she felt as confident as she sounded. Would she really be able to care for an invalid, along with handling her other responsibilities?

"Go," she said, "and be with her. Tell her I am praying." Beth paused, then added, "I will pray for you, too."

Another laugh crackled through the phone wires. "Me? Why me?"

"Because I have a feeling she will not take it well, once you explain that she cannot go home, and how things will have to be."

"I'm not worried," he said. "Except for those hours when Sam was missing, I haven't been worried since you stepped off that train."

She'd carry those affection-laced words in her heart until she saw him again . . .

. . . and long, long afterward.


In the week that had passed after he brought Esther home, Aaron found himself apologizing frequently. When their mother's short-temperedness hurt Stella and insulted Karl, he tried to smooth their ruffled feathers. When she demanded that the children play outside because the sound of their "loud voices" was driving her to distraction, he'd told them how sorry he was. He'd asked the bishop's forgiveness for the ungrateful way she'd reacted to his wife's gift of baked goods and Fisher's sincere offer to pray with her. He apologized most often to Beth, who hadn't even looked cross when Esther threw bowls and spoons at her, or deliberately allowed juice and soup to dribble from her mouth, or scolded her for tea that wasn't sweet enough, soup that wasn't hot enough, or bread that hadn't been sufficiently buttered.

He felt guilty for spending so much time at the mill. Felt bad about dozing off in his chair because his mother's loud grumbling kept the family up all night. Aaron could have tolerated it all—even the cutting insults aimed Beth's way—if only he could see a light at the end of the proverbial tunnel. But Esther flat-out refused to take the medications or perform the exercises the doctor had prescribed.

That night, exasperation had him up, pacing their bedroom floor. "How long can I ask you to put up with her behavior?"

"You never asked. I offered, remember?" She threw back the covers, patted the mattress, and invited him to come to bed. "You need your rest."

Aaron complied, because he did need rest . . . in her arms again.

"You are not to blame," she said when he nestled close, "for anything your mother says or does. It is the injury to her brain making her act this way."

Then, as she had at the end of every arduous day, Beth recited the litany of reasons to stay the course: Esther would eventually tire of having no privacy, of being treated like a helpless infant, and seeing frustration in everyone's eyes. "When she has had her fill of all that, she will cooperate, get better, and go home."

He quoted an age-old cliché. "From your lips to God's ears."

And promptly fell asleep.

# Chapter Fifteen

The aroma of fresh baked bread filled the house, and under other circumstances, it would have been a warm welcome home. But the minute he walked into the parlor, his mother began complaining: The soup Beth fed her for lunch had been cold, and the sponge-bath water too hot. The seams in her socks were irritating her feet, and so were the folds in the top sheet.

"And she hasn't delivered fresh water in nearly an hour."

"Where is she now?"

"In the basement, doing laundry, I expect." Esther glared at the quilt Beth had draped across her lap. "That wife of yours is so stupid, and she must be blind, too." She held up an arm, so that he could see the sleeve of her nightgown. "Just look at all the wrinkles she missed!"

His mother had always been fiercely independent, so Aaron understood that frustration had motivated her attitude. For her sake as well as Beth's, he had to at least try to reason with her.

"Maem, Beth has been nothing but good to you. She's up every morning at four trying to anticipate the children's needs so that she can devote the rest of her day to you. Every meal is prepared, every task performed with your best interests and comfort in mind. It isn't easy for her, racing around on that bad leg, and by bedtime, she's limping. But she does it because she cares about you."

"I noticed no limping."

*You wouldn't,* Aaron thought. And immediately felt bad. The always strong-willed Esther must hate being told what to do and when to do it, even by someone as loving and well-intentioned as Beth.

"I realize this is hard for you, being here instead of in your own home. But you heard what the doctor said. Because of the stroke, you cannot be left alone. When I told Beth that he wanted to put you in a nursing home, she wouldn't hear of it."

"Nursing home!"

"Yes. Seth and Stella and I agreed that you'd be safest in a rehabilitation facility, where the staff could feed and bathe you, help you exercise to build muscles weakened by the stroke. Beth said yes, they'd do all that, not because they love you, but because they're being *paid* to. She knows you'd rather be in your own home, fending for yourself. That's why she has tried so hard to get you to follow doctors' orders about exercise . . . so you can recover more quickly and get back to life as it was before the stroke."

His mother answered with a grumpy *harrumph.*

"This house is as much hers as mine, don't forget, and you're here because that's the way she wants it. All I'm asking is that you show her a little respect."

"Respect?" She harrumphed. "The Bible says 'Honor your father and mother.' Is this the way you honor me?"

"Scripture also says that man should leave his mother and father and hold fast to his wife. . . ." In other terms: *Please don't force me to choose, Maem.* "I love you."

"I know this." She paused, picked at a loose thread on the quilt. "And I love you, too."

All his life, she'd hammered home the concept that love was proven by action, not pretty speeches. He could count on one hand the number of times she'd said the words and have fingers left over. Hearing them now made him realize exactly how helpless and afraid she must feel.

The basement door opened, and Beth walked into the kitchen, a basket of laundry balanced on one hip. She put it on the table and joined them in the parlor. Her tentative smile told him she'd sensed tension between him and his mother.

"You're home," she said. "Good. You were at work earlier than usual, and you need your rest. I am about to fix your mother a cup of tea. Sit. Put your feet up. I will fix one for you, too."

He wasn't surprised by the offer, or by the sweet-tempered way she'd made it.

Aaron would have been surprised, though, to learn that because of the open heating vent between the parlor floor and the basement ceiling, she'd heard every word.


While waiting for the water to heat up, Beth dumped the basket's contents onto the table and began folding. Soon, it was full again, this time with tidy stacks of clothes, one for each family member. She was torn between feeling pity for Esther, whose life had been so crudely disrupted by the stroke, and gratitude toward Bontrager, who'd defended her in such a loving, supportive way.

The teapot whistled, and she prepared two mugs. Extra sugar and milk for Esther, plain black for Bontrager. "Sit with us," he said when she delivered them.

Their talk had ended on a positive note, and she believed they could use more time alone, to cement the positive feelings. So Beth used putting away the laundry as an excuse to decline, and kept herself busy with supper preparations.

Their talk must also have hit a nerve with Esther, who behaved so well during supper that the children decided to pass the time before bed in the parlor. Sam read his book aloud to her, while Matthew and Molly acted out the story. Even Traveler joined in, spinning in circles and yipping quietly each time he heard his name. It warmed her heart to see Esther smiling, applauding, thanking them with hugs. Her behavior must have impressed Bontrager, too, because he stayed with her after the kids went to bed.

His long day finally took its toll, and after half a dozen expansive yawns, his mother said, "Go to bed before you inhale every ounce of oxygen from the room!"

On his way upstairs, he bent to kiss her forehead. "Sleep well, Maem."

Beth carried her knitting into the parlor and sat in the rocking chair. She reached for the lamp's switch, but paused before turning it on.

"Will the light bother you?"

"Not at all. I'm happy for the company."

In the week she'd been with them, Esther hadn't said one pleasant thing to anyone. Beth sent a silent thank-you to her husband and picked up her project.

"What are you making?"

"A sweater, to give Mr. Bontrager for Christmas." She held it up. "Cable knit. I only need to add the collar and cuffs."

"It looks good, like all your work. And big enough, too."

"This is my second attempt. The first time, it would have fit like a second skin!"

Esther laughed, too. "Then I'm glad you tried again. But . . . Christmas is a long ways off."

"Two months will pass quickly."

"I suppose." Esther paused. "May I ask you a question?"

Beth automatically tensed. Only the good Lord knew what might come out of her mouth.

"You have been married for what, four months now? Why do you call my son Mr. Bontrager?"

"It is a sign of respect. My mother referred to my father that way, and her mother called my grandfather by his surname. Plus . . . it is a good strong name. I like saying it."

"Sounds too formal to me. He is a big-hearted man. I think he'd like it better if you called him Aaron. Even *husband* would sound less cold."

Cold? Beth had never thought about it that way. At first, when they'd still been strangers, it had seemed the only choice. In time, it had become a habit, one that, until now, she hadn't even considered breaking.

"I will practice calling him Aaron, starting tomorrow."

But Esther didn't respond, because in those few moments, she'd fallen asleep. Beth put away her knitting and positioned chairs beside the bed to act as guard rails.

Then, lights out, she went upstairs and found Bontrager sound asleep.

The outside temperature had dropped into the mid-twenties. Thanks to the woodstove, the house was toasty warm. He'd closed the bedroom door, blocking out the heat. On his side, with one leg hanging over the edge of the mattress, he clutched the balled-up blanket to his chest.

*Aw, he is cold. . . .*

Beth tiptoed to the closet and dragged a quilt from the shelf. Standing on her side of the bed, she gave it a flap, and let it float onto the bed. He exhaled a sleepy sigh and rolled onto his back. Now, he was fully covered, except for his face and the fingertips that curled over the quilt's top hem.

After changing into her nightgown, Beth got into the bed. On her side, facing him, she studied his magnificent profile. The patrician nose. The long eyelashes. The strong jawline and slightly parted lips. Lips that had kissed her forehead. Her cheek. But never her own.

*Count your blessings, not your wishes,* she thought, and closed her eyes. Heart thumping with tenderness, she whispered, "I love you, Aaron Bontrager," and promptly fell asleep.

# Chapter Sixteen

He woke to a cold, wet nose bumping his cheek.

Aaron reluctantly opened his eyes, and met the shining, chestnut-colored orbs of a furry white face. As the fuzzy eyebrows twitched, first the left, then the right, he suspected something was wrong, because the dog had never come right up to the bed this way. He slipped out of bed slowly and followed Traveler into the hall, then closed the door behind him.

"What's up, pup?" he whispered.

The dog ran downstairs and, stopping at the foot of Esther's bed, whimpered.

Heart hammering, Aaron approached, heard her labored breathing. The doctor had said several factors could further complicate her condition. Such as blood clots that formed in the brain, lungs, or an artery leading to a vital organ.

"Maem," he said, shaking her arm, "are you in any pain?"

She opened her right eye. Opened her mouth, too, and tried to say, "Yes."

"Can you tell me where?"

"Mmm . . . Nnn . . . Www . . ."

Aaron had no idea what that meant. He hurried into the kitchen, started dialing the clinic. But it was barely past five in the morning. Neither Emily nor Willa would be there at this hour. He called 911, but had no idea how long it would take an ambulance to arrive.

"Beth!" he yelled, dialing Emily's home number. "Beth . . . come downstairs, please!"

Emily had just said a groggy hello when Beth came downstairs, still belting her robe. "What is it?" she asked. But one quick glance at his mother, and she knew.

Yes, he told the doctor, he'd called 911—in her condition, he couldn't very well put his mother in the truck and drive her to town—and no, he hadn't noticed any convulsions. "She's struggling to breathe, though. Any way to find out how long it'll take the ambulance to get here?"

"What did the dispatcher say?" Emily asked.

"Ten, fifteen minutes out," he answered.

He looked up, saw that Beth had gone back upstairs, probably to get dressed. Then he looked down, at his own bare feet sticking out from his T-shirt and undershorts. *Can't go with her to the hospital looking like this. . . .*

Aaron heard Emily say, "I'll meet you at the hospital."

And he responded with a wooden, "Good. Yes. Thank you."

He hung up and took the steps two at a time.

Beth was already dressed when he lurched into the room. "Will you ride with her in the ambulance?" she asked.

"If they'll let me." His hands were shaking as he

stepped into his trousers, hard enough that he could barely fasten the buttons.

"Let me," Beth said.

"Will you call Stella, let her know what's going on?"

"Of course," she said, buttoning his shirt. "I will ask Karl to bring the twins here, too."

"Call Rachel instead. In case I need you."

She slipped the suspenders over his shoulders. "All right."

"I raked her over the coals yesterday. This is my fault."

"It most certainly is *not*. Emily told us that the chances of a second stroke are highest in the days immediately following the first."

He tried to remember what Sam had told her on his first night home from the hospital, something about feeling relieved that everything was all right "because Daed doesn't handle things like this very well."

"Emily also said to keep her calm." While lacing up his boots, he looked up at Beth. "I'll stay with her until the ambulance arrives. Maybe you should wake the kids. They'll be scared enough without waking to the sound of sirens."

She wrapped him in a fierce hug and held on tight. Years ago, he'd read an item in *The Budget* reacting to the Englisher belief that the Amish were standoffish, cold, that they felt physical demonstrations of affection were worldly, and therefore sinful. Hugs, the piece said, were healthy, good for body and soul, a cure for what ails you, medicine for the mind. Right now, standing in the protective circle of her arms, he believed every word.

Traveler leaned against his leg, and Aaron squatted. "This guy," he told Beth, "knew something was wrong with Maem. He woke me up, poking that cold black nose into my face, and wouldn't let up until I followed him downstairs." He gave the dog a well-deserved hug. "I'll find a way to thank you properly once Maem is home again."

# Chapter Seventeen

"The paramedics tried to revive her, but . . ." Anguish had deepened his voice. "She's gone."

"Oh, Aaron. I am sorry, so very sorry. I wish I could be there with you."

"I wish you could, too, but the kids need you more than I do. How are they doing?"

"They are handling things well, considering."

She heard his sharp intake of air. Heard the shaky exhale, too.

"So much to do," he said.

"You have a brother and a sister. Let them help. It will make them feel needed, and give them something to think about besides . . ."

"Yeah. Besides." Another deep breath, and then, "I'm not sure when I'll be home. They want me to sign some papers. Invoices, so the hospital and ambulance company will know where to send the bills. Can I bring you anything on my way home?"

"We have everything we need . . . except you . . . Aaron."

"I . . ." Aaron cleared his throat. "Soon as I find out when they'll release her, I'll give you a heads-up."

"Be careful driving home."

"I will. See you soon," he said, and hung up.

He didn't need to know that the children had cried, Beth thought. They'd chastised themselves that they should have spent more time with her, before the stroke. Molly had wanted to know if, when the ambulance took her grandmother away, Esther had been scared. Sam asked if she was in pain. And little Matthew . . . "Do you think she knew that we loved her?"

"Yes, sweet boy, she knew."

"But how? We didn't tell her."

Oh, but they had told her. Beth had been present, dozens of times, when they'd said it. But Esther's "show, don't tell" mentality had made it seem as if she hadn't heard. *From this day forward, they will hear the words, often!*

"You did better than tell her. You *showed* her, by reading and singing to her, bringing her favorite snacks, listening to her stories about the good old days."

For the time being, it seemed her words had satisfied them, enough to keep them from seeking answers to their other questions. But if they had asked? Beth would not have told them the truth. In her opinion, they didn't need to know that she'd seen Esther's face, contorted by fear and pain. It would be hard enough for them to submit, yet again, to the long-held Amish belief that grief was not to be expressed in public.

"So much to do," Aaron had said. Beth could still hear the fatigue, the anguish in his voice. The same defeated tone she'd heard when he blamed himself for the stroke.

Yes, there was a lot to do. And it all had to be done within three days.

She made a mental list of the ways she could help him:

Ask the bishop for permission to hold the viewing in the church. She'd appeal to his logical side by stating that everyone would be more comfortable, since the house wasn't large enough to accommodate mourners. She'd also ask his advice about finding four strong men to carry the casket from the church to the cemetery. And another four to dig the grave.

The undertaker, who'd supervise the building of an un-lined, handleless pine coffin, would be next, followed by the stonemason. No need to trouble Aaron, Stella, or Seth for Esther's birth year since the information had long ago been penned onto the opening pages of the family Bible. The stonemason would chisel the names of Esther and her departed husband into a slab of granite that exactly matched every other headstone in the graveyard.

It wasn't likely she'd find a white dress in her mother-in-law's closet, but if she got started now, she could make one and have plenty of time to collect clean clothes for Aaron and the children.

Speaking of the children . . .

Beth had an idea, but to implement it, she'd need their cooperation. She gathered them in the kitchen, and while they sipped whipped cream-topped cocoa, she encour-aged them to talk about Esther . . . their fondest memo-ries, things she'd said that made them laugh, favorite recipes. . . .

The cocoa was gone long before they ran out of things to say, and that's when all three grew quiet and contem-plative.

"Sam, how long would it take you to make a book

about your *groosmammi*, like the one you wrote about Traveler?"

"Couple hours, I guess. Why?"

"I think it would mean a lot to your father, to see with his own eyes that you will miss his mother, too."

The hidden meaning beneath her suggestion wasn't lost on them. They'd lost their own mother, and although it had been nearly three years ago, the memory of it was still fresh in their minds and hearts.

"Ca . . . *may* I help, Sam?"

"Me, too?"

He quickly said yes and, as he shoved back from the table, began delivering instructions:

"Molly, you get the paper. Matthew, find some more of that wood. And bring me that can of shellac while you're out in the shed."

"What are *you* gonna do?" his sister asked.

"Start a list, that's what, of things we will put in our book."

*Our* book. It pleased Beth to hear that he understood that, for Aaron's sake, it should be a combined effort.

"Will you be all right here alone for an hour or so?" she asked. "I need to do a few things."

"What things?"

It didn't make sense to keep this truth from them, so she said, "Talk to the bishop and . . ." Beth hesitated to say more. They were coping well with Esther's passing, but words like *undertaker* and *coffin* and *funeral* might be more than they could handle right now. "Your father will be tired when he gets home. Tired and—"

"Sad," Molly finished. "And because he's Amish, he isn't allowed to say so."

"Yeah," Sam agreed. "That was hard when Grootvader Bontrager died. I really liked spending time with him. It was even harder when Maem died."

"That was my fault."

Everyone looked at Matthew.

"What do you mean, sweet boy?"

"She caught my cold, and it got worser and worser and turned into pamonia."

"Pneumonia," Molly corrected.

Sam cut her a dirty look. "Hush, Molly, and let him talk."

"Oh, so you can correct us when we make mistakes, but I can't?"

His brow furrowed, and in that moment, he looked like a younger, smaller version of his father.

"Not at a time like this." He faced Matthew again. "Go ahead, li'l brother. Finish what you were saying."

"She got *pneumonia* from my cold. And . . . and . . . and . . ." He'd started to cry, but managed to say, "And the day before she died, I told her she was faking, to get out of emptying the trash so I had to do it."

"You *did*?" Molly said.

Sam was stunned, too. "Whoa . . . And then what?"

"And then . . . and then she started coughing really bad. Blood came out and she said I should never say things I didn't mean because . . . because . . . because . . ." He was crying harder now. "Because words hurt, and someday, I might be sorry." He buried his face in the crook of his elbow. "She was right."

Nodding slowly, Sam said, "So *that's* why you stopped talking."

"Kinda," the boy said, his voice muffled. "That's when she got even worser, and she couldn't talk anymore. And I felt real bad, 'cause I was so mean. I told her if she wouldn't talk, I wouldn't either."

*And then she died,* Beth realized.

"The pneumonia was not your fault, Matthew. Neither was your mother's catching your cold." She thought about saying it was God's will, but in this moment, the words that had been drilled into her head since childhood seemed callous and insincere.

"People get sick every day. Some with serious illnesses, others with things that are not. But in either case, no one is to blame."

"Then why do they get sick?" Molly wanted to know.

"Their bodies just aren't strong enough to fight off the sickness."

"Like Maem," Sam said. "She was sneezing and coughing and weak for a long time before the pneumonia."

"Yet none of you got sick," Beth said, "right?"

All three children shook their heads.

"Because your bodies were young and strong."

Now, they nodded.

"At the funeral," Molly said, "Bishop Fisher said it was God's will."

It was something Beth had wondered about, many times, including the day they'd buried her own mother. "I will tell you what I believe," she began, "and you can think on it and pray about it, maybe even talk with your father about it . . . later. . . ."

*Should I tell them what's in my heart, Lord? Guide my words. Please, guide my words!*

They sat there, wide-eyed and silent, waiting for her to tell them what she believed.

"I have always viewed God as a loving, caring being. Powerful, yes, but also merciful. So I have never been able to accept that all things, good and bad, are His will. That would mean He arranges the good and the bad. But why would He do that? He has told us to come to Him, to ask, and we will receive. Who would ask for bad things!"

They looked confused, and who could blame them!

"Storms. Droughts. Accidents. Sickness. God does not *make* those things happen. He allows us to survive them, perhaps to teach us that all we need to do is trust that, in good things and bad, He will do what is best for us, always."

"I think I get it," Sam said. "'God's will' is just another way of saying 'have faith.'"

"That is what I believe. But I must admit . . . many, *many* people have disagreed with me."

"That's okay," Molly said. "If we all felt the same way about everything, the whole world would be Amish!"

Beth got up, gave each child a hug, and kissed their foreheads.

"God blessed me richly, sending me to Pleasant Valley. I love all of you so much."

"Oh brother," Sam droned, "happy tears again." But he said it with affection and tenderness, and it touched her, deeply.

"Well, the sooner I get started, the sooner I will be

finished." She moved toward the door. "I promise to hurry, and when I get home, I will make your favorite supper."

"I'm not really hungry," Molly said.

"I am not hungry, either, but we might be by the time I get back. But even if we are not, we must try to eat a little something, to keep up our strength."

"So our bodies can fight off germs," Matthew said.

"Yes, sweet boy, exactly."

Beth had taken a huge risk, sharing her opinions with the children. Some in the community might hear her words as blasphemous, as grounds for a shunning. She should be afraid. Terrified, in fact. Instead, Beth felt calm and at peace.

Did it mean God approved of what she'd said?

*Have faith, Bethel, and trust Him to do what is best for you, always.*


It was cold there in the cemetery. Cold and windy enough to induce mourners to turn up their collars and hide gloved hands deep inside woolen coat pockets.

And yet time seemed to crawl by at the pace of a slug, crossing hot blacktop on a muggy midsummer day.

Aaron, feet planted shoulder-width apart, stared straight ahead and listened, like all those assembled near the deep rectangular hole, to Micah Fisher's gravelly voice.

"*There is no death, though eyes grow dim,*" he sang, alone. "*There is no fear when I'm near to Him . . .*"

Across the way, two fellow parishioners mouthed the words, heads bowed, eyes closed. The rest drew closer to their families.

*"I'll lean on Him forever, and He'll forsake me never . . ."*

Families . . .

His own—what was left of it—was right here with him, making the dreadful gray day a little less so. The children, side by side, stood in front of him. At his side was Beth, one mittened hand on Molly's shoulder, the other on Matthew's. Aaron completed the chain . . . left hand on Sam's shoulder, right hand on Matthew's.

The pallbearers lowered the coffin into the ground, and Aaron lowered his head. *Lord, but I'm tired,* he thought.

And as if the Lord had heard and answered, Fisher started a new hymn.

*"When my hands are tired and my step is slow, walk beside me, give me the strength to go . . ."*

Clods of dirt thumped against the pine box, one after the other.

*"Fill my face with Your courage so defeat won't show, pick me up when I stumble, so the world won't know . . ."*

The wood wasn't visible any longer. Just dirt. Black, rocky, Allegheny Mountain dirt.

*"Lead me, Father, with the staff of life, and give me the strength for a song . . ."*

"Are you all right?"

Beth. Sweet, caring Beth. "Yeah," he whispered back. "Freezing out here, though." A sob ached in his throat, but he wasn't supposed to show emotion. Death, like birth and everything in between, was God's will. What could a man do but accept that?

She smiled up at him and patted the hand that rested on Matthew's shoulder. "It will be over soon. Just one more hymn, I think."

*Sweet, loving Beth.* He was barely holding it together. If she didn't stop trying to console him, he'd lose control. And how would he explain that to the bishop?

"Thanks for all your help today. And yesterday. And the day before." He held her gaze for a long time, then confessed, "I don't know what I'd do without you."

She blushed—or had the wind chafed her cheeks?—and shook her head. "Aaron. Hush. Or the bishop will punish us with yet another hymn."

The aching sob eased, and he smiled, because . . .

. . . family.


A month after Esther's passing, a newly married couple approached Karl after services and asked if the family might consider selling her house. After days of discussion, Seth, Stella, and Aaron decided to let it go.

Beth and Karl took charge, cleaning and painting, repairing and reorganizing to spare the siblings from having to go through all her things. And today, six weeks to the day since the funeral, the new family moved in.

Aaron had to drive right past the house on his way home. He must have seen them hauling their belongings inside because, when he walked in, he seemed restless.

"Where are the kids?"

"Upstairs in their rooms. Sam is writing another book, Molly is knitting, and Matthew is teaching Traveler how to roll over."

"Then we have a few minutes, alone?"

Although she didn't like the sound of that, Beth said yes. "I know you have something on your mind. That you've *had* something on your mind since your first day in Pleasant Valley." He pulled out a kitchen chair, pointed at its seat. "Let's get it out in the open, once and for all."

"It is true," she said, sitting beside him. "But every time I tried to tell you, something got in the way."

"Then aren't we lucky." His arm swept around. "There's nothing in the way."

Beth wondered why she hadn't thought to rehearse the speech, so as to prevent stuttering, stammering, and long pauses.

"Where to begin . . ." she said.

"I think you know what I'm going to say."

"At the beginning," they said together.

That, at least, made him smile. But she snuffed it by asking, "Why now, Aaron? If you knew all along that I was keeping something from you, why did you not bring it up before now?"

"I kept hoping you'd come to me on your own."

His voice was unemotional, but by the look on his face he was anything but.

"You will think I am conceited. Or, at the very least, forward."

"Why don't you let me decide how I'll feel?"

"All right, here goes . . ."

He'd leaned forward, and now balanced elbows on knees. What a convenient way to avoid looking her in the eye, she thought, and continued. "Just as you kept hoping I'd come to you on my own, *I* hoped you would come to me . . . as a husband comes to his wife."

He looked up at that!

But she couldn't let his big, worried eyes distract her.

"In a way, it was good that you didn't. If you had, I was worried about how I might react, because . . ."

He grabbed her hands, sandwiched them between his own. "Stop. I'm sorry. I didn't realize it would be this hard. So how about this? How about if I toss out a few guesses, and you tell me if I'm right?"

She released a breath and nodded.

"It has something to do with your father and your brother?"

Her heart was pounding so hard, she wondered if he could hear it.

"They were rough with you? Shoved, hit, things like that?"

Beth nodded.

"Rough, and a whole lot more, am I right?"

Another nod, which infuriated her, because he'd earned the right to hear the truth. All of it. Every ugly element.

"I thought so. And I'm sorry you had to go through that. In my opinion, there is no greater sin. A father's duty to his daughter is to shelter her from men like that, not *be* a man like that."

If there had been any doubt that he understood, all of it, that doubt was gone now.

"I am sorry, Aaron."

"For what?"

"That you purchased damaged goods."

He got up so quickly the chair fell backward and landed with a clatter. He must have seen that his sudden move scared her, because Aaron knelt in front of her, pulled her close, and, resting his cheek against her chest, said, "Don't ever say such a thing again. Nothing could be further from the truth. What they did . . . no one can hold you accountable for that!"

"But—"

"Money exchanged hands, that's true, but I never felt as though I'd *purchased* you."

"Then what? And why?"

"I needed help, and when I finally admitted it, I'd run out of options. And he wouldn't let you go unless I made it worth his while."

She stroked his hair. "You did not know it, but you saved me."

"No, Beth, it's you who saved me."

The thunder of children running down the stairs made it clear that this discussion was over, at least for now. He got to his feet, brought her with him. His lips were touching hers when he ground out, "All that really matters is that we're together now . . ." He kissed her, and pulled back a bit to add, ". . . and forever."

# Chapter Eighteen

"Sounds like a lot of work," Aaron said.

"I will have help. Stella, Emily, Willa, and Molly, of course."

It would be the first major holiday without Esther, and Beth wanted it to be special.

"So let me get this straight: You're baking the turkey and making the stuffing, and that's it?"

Laughing, she said, "No, I will make mashed potatoes and gravy, biscuits, and pumpkin pie, too."

Now Aaron laughed, too. "Doesn't leave much for your helpers."

"Only broccoli salad, baked beans, sweet potatoes, and a few other desserts."

"The table will collapse under the weight of it all. Speaking of which, how do you hope to seat all of these people?"

"Karl said he would loan me some sawhorses and plywood. If we put them in a straight line with our table, we can easily seat eighteen."

"Do we have that many chairs?"

"Chairs . . . I hadn't thought about that."

"We have benches in the shop. I'll bring some home the day before."

"It is exciting, yes?"

He pulled her into a hug. "*You* are exciting."

"I can hardly wait to see the house filled with friends and family, laughing and talking and—"

Aaron silenced her with a kiss, then turned her loose. "I need to get to the mill. Moses will need help, typing things into the computer."

"I thought he would have returned to the shop by now."

"He would, except that he's more help to us in the office. Who knew he could balance the books, mail invoices, make bank deposits, and schedule appointments."

"And he is happy? He does not miss working with the big equipment?"

"Apparently not. You should hear him, whistling and humming. Perfect timing for his move, since David's son is old enough to work the machines now."

Things had settled down quite well at the sawmill. It was remarkable, really, what a change Moses's help had made in her husband's personality.

"I'll be home by five," he said, pulling the door shut behind him.

"And I will be waiting," Beth said to herself.

If she'd ever been happier, she couldn't remember when.


Aaron had never been fond of winter. Slick, wet, cold weather wasn't good for chainsaws. For dozers or logging trucks either. But hearing Beth talk about snow had changed his mind, and his attitude.

"It is not just white. When the sun hits just right, it is pale blue, or pink, light yellow. And at night, the moon turns it silver."

Walking from the truck to the office, he remembered something else she'd said. "It creaks underfoot. And if you listen really carefully as it falls, you can hear the sound of every snowflake landing on top of the one before it."

Yes, it was cold, she'd agreed, "But what better excuse do we need for a warm fire in the woodstove!"

He didn't realize he was smiling until he walked into the office and Karl said, "Well, aren't *you* in a good mood this morning."

"It's a nice day."

"Nice day? They're calling for blizzard conditions, and you hate snow!"

"Past tense." He straightened a picture on the waiting room wall. "I've always liked this photo."

"Which one? The aerial shot of the mill?"

"Yeah. I figure that's how it looks to God, how everything down here on earth looks to Him."

Karl looked from Aaron to the picture and back again. "Have you been drinking?"

"Me?" He laughed. "Alcohol has never passed these lips, and you know it."

"Well, *some*thing's got you awfully poetic all of a sudden," he said, walking through the door to the shop.

"Poetic," he said to himself. "Me. Ha-ha."

"What's that, Aaron?"

The sudden sound of Moses's voice startled him, and he nearly tipped over his wheeled desk chair. *Now you know how Beth feels every time you sneak up on her.*

"Left a phone message on your desk. Two, actually. One from McCartney, one from Gibson."

One new client, one old, Aaron thought, looking at the pink slips. He picked up the phone and had started to dial Gibson's number when Karl burst into his office.

"Heads up," he said. "It's my uncle and my cousin."

"I wasn't aware you had any relatives in Pleasant Valley."

"I don't. They're here from Nappanee."

The man looked downright panicky. Surely he didn't mean . . .

"Beth's father and brother?"

"Yep. Saw 'em getting out of a cab. Driver must have gotten confused, dropped them out back. When I saw them talking to David, I came straight in to warn you."

"What do you suppose they want?"

"Money would be my guess." Then, "David gave them directions. They'll be walking in that front door any minute."

Karl opened the shop door again. "If they ask where I am—and that isn't likely—tell 'em I'm busy."

The door had no sooner clicked shut than two men walked into the waiting area, stomping snow from their boots and shaking it from their shoulders.

"We're here to see Aaron Bontrager," said the older of the two.

Moses pointed toward Aaron's office. "Right there he stands." Moses frowned, a sure sign that he sensed something was awry with these two.

"Edward Mast," the older one said, walking into the office. "Bethel's father?" He extended a hand. "We spoke on the phone?"

*Six months ago*, Aaron thought. She'd been here for six months, and they hadn't been in touch once. Not to make sure she arrived safely. Not to see if she was happy. Not to make sure she wasn't being mistreated.

He ignored the hand, and after a second, watched Mast drop it to his side. "Moses, give us a few minutes, will you please?"

The frown deepened as he said, "All right, boss."

When he left, the younger one said, "That is one big man!"

"And that's one big winter outside," Beth's father said. "We see plenty of snow in Nappanee, of course, but not this much, or this early in the year."

"Sometimes we do," said the young one. He took a step closer. "Vernon Mast. Bethel's brother. We have not spoken, but my father told me about your discussions with him."

"Hmm. Is that so." He gave them the once-over. If they thought he intended to ask them to make themselves comfortable, they were mistaken. "What can I do for you?"

"It is Thanksgiving soon," Edward said. "We thought, what better time of year to visit Bethel?"

"We didn't expect to arrive in the middle of a snow-storm."

"Where is she?" her father wanted to know.

"Home, with our children."

"Ah yes. I'd almost forgotten. They are the main reason you hired her."

The children had been the only reason, seven months ago, when they'd first talked. But that wasn't true anymore.

"Quite the business you have here," Edward said, looking around. "Quite profitable, I imagine."

"We do well enough to keep the wolf from the door."
*Until now* . . . He couldn't have been more than six when
he'd gone to town with his father and, while waiting outside the bank, seen a one-man band performing *Peter and
the Wolf.* The musician had played the violin to represent
the boy, the oboe, clarinet, and flute to portray various
birds and animals, and pounded a gigantic drum to sym-
bolize the hunters' rifles. Most memorable of all were the
eerie, ominous notes of the French horn . . . the malicious
voice of the wolf.

"I have meetings scheduled," Aaron said.

"I am a businessman, too, so I can appreciate the im-
portance of that. If you will tell us where to find Bethel,
we will wait to talk to you there."

"Talk to me? About what?"

"My daughter, of course. She has not reached out to us,
not once, since we put her on that train."

*And why would she?*

"Not that we are surprised. Bethel never was a very
loyal person."

Aaron bristled. Six months without a word from them,
and now that they were here, they still hadn't asked about
her welfare.

"Why not save us all a lot of time, Mast, and get to the
point."

"The point?" Vernon asked.

"You came a long way just to *talk.* Name your price."

At least the man had the good sense to pretend shame.

"We can see you are too busy to drive us to your house.
An employee instead, then?"

"Speaking of employees, who's minding your store?"

"We . . . it has been sold."

Aaron barely knew the man, but he could spot a liar when he saw one.

"The taxi driver told us he has passed your house many times on his way into and out of town. From what he said, we know it is not far."

"Yes," Vernon said. "We can walk."

They headed for the door, but Aaron blocked their path. No way he'd allow them anywhere near Beth!

Both men saw his fists, doubled up at his sides. And both men smirked. "Even New Order Amish avoid physical violence," Mast said.

"Two things in this world would make me violate the Ordnung." He held up a forefinger. "If my children were being threatened . . ." The middle finger popped up beside it. "Or if Beth was in danger."

"Danger?" Mast laughed. "From me? I am her father. What makes you think—"

"She is disloyal," Vernon interrupted, "and if she has told you bad things about us, she is a liar, too."

Even before they'd walked in, Aaron had decided not to give them a dime. But if money would get rid of them . . .

"Name your price," he said again.

"How crude these New Order Amish are, thinking only of money," Mast said.

His son agreed. "You could at least invite us to Thanksgiving dinner before you throw money at us."

Thanksgiving was two days away. He wouldn't allow them to hang around town that long, waiting for a free meal.

"How about this, then?" Mast began. "At least let us say a last good-bye to Bethel before you send us away."

Aaron pictured her face as she had described what they'd done to her. He'd promised to protect her, and he aimed to do just that. He was about to ask them to wait while he had Moses fetch the petty cash box when Karl entered, red-faced and out of breath.

"I need to speak with you," he said, and grabbed Aaron's arm. "It's important."

"I won't be long," he told the men, and followed Karl into the shop.

He slammed the door and said, "I knew they meant to cause trouble, so I called the Nappanee postmaster, one of the only businesses there with a phone. Asked him to get the bishop on the line. Short walk," he added, "since the post office is next door to his house. Lantz said those two were shunned."

"Why?"

"Vernon attacked a young girl, and according to her, Edward watched . . . and when the girl's father got the bishop involved, they both denied it. Only took one meeting for the elders to decide they had to go. Evidently, it wasn't the first accusation of its kind. Anyway, the community bought the shop and two first-class tickets to Phoenix. Lantz said it didn't surprise him at all to find out they traded the tickets for coach seats to Maryland."

It was reliable, if not shocking information. Aaron thanked Karl and returned to his office.

"Remind me . . . who's running your store?"

"No one. I told you, we sold it. Didn't get quite what it's worth, but . . ." Edward shrugged.

Aaron stepped up, nose to nose. "I know a little something about Englisher law. Now that you've both been shunned, the community can't protect you from your crimes."

"Crimes?" Vernon laughed. "What crimes?"

"Rape . . . assault . . . crimes that, out there, in the Englisher world"—Aaron pointed into the parking lot—"will put you behind bars for a long, long time." He walked to his desk, where a promotional calendar bore the number of the taxi company. He'd just picked up the phone's handset when Vernon said, "It's our word against those girls'."

"Girls? There was more than one?" He slammed down the phone and called for Moses. When the big man appeared, Aaron said, "Keep an eye on these two for a minute."

"Happy to, boss."

Aaron stomped into the storeroom, hands shaking while he spun the dial on the safe. He'd give them five hundred dollars, enough for taxi fare to the station and train tickets to Chicago.

"Is this all she's worth to you?" Mast said after counting the money. "A lousy five hundred bucks?"

"You could gather up all the money in the world and it wouldn't equal her value. She's the best thing that ever happened to me. That money," he said, pointing at the stack of bills in Mast's hand, "is insurance, against your ever coming back here. Because if you do, I'll forget I'm Amish for a half hour, and then I'll call the cops."

A white taxi pulled up beside the front door.

"While I was watchin' 'em," Moses said, "I took the liberty of callin' a cab."

Karl, Moses, and Aaron watched father and son climb

into the taxi's back seat. Watched them glare as it pulled away from the curb.

"So who's ready for Thanksgiving?" Karl asked, patting his trim belly.

Aaron thought of everything he was thankful for, and Beth topped the list. She was safe. So were the kids. These men beside him were more than employees; they were loyal friends. He'd lost his mother, but she was in a better place. And in his gut, he knew that, despite their bravado, the Masts would not return.

"I am now," he said. "I am now."

# Chapter Nineteen

He wore the sweater Beth made him for Christmas several times a week. He'd wear it every day if she didn't insist on washing it weekly.

She was in the garden when he got home one early spring day, doing her best to figure out the post hole digger. "Those deer won't get into *this* garden."

"Why do you insist on doing jobs like this all by yourself? I'm happy to help . . . if only you'd ask."

"I know that. But I like the work. And I like a good challenge, too." She jabbed the digger's blades into the soil, and they barely penetrated an inch.

"Give me that thing," he said, laughing as he grabbed the handles.

They made quick work of clearing the holes and adding a few inches of pea gravel. Then, as she held the posts, he made sure they were plumb and dumped in the dry concrete. All that was necessary after adding water was the patience to allow the cement to dry.

"Isn't it too early to plant vegetables?"

"Out here, yes." She shoved windblown hair back into place and left a muddy streak on her forehead. "But my intention is to start them in the shed. I have already cleared a space for the peat pots."

"Where?"

"On your work bench."

"On my . . . Where are my tools?"

"On the pegboard above it, where they belong."

Would he ever get used to hearing that? She said it when one of the kids misplaced a toy, or he couldn't find his keys. It was her stock answer to just about anything that went missing.

And he loved it.

"When will you go into town next?" she wanted to know.

She'd need plants, and although he'd offered to teach her, Beth hadn't yet learned to drive.

"Tell you what. Let's go tomorrow. I'll leave work early and pick you up. We'll have lunch first, then hit the nursery."

"But the children—"

"Are old enough to stay home alone for a couple of hours." He lifted her apron hem and wiped the dirt from her face. "Great opportunity to get you behind the wheel."

"All right then, it's a date. Except for the driving part."

"Chicken."

"Bawk-bawk."

He slung an arm over her shoulders. "Well, at least you're honest," he said as they made their way to the house.

The following morning, he was at his desk by six. With the paperwork and meetings behind him, he arrived home in time to have lunch with the kids, who suggested that— if they felt like stopping, of course—buying ice cream on the way back would sure be nice!

During the first moments of the drive into town, they enjoyed a compatible silence. Aaron broke it by saying, "What kind of plants do you have in mind?"

"Tomatoes," Beth said, and started counting on her fingers. "Cucumbers. Spring onions. Green and red peppers. Some leaf lettuce. Zucchini, of course . . ."

"Of course?"

"I cannot bake zucchini bread without it."

He loved seeing her this way, rested, calm, happy, and pink-cheeked. "What are you in the mood for?"

She sent a flirty grin across the console and wiggled her eyebrows.

"Food, Mrs. Bontrager. What kind of *food* would you like for lunch?"

"Something cheap and quick. But not a drive-through restaurant."

"Are you brave enough to try Mom's again?"

"That will give you a chance to *really* visit with your friends, without interruptions."

"Yeah, 'cause what are the chances that rude woman will be there again?"

They chose a table near the windows, and within minutes, Gladys marched over. "I'm so glad to see you!" she said, giving him a sideways hug. "Allie told me why you left the last time you came. We're all sorry, so sorry, your family had to go through that. I wish I'd known. I would've booted that harpy out on her bee-hind. Would've told her never to come back, too."

"Aw, thanks, Gladys. But there's no reason to cost yourself business. No harm, no foul."

"If we ever get so desperate that we allow people like *that* to harass people like *you,* we have a whole lot more to worry about than money." She slid an order pad from her ruffled pink apron and smiled at Beth. "What can I get you, cutie-pie?"

Grinning, Beth said, "Something completely unhealthy. A hot dog with everything—except chili—and fries on the side. A root beer." She put down the menu. "Do you have hot fudge?"

The woman's jovial laughter filled the space and, because of the day and time, echoed from every hard surface. "Now really, what kinda diner would this be if we didn't!"

"Then I will have a hot fudge sundae for dessert."

"Good golly Miss Molly, where will you put it all, tiny as you are?"

"Believe me, Gladys. She can out-eat a truck driver."

"And what're you in the mood for, handsome?"

Aaron looked at Beth, who, as she'd done earlier, wiggled her eyebrows. And winked. *Winked!*

"How about a burger, with onion rings and potato salad. And sweet tea, no lemon."

"You got it, kids." She pocketed the tablet and tucked the pencil behind her ear. "Back in a jiffy. And I'll bring Homer with me."

"She's a card, isn't she?" Aaron said.

"Is her husband like her?"

"Yeah, only more so." He laughed.

"Then I can see why you like them."

The awning that boasted the diner's logo kept the sun's rays at bay, but its glow still radiated from her face. "You look especially pretty today."

"Aaron Bontrager, you know better than to say things like that."

"Hey. Just because I live Plain, I can't compliment my gorgeous wife?"

"Well, you can. But you should not. You would not like a *conceited* wife."

"Bah. That'll never happen." He reached across the table, took her hands in his. "Because you're more beautiful inside than out."

Movement outside captured her attention. Whatever it was changed her mood as surely as a window shade blocks the sunlight. Her cheeks turned pale and raw fear widened her eyes.

"What is it?" he asked and followed her gaze to the gas station on the opposite corner, where a scruffy man had just inserted the gas nozzle into his tank.

He barely heard her husky whisper. "Vernon."

Sure enough, Mast was the man at the gas pump. *Of all the unmitigated gall . . .*

Aaron slid out of the booth, leaned close to her face and said, "Promise me you'll stay right here."

She nodded, but he wasn't convinced.

"I mean it. *Stay. Put.* Understand?"

"Yes."

Aaron half ran across the street and, when he reached the gas pump, said, "I told you to stay away from her."

Vernon smirked. "You can't tell me what to do, Bontrager." He scanned the station's small parking lot. "Where'd you come from, anyway?"

"Pay for your gas, get in your truck . . ." He inspected the nearly new pickup. "Rapes. Beatings. Now car theft?"

"I borrowed it from a friend, who was kind enough to teach me to drive it." He dangled the keys in front of Aaron's face. "See? The tag says 'If lost, return to . . .'"

Aaron didn't believe him, but ownership of the vehicle wasn't his concern. Beth's well-being, however, *was*.

"I told you two things before Thanksgiving. Stay away from Beth. And *no. More. Money.*"

"I'm not here for money."

"Then what? Beth sure as hell doesn't want to see either of you!" He leaned slightly, to look around the man. "Where's your father?"

"Dead."

The word hit him like a slap. He hadn't known what Mast would answer, but certainly not *that*.

"Beth needs to know. You might not agree with his paternal methods, but he was her father."

"Heart attack?"

Vernon gave a slow nod. "He was upright and talking one minute . . ." He snapped his fingers. "Flat on his back and gone the next." Mast looked over Aaron's shoulder. "Is she over there? In the diner?"

Aaron looked toward the diner, too, and thanked God that the sun's glare made it impossible to see her at the table near the window.

"You're right. She should know. But she doesn't need to hear it from you."

"Like I said, Bontrager, you can't tell me what to do. I'm not leaving until I talk to her."

"Fine. How much this time? A hundred? Two?"

"I don't need your money, *brother-in-law*. I have a good job. With a sanitation company in Morgantown." He replaced the pump handle and slammed the gas tank's cover shut, then took a step, as if to walk across the street. "I'll say it again: I'm not leaving until I tell her, face to face."

Aaron filled both hands with the man's corduroy jacket

collar. "You're not going anywhere near her," he said, molars grinding together, "so *I'll* say it again: Beth needs to hear it, but not from *you*."

"I need to hear what?" Unnoticed, Beth had crossed the street and put herself between the two men. "Aaron," Beth said, tugging his wrists, "stop this. Please."

Reluctantly, he released her brother, who straightened his clothes. "Marriage agrees with you, sister. You look wonderful."

"What are you doing here, Vernon?"

She might as well have said *snake*. Her voice held no warmth, no relief at seeing him after so many months, not a trace of love. Aaron had never seen that indifferent look on her face before, either.

"Our father is dead, Bethel."

She blinked. Licked her lips. Swallowed. "When? How?"

"His poor heart gave out, three days ago."

"So he's in the ground already, then."

"He is."

Beth linked her arm through Aaron's. "All right," he said. "She knows. Now you can make your way back to Morgantown."

"Morgantown? West Virginia?"

"He has a job there. His boss was kind enough to loan him the truck, so he could tell you, face to face."

"But . . ." Brow furrowed and eyes narrowed, she looked at her brother. "Why not Nappanee?"

He hung his head. "We, ah, the store was sold."

"I'm sorry for your losses."

He looked up quickly. "Losses?"

"Daed, the store, your right to live Plain . . ."

"Just how long have you been standing there?" Aaron asked.

"A second or two," she said to her husband. To Mast, she said, "Thank you for delivering the news. And again, I am sorry for your loss."

"*My* loss?" Mast thundered. "He was *your* father, too!"

"He kept a roof over my head, food in my belly, and clothes on my back—I will give him that. But nothing else he did qualifies as fatherly. I will miss the man he could have been, *should* have been, but I will not miss *him*."

She started walking, and Aaron went with her. On the other side of the road, he said, "How long have you known about the shunning?"

"Since Thanksgiving. I overheard you and Karl, talking on the porch after dinner."

"And you didn't say anything?"

"Why would I? You sent them away. It would have made me sound heartless to say I was glad." She patted his hand. "I imagine Gladys has delivered our food by now."

"Would you mind very much if we skipped lunch? I've suddenly lost my appetite."

"Me, too."

"Want to come inside with me, so I can pay the tab?"

She watched Mast's truck, heading north on 219. Two hours from now, Aaron thought, the man would be back in West Virginia . . . where, hopefully, he'd stay.

"You go ahead," she said, patting his hand again. "I will wait for you in the truck."

He turned to go inside, but she stopped him, threw

herself into his arms, and pressed a long, passionate kiss to his lips.

"Thank you," she said when it ended.

"I enjoyed it, too," he said, chuckling, "so thank *you*."

"No, silly. Not for the kiss. For being a man of your word. You said you'd protect me, always and from everything. I believed it for no reason other than you are a good and decent man. But just now? You proved it."

She kissed him again, a shorter, but no less passionate kiss, and walked away.

A man opened the diner door, held it for the woman behind him. "'Scuze me, pal," he said.

Still somewhat dazed, Aaron said, "Sorry," and stepped aside.

The couple linked arms as Aaron entered the restaurant.

"Isn't that the fellow who was roughing up that other Amishman?" the woman asked.

"One and the same. And you know what? If the woman hadn't walked up when she did, he might've snapped the big guy's neck."

"I thought those people weren't allowed to fight."

"Guess not all of those people follow all of the rules, all of the time." He laughed, and the woman laughed with him.

"Strange," she said.

"Yeah, strange."

By now, the door had hissed shut, and Aaron crossed to the table near the window. He'd always felt a bit out of place in town, even though he used a cell phone and drove a pickup, same as the Englishers. But he wore the beard, the hat, and the clothes that marked him as Amish.

Funny, he thought, placing thirty dollars beside the napkin holder on the table, that the man had seemed impressed by what he'd witnessed. He'd ask God's forgiveness later, during his devotions.

# Chapter Twenty

Beth sat up alone in the darkened parlor, thinking . . . about the fact that her father and brother had come to the sawmill under the guise of reuniting with their long-lost relative. When the time was right, she'd let Aaron know that, although she understood why he'd done it, he had been wrong to keep it from her.

Thinking, too, about today's sudden appearance of her brother. What were the chances that she'd see him in Oakland, of all places?

*So you're officially an orphan,* she thought. *Shouldn't you feel something other than relief?*

It was definitely a matter for prayer.

Beth went to the small desk near the staircase, lifted its roll-top lid, and retrieved her mother's Bible, the one treasure she'd managed to hide from her father. Elizabeth had accumulated a few nice things over the years, but one by one, Edward had destroyed them all. The stoneware that had belonged to *her* mother. Hand-thrown vases. Cookbooks. Every dress in her closet . . . except the blue one they'd buried her in.

Beth flicked on the lamp and sat in the mahogany

chair—the most ornate piece of furniture in the house—and opened to the first page of the Good Book. There, written in German, were listed the Rebeccas and Hannahs, Noahs and Samuels that had taken the Stetzler name back as far as the late 1800s. The list ended with her mother's beautiful curlicue script, and the things she'd written beside her own name: Marriage to Edward, the birth of her son and daughter, and the dates that marked the events. To the right of the names, another column—blank—to record each Mast's death. And under Beth's name, a dozen blank lines.

She opened the narrow drawer at her waist, withdrew the ballpoint Aaron used to balance the household budget, and next to her name, penned "Married Aaron Bontrager," and their wedding date. She added the children's names and birthdates, too . . . black and white proof that in her heart, they were hers.

Beth's fingertip slid up the page, stopped on her father's name. And with trembling hand, she wrote down the date of his death.

Now, as tears stung her eyes, she felt something. Resentment, for the way he'd treated her mother. Bitterness, over what he'd done to her. Regret, for the time he'd wasted on violent actions and hateful words, like those he'd hurled at her as she boarded the train in Fort Wayne: "Good riddance. You were only good for cooking and cleaning, stocking the shelves and . . ."

She couldn't bring herself to complete the slur. Couldn't stop the tears, either.

Beth closed the Bible and returned it to the desk, then rolled down the cover and returned to her rocking chair. *Her* rocking chair, the one Aaron had given her for Christmas, so she wouldn't have to feel as if every stick of furniture, every pot and pan, every knife and fork had first belonged to Marta. He didn't realize it, but he had, quite literally, rescued her. Not only from the abuse, but from a future without hope and a life without love. Everything he'd done, from reserving that special train car to threatening Vernon, had been out of concern for her. So why was she crying over a dead man, a man who'd hated and hit her for years, instead of thanking—

She had been so busy feeling sorry for herself, Beth hadn't heard him come downstairs. Hadn't noticed when he knelt beside the rocker . . . until he slid one arm behind her back, the other under her knees, and lifted her from the chair.

Aaron didn't ask why she was crying, or tell her that everything would be all right. Instead, he kissed her, softly, slowly, lovingly, and carried her upstairs.


She'd fallen asleep quickly, nestled in the crook of his arm. Aaron would kiss her face, her throat, her lips . . . if he thought he could do it without waking her.

Silhouetted by the moonlight, propped on pillows and huddled under a thin blanket, his sleeping wife was beautiful. Finally, Beth looked at relaxed and at peace.

"What are you staring at, Mr. Bontrager?" she asked, her voice whisper soft.

He answered with a kiss, and she met it with equal ardor. His only regret since bringing her to Pleasant Valley had been waiting so long to tell her that he loved her.

He said it now. "I love you, Mrs. Bontrager."

She said it, too.

And they fell asleep together, tangled in one another's arms.

# Chapter Twenty-One

September was still delivering sticky temperatures when the parishioners gathered behind the church. Boys and girls raced around a rough but serviceable baseball diamond, shouting "I've got it!" and "Throw it to first!" after the crack of the bat. Women sat together at the picnic benches neatly arranged in the shade of maple trees, swapping recipes and scolding youngsters who nearly overturned pitchers of iced tea and lemonade. The men gathered near the food tables, discussing crops and livestock and how the weather was impacting life in Pleasant Valley.

Aaron had waved their friend Max over, and as they leaned on the white split-rail gate of the churchyard, Seth joined them, too.

"Ah, the Bontrager brothers," Max said. "What can I do for you today?"

"We shouldn't talk business on a Sunday, but between your schedule and mine . . ."

"I won't tell the bishop if you don't," Max said, laughing.

"I want to hire you to build an addition for the house. Something like the one you built for the Bakers."

"The whole back side of the place?"

"Yup. Two bedrooms upstairs, a larger parlor and dedicated dining room downstairs."

"Don't forget about Beth's dream porch," Seth added.

"Let me guess," Max said. "A covered, three-sided wrap-around, with spindles, not pickets."

"Hey, this is supposed to be a surprise. When did she talk to you about it?"

"She didn't," the carpenter said.

"Then how did you know, right down to the spindles?"

Max chuckled. "Let's just say my hammer an' me have made more than a few porch dreams come true." He paused. "Why the sudden drive to expand?"

Seth said, "With our mother's house sold, there's a lot of furniture piled in Aaron's garage."

"I've always wondered," Max said. "Why didn't you keep the house, Seth, instead of selling it to the Weavers?"

"Too big. Too much to take care of. I'm not married, and have no plans to be. Ever. So my three-room cottage is perfect."

Max and Aaron shared a knowing grin.

"Spoken like a true confirmed bachelor," Max said.

"Who's just announced to every unmarried woman for miles around . . ."

". . . that he's ripe for the pickin'," they said together.

"I give him two years before he and some pretty young thing are published."

"More like one," Max said, "and we'll hear the bishop make that announcement in church."

"You're pretty far afield from talking about the house addition," Seth said.

"He makes a good point," Aaron said, and gave his brother a playful shove.

"Any drawings yet?" Max asked.

"Yeah, but I'm keeping those close to the vest. I want Beth to see them first, so if she wants to make any changes . . ."

Max laughed. "If? Biggest li'l word in the English language. If I was a betting man, I'd wager she'll change everything *but* those porch spindles."

The men shared a companionable laugh, and afterward, Aaron asked about Willa, Frannie, and the baby. "Doing well," he said. "Really well."

Judging by the look on his face, Aaron believed it.

"I have to warn you, a project like this takes a couple of months, and that's if the weather cooperates. It's a huge mess, and noisy, too."

"I built the place," Aaron reminded him, "so I remember. We'll get it done faster than you think, with Seth here, and my crew helping your men."

"So what's behind this big addition? Are the boys tired of sharing a room?"

Now, Seth gave Aaron a good-natured shove. "He isn't just adding to the house. Ol' Aaron here is adding to his brood."

Max whistled. "No kiddin'? Congratulations. That's great news."

"I couldn't agree more, Maxwell. Couldn't agree more."

Aaron caught Beth's eye, over there under the maples. She smiled, wiggled her fingertips in a girlish wave that sent shivers up his spine . . .

. . . and made him want to whisk her away from here, and take her home.

* * *

They spent their first hours after the gathering catching up on homework. Beth helped Molly with a book report, while Aaron guided Sam through his latest lessons in fractions.

"How come I get stuck with writing the alphabet over and over, instead of cool homework like that?" Matthew demanded.

"Patience, son. Next year, you'll be complaining because you're *not* writing the alphabet."

Since arriving home, Beth had been quieter than usual. Sweet and friendly, just not as talkative. And as soon as the kids were in bed, he intended to ask why.

"They've already started talking about the Christmas pageant," Matthew said. "I volunteered to play the shepherd boy." He pretended to hold a long staff, pretended to use it to poke Traveler. The dog yipped and bounced happily around him. "We're gonna dress Traveler up like a sheep. Good thing I have some time. I need to teach him to sit quiet while we're all standing around the manger."

"I am happy to help with the costumes," Beth said. "Seems a shame for all those bolts of fabric we found at Esther's to go to waste."

"I'll tell Miss Zook." He poked out his lower lip. "But she might not be our teacher after Christmas."

"Ah, getting married, is she?" Sam said. "Too bad the bishop doesn't make a new rule saying schoolteachers can work until they have children to take care of."

"When they get married," Molly said in her best lecturer voice, "ladies have to start taking care of their husbands, right off. It's practice, I guess, for when they *do* have kids."

She dusted eraser shavings from her paper. "I'm sorry, Beth, that you didn't get any time to practice. You got here, and *pow!* you became an instant mother."

"There is absolutely nothing to be sorry about," Beth said. "Right from the start, I loved taking care of you, Sam and Matthew, too."

"And Daed?"

She met his eyes across the table and smiled. "Especially your *daed.*"

If pride was a sin, he'd be asking the Almighty's forgiveness every day for the rest of his life, because he was proud of this woman. Proud that she'd married him. Proud she was carrying his child.

And Lord help him, proud to look into that beautiful face for the rest of his days.


The children had been upstairs for nearly an hour, and all was calm.

"I love this time of day," she said, "when the day's work is done and the house is quiet."

Aaron took her in his arms. "Quiet, and alone." He kissed her forehead. "Just you and me." Placing a hand on her stomach, he added, "And for the time being, this li'l fella."

"Hmpf. It could be a girl, you know. Molly would just love a little sister."

"I suppose she would. And to be honest, I wouldn't mind having another girl around the house." He faked a thick southern drawl. "Females tend to civilize a territory."

She rested her cheek on his chest.

"Something on your mind?"

"Yes. No." She took his hand, led him to the sofa, and patted the cushion beside her. When he sat, Beth said, "Do you ever worry that the baby might . . ." She looked at her foot, and the thick-soled shoe that covered it. "What if it inherits . . . *this*?"

"It won't. But Beth, even if it does, doctors can work medical miracles these days. Didn't you say that if your parents had taken you for that operation, the surgeons might have been able to fix your limp?"

She nodded.

"That was years ago. Imagine all the new procedures they've discovered since then."

"It would be expensive."

"We have money in the bank. More than enough for something like that. Maybe Emily will know about a test of some kind, to tell us what to expect. If there's a problem with the little one's foot, we'll start a savings account, right now. We'll call it the Peace of Mind Account."

"I like that."

He got to his feet, led her back to the kitchen. "Sit down for a minute. I have something to show you."

Aaron grabbed a long tube of papers that had been leaning in the corner of the mud room. As he approached the table, he slid off the rubber band that held the papers in place. It bounced a time or two, hitting the table, and he shoved it aside. Moved the salt and pepper shakers, and the napkin basket, too, to make room for the drawings that he spread out.

"Aaron, what's this?"

"House plans," he said. "For an addition we'll build out back." He wrapped her hand in his, guided her forefinger across the thin black lines. "A bigger parlor, a brand-new dining room. And upstairs, Matthew will have his own room. The baby, too." He moved her hand until it followed the marks at the far edge of the page. "A wrap-around porch. It will go around the front and both sides of the house. I'm giving a little thought to going whole hog, having Max connect it to the back porch, so that you can walk clean around the house, outside, with a roof over-head. We'll buy a bunch of rocking chairs, so you can watch the sun rise *and* set." He showed her the spec sheet. "And look here. Railings with spindles, not pickets."

"Aaron, it's . . . I . . ." She bit her lower lip. "Can we afford this?"

"For your information, pretty lady, I started a Make the House Bigger Account two weeks after we got married. So yes, we can afford it. We'll use some of Maem's things, if we can, but you'll want new furniture, a rug or two, rocking chairs—for the porch, and to go with the baby's crib and bureau. Plenty of time for all that, though."

"It will be quite a house."

"It has to be, because it's for quite a woman."

How many years would it take, she wondered, before he grew tired of plying her with compliments? And how many years until her heart stopped pounding like a parade drum when he delivered them?

Tomorrow, first thing, she'd call Emily, find out if, as he'd suggested, there might be a test to determine whether or not their child had inherited her condition.

For now, she intended to show her husband how grateful she was, how blessed she felt to be married to this fine man.

"Thank you, Mr. Bontrager. I love you."

\* \* \*

Beth could hardly wait to share the ultrasound printout with Aaron, and show him how to identify the toes, the tiny fingers, and facial features. In another month, Emily said, they'd repeat the test for a clearer image that would reveal gender, and whether or not they'd need to start that Peace of Mind Account.

She felt good. Healthy and happy. And according to Emily . . . Beth pressed a hand to her stomach, remembering something else Emily had said. . . . "Some women notice movement as early as thirteen weeks, but sixteen to twenty-two is more the average."

How odd will that be, she thought, feeling the flutter of life inside her!

The children were just finishing up supper when Aaron got home, but they hung back, to sit with him while he ate. Their happy chatter was a wonder to behold, especially compared to the sullen, sarcastic sounds that had come from them when she'd first arrived.

How would they react to learning that their family was growing?

*Lord, let them be happy.*

For as long as she could remember, everyone, including her mother, had believed she'd never have children. Finding out otherwise, well, Beth didn't know how a woman could be happier!

Was everyone taking longer than usual to get ready for bed tonight, or did it just seem that way because she was excited to show Aaron the grainy photograph she'd hidden under the buffet doily.

Once they'd finally settled down for the night, he spread the blueprints across the table again. "I have a surprise for you," he said, tapping the drawing. "See this?"

She leaned in close, squinting to see what he was pointing at.

"This right here? It's a potting shed. Big enough to hold buckets of dirt, pots of every size and shape . . . I'll ask Max to install shelves, to hold seed packets, fertilizer, peat pots . . . And see? A window, so you won't have to traipse all the way out to the shed to check on your plants."

"When did you come up with this idea?"

"This evening, when I went out there to fetch the hose, to wash the mud off my boots. Which reminds me." He tapped the drawing again. "A sink, with running water."

"I am the most fortunate wife in all of Pleasant Valley." She pressed a kiss to his whiskered cheek. "I have a surprise for you, too."

Beth hurried into the dining room, came right back carrying the envelope that held the ultrasound image.

Aaron slid it out, turned it right and left, upside down, right side up again. "What in the world *is* it?"

"An ultrasound. Beth has a new machine at the clinic. I went to see her this morning, to find out if, as you suggested, there might be a test that will tell us whether or not my issue is hereditary."

He still hadn't figured out which way was up, and squinted at the paper.

"In a month, we will repeat the test, but from what she could see here, everything is as it should be."

"So . . . this is a picture of our baby?"

She helped him decipher top from bottom.

And pointed at the image's right side.

"Feet. Hands. Belly. Head."

She pointed again, this time at the left side of the image. "Feet. Hands. Belly. Head."

His brow was furrowed when, finally he looked up. "Did the machine malfunction?"

Beth shook her head.

"Then why . . ." His eyes widened. "You mean . . . This . . ." He tapped the paper. "This is . . ."

"Twins."

"No."

"Yes."

"You're sure? Emily is sure?"

"Yes, and yes."

"Twins," he said again, staring at the picture. *"Twins!"*

"Come here."

Aaron hugged her tight, then stepped back. "Are you all right? The babies—I can't believe I'm saying *babies*— is everything all right?"

"Yes," she said again. "Everything is all right."

He pulled her close again, and again, stepped back. "That means two of everything." Aaron pecked the keys of an imaginary calculator. "Two cribs. Two bureaus. Two high chairs . . ."

Beth pretended to steal the calculator and hit its imaginary OFF button. "By the time we need all of those things, Mark and Micah will have outgrown everything. I am sure Stella will let us borrow her baby stuff. Until she needs it again, that is."

"My legs are weak," he said, dropping onto a kitchen chair.

She sat on his lap. Kissed his temple.

"Twins," he said yet again.

"I shouldn't be surprised, really. Life—everything about life—is twice as good as it ever was." He laughed, and the sound of it echoed in her chest. "So why not twins, right?"

Beth held his face in her hands. "Right."

"And you're sure everything is all right, with . . ." He laughed again. ". . . with all three of you?"

"I am sure. Next time I see Emily, you can come with me, hear the good news firsthand."

"Remarkable. Amazing. Shocking. *Wonderful.*"

"We need to decide when to tell the children."

"Let's wake 'em up right now." Again, he laughed. "Why should I be the only one who sounds like a blithering idiot, chanting twins, twins, twins."

"I think it can wait until morning."

"You're right. As usual."

All of a sudden he looked worried. "Are you tired? Should we hire a housekeeper?"

It was Beth's turn to laugh. "No! I am *fine.* Honest!"

His lips were touching hers when he said it again. "Last time, I promise."

"I won't hold you to it."

"Good, because . . . *twins!*"

Aaron inhaled a huge breath, let it out slowly, then kissed her soundly. When it ended, he took another deep breath. Released it. And said, "Well, that's what I get for loving Mrs. Bontrager."

**Don't miss any of the Amish romances
in Loree Lough's
A Little Child Shall Lead Them series!**

*USA Today* Bestselling Author
Loree Lough's

**ALL HE'LL EVER NEED**

*Out of the hearts of babes.*

**Among the New-new Order Amish
of Oakland, Maryland, children bring
precious hope, joy—and sometimes
an unexpected second chance at love . . .**

For Amish widower Phillip Baker,
providing for his family in the wake of his wife's death
means back-breaking work and renewed dedication
to his faith. Still, his strength can't help him relate
to his little son's struggles. It seems a godsend
when new doctor Emily White is able to treat Gabe's
shyness and fear even as she helps heal him.
But no matter how strongly Phillip is drawn
to the caring Englisher from the city, their differences
may be too great to overcome . . .

Reeling from her own tragic loss,
Emily keeps loneliness at bay through her clinic work.
Somehow, though, Gabe and his gentle,
sad-eyed father are making her want to risk
opening her heart again.
But can she find acceptance
in their Plain world—and a way to turn their
separate lives into a family forever?

# HOME TO STAY

*USA Today* **Bestselling Author**
**Loree Lough**

*New hope is always precious . . .*

**In the New Order Amish community
of Pleasant Valley, a helping hand is never far away,
and a baby's smile can be reason enough
to start over—and risk love again . . .**

Since losing his family in a tragic accident, building
contractor Max Lambright can't seem to find purpose
in anything but hard work . . . until he meets feisty
newcomer, Willa Reynolds. As she struggles to make a
new life for herself and her baby girl, she challenges
him in just about every possible way. Dare he hope that,
alongside this spirited woman, he might rekindle his lost
faith, and find the path to love and the family he craves?

Poor choices and a difficult past have inspired
Willa to make better decisions for her precious Frannie,
even if it means leaving the familiar behind
and starting over . . . among strangers.
As she adapts to the Amish ways, she learns about
Max's generous and steadfast nature. The loneliness he
tries so hard to mask can't be hidden . . . not from a
woman with something to prove: Together, they can
build their friendship into something that will forever
stand as the cornerstone of a happy family . . .

# Connect with U(s)

Visit us online at
**KensingtonBooks.com**
to read more from your favorite authors, see books
by series, view reading group guides, and more.

Join us on social media

for sneak peeks, chances to win books and prize packs,
and to share your thoughts with other readers.

facebook.com/kensingtonpublishing
twitter.com/kensingtonbooks

## Tell us what you think!

To share your thoughts, submit a review,
or sign up for our eNewsletters, please visit:
**KensingtonBooks.com/TellUs.**